FOUND

SAMANTHA KAY

For Adam, always x

PROLOGUE:

Their limbs tangled together like strands of spaghetti as they clung to each other on the narrow single bed. Their bodies were warm and their breathing still fast. He took her hand in his and kissed it gently before lacing his fingers into hers.

It was certainly morning, but neither was sure what time exactly. The curtains were drawn lazily across the small window next to the bed, the gap between them allowing a sliver of dawn light into his cramped room.

Exhausted, they rested their heads on the same thin lumpy pillow and stared into each other's eyes with the innocent joy of hopeful teenage lovers, neither having a care in the world beyond essay deadlines and what to have for breakfast.

'I need to go. I need to have a shower before I head to my mum's,' Carly said quietly, reluctantly slipping herself out from under him.

'No, no, you smell lovely. Don't go. Stay, just a little longer,' pleaded Jack, his voice muffled as he buried his face in her neck, inhaling her sweet scent of last night's perfume and hairspray as he gently kissed her skin.

Not wanting to leave his warm embrace, she succumbed to his plea in record time, allowing her body to lovingly fold back into his.

It was past lunch time when Carly finally arrived back home, somewhat later than she had originally planned.

Happy to return to familiar surroundings, she tossed her keys into the glass bowl that lived on the side table by the front door and practically skipped her way down the hallway.

'Mum! I'm home!' she bellowed en route to the kitchen, where she found her straight away, sitting at the small wooden table, which was littered with unopened mail, well-read newspapers and a small empty crystal glass, of the type that was only ever used for brown spirits, and even then, only on the rare occasions they had guests.

Carly's mum smiled brightly, happy to see her only daughter had returned safely home, even if it was just for one Sunday afternoon.

Carly stood behind her mum and wrapping her arms tightly around her frowned down at the out-of-place glass. As she clung tightly to her mother, Carly caught the subtle hint of brandy on her breath.

'You all right?' she asked, concerned.

'Sit down, darling, we need to talk,' said her mum, pointing to the chair opposite.

'Is everything okay?' asked Carly, releasing herself from her mother and pulling out a chair.

Carly's mum looked up at the ceiling as her grey-blue eyes filled with tears. Trying to compose herself, she looked straight back at her daughter as she brushed her hand through her long blonde hair and sighed heavily.

'I got my results back from the doctor ... It's ... it's not good news,' she said as her bottom lip quivered and her voice began to break.

Carly struggled to tune in to the words. She understood the severity, but was finding it hard to absorb what she was being told. Her own grey-blue eyes that were just like her mother's welled with tears and they both sat crying at the kitchen table, unable to comprehend the tragic news that had caused their whole world to crumble.

CHAPTER 1:

It wasn't the best wedding Jack had ever attended.

Sure, it had been somewhat pleasant to see
some old faces, and it was clear a lot of money
had been spent on Michael and Fran's big day, but
Jack was more than ready to call it a night, even
if it was only 8.30 p.m.

The day had been a long one, not to mention
exhausting. He'd had to answer a constant barrage of questions: Where are you working now?
Where are you living? And the most dreaded of
them all: Are you seeing anyone at the moment?

The fact that Jack was attending a friend's
wedding minus his plus-one really should have
been a dead giveaway, but that didn't seem to
stop people from asking. Ordinarily such a question wouldn't bother someone with as much
moxie as Jack, but what with it being a mere
three weeks since Jess had flung her engagement
ring at him across the kitchen, the question was
starting to wear a little thin, not that anyone
could tell, of course.

Jack stood at the small bar of the Princess event room and looked out at the wedding party. The room was becoming crowded as the evening guests arrived in their droves and the sound of Mark Ronson's Up Town Funk blared out. Jack watched as a large, mainly female gathering took over the small dance floor. On any other day Jack would have been more than happy to throw himself into the thick of it, using his effortless charm and smart one-liners, his trusted method of getting any woman he wanted into bed, but tonight he wasn't in the mood. Not only were most of the female guests past their best, but also now that the thrill of getting caught was gone he simply couldn't be bothered.

Right now Jack was just grateful finally to have some peace and quiet.

Brad's wife Holly was in amongst the crowd on the dance floor, and Jack was sincerely hoping she stayed there. A nice woman, but she possessed a high-pitched shrill of a voice. Every word she spoke was at such ear-piercing volume, with such enthusiasm and such neck-breaking speed that Jack was sure she must've taken some. He simply found her annoying and was happy to have his friend and former colleague to himself for a while.

'Same again?' Brad yelled into Jack's ear over the music.

Jack brought his short-glass to his lips and

poured the remaining whisky down his throat, then nodded towards his friend. Brad turned to the barman to order himself and Jack a drink.

While Jack waited, he knew that now might just be the right time to suggest they both get a little 'fresh air'.

'Cheers. Fancy stepping out for a bit?' he asked as he accepted the fresh glass from Brad. He opened his suit jacket and dug his hand into the inside pocket, lifting out a white ready-rolled joint, giving his friend a quick glance at it before quickly dropping it back into his pocket.

'Where'd you get that?' asked Brad, his brown eyes wide with excitement.

'I confiscated it last week from one of my year 11s. Call it a perk of the job! You coming?' asked Jack, nodding towards the exit before taking a sip from his whisky.

'I dunno, mate, Holly'll go mad!'

'I won't tell her if you don't,' shrugged Jack, before confidently walking through the crowd of dancing women, along the back of the room and out towards the exit and the venue's open grounds.

Outside in the chilly autumn air, Jack made sure to avoid the other smokers or fresh-air breathers, choosing a more private area that still provided some seating. He pulled himself out one of the white iron chairs, placed his glass on the small matching table and sat himself down, unconcerned as to whether Brad would be joining him or not. He reached for the inside pocket of his smart suit jacket and took out the joint, holding it between his fingers as he dug a little deeper for his lighter.

Jack placed the joint between his lips and shielded the end with one hand as he flicked on the lighter with the other. After a couple of tries the joint eventually caught alight and Jack wasted no time in taking one long pull on it before he'd even leaned back in his chair. It had been a while since Jack had smoked weed and he instantly felt a small head rush as he held the smoke inside his mouth.

'You really are a terrible influence!' said a voice to his right.

Jack turned his head and smiled at Brad, happy, if a little surprised, that his friend had chosen to join him.

'No one's twisting your arm to be here,' replied Jack, his voice strained as he tried to stop the smoke from escaping his mouth.

Brad sat down beside him.

Jack exhaled the smoke and handed the joint to his friend, watching as he inhaled.

'Whoa, that's strong,' said Brad, suppressing the urge to cough. 'I can't even remember the last time I smoked this stuff.'

'I can. About three years ago at my cousin Will's wedding.'

'Sounds like a good wedding?'

'Far from it. Incredibly drab. I caught my grandmother smoking outside in the gardens. Turns out she likes this stuff, helps her with the arthritis in her wrists, or at least that was her excuse,' chuckled Jack.

The two friends sat in a relaxed silence, leaning back in their chairs while the weed helped them both wind down after the long day, both lazily tuning into a muffled blend of music from their attended wedding along with the music from the other party being held upstairs.

The voice seemed to come out of nowhere.

'SERIOUSLY, BRAD, WHAT THE FUCK IS WRONG WITH YOU!' screamed Holly, scaring the bejesus out of them both. Holly stood before them with her hands on her hips and with a look of sheer anger plastered across her chubby red face.

Brad sprang up from his seat and forcibly handed the joint to Jack.

'It's not mine, I swear, it's Jack's!' he exclaimed in a panic, disappointing, but by no means surprising, Jack.

Not minding what the annoying Holly thought of him, Jack didn't move from his chair.

'We're supposed to be trying and here you are, weakening your sperm count with this – this illegal activity – like some kind of fucking addict!'

Jack couldn't help but scoff a laugh, finding it humorous that Holly was being so melodramatic.

'Oh Jesus, calm down, Holly. It's hardly crack! It's just a bit of puff!'

'Oh piss off, Jack!' snapped Holly, her words along with the weed making him laugh even more.

'Eloquent as ever,' Jack responded in his usual deadpan manner before brazenly taking another long pull on the neatly rolled joint, knowing just how much it would annoy Holly.

'You know, Jess was right about you. You're nothing but a selfish, irresponsible man-child!'

Jack didn't flinch. Even if the mention of Jess's soiled opinion of him did cut like a knife, he wasn't willing to let Holly see it.

'There is only one thing in life worse than being talked about, and that is not being talked about – Oscar Wilde, in case you were wondering, Holly,' declared Jack in the most condescending tone he could muster as he exhaled the smoke.

Holly stared hard at Jack, far too angry to string together a sentence. Jack knew that if looks could kill he would've been dead on the spot, but he didn't care, and continued to stare back at Holly with a large unnerving grin.

'Come on, Brad, we're going home,' Holly said quietly, promptly marching away in the direction she had come from.

'Cheers for that, Jack!' said Brad. He sighed heavily, then turned to follow his stroppy wife who had already disappeared around the corner.

Jack did feel bad for his friend, but he didn't envy him.

Jack knew the routine of the pissed-off woman all too well. Silence in the cab home, while she mulled over all the verbal abuse she would hurl at you the moment you both stepped through the front door. Although gutted he was now alone, Jack was content to remain sitting outside to enjoy the rest of his joint, using its effects to take his mind away from the horrible feelings of guilt that had been festering in him over the past three weeks.

As Jack went back over the memory of Jess throwing her ring at him, as well as countless personal insults, he was interrupted by the sound of human vomiting coming from the other side of the wall.

As truly vile as the sound was, Jack was good-humoured enough to recognise that it was also the sound of someone having a much better night than he was.

'Oh no, I've been sick all over the flowers,' said a concerned, if a little common, female voice, followed by a filthy cackle.

'It's only sick, a bit of rain will wash it away,' said another woman, her voice soft and calm.

'Can you smell that?'

'Your sick? Unfortunately, yes.'

'No no, someone is getting high out here,' said the vomiting woman in a hushed voice, but still loud enough for Jack to hear.

He sat up straight in his chair, trying to make himself look effortlessly cool and relaxed as the clanking sound of high heels got ever closer.

'Lauren, where you going?' said the softly spoken voice, concerned about the trouble her friend seemed to be seeking.

'Well, hello, kind sir!'

Jack turned his head to see a very pretty blonde standing before him. She looked a damn sight better than she had sounded, wearing a very clingy knee-length black dress that showed off her curves nicely. Her thick blonde locks looked a little bedraggled, and her stance a little wobbly, but she displayed a very naughty grin at the sight of Jack, staring intently at the joint in his hand, making her intentions very clear.

'Take a seat,' said Jack, and so she did, instantly slumping herself down on the iron chair recently vacated by Brad.

Noticing the joint had gone out, Jack dug back into his jacket pocket for his lighter.

'Lauren, what you doing?'

'Carly, meet my new friend—'

'Jack,' said Jack, keeping his focus on the joint as he flicked his lighter.

'This is my new friend, Jack.'

Jack looked up at Lauren's friend and instantly froze.

She looked stunning.

She was wearing an emerald-green knee-length dress that showed off her slim figure, and she certainly looked a lot steadier on her feet than her friend, retaining her elegance and poise. Her light ginger hair ran well past her shoulders and down her back, her hair being her signature feature and what had first drawn Jack to her all those years ago.

Carly's pretty grey-blue eyes scanned Jack's face as she smiled at him nervously, confused as to why he was staring at her so intently.

'Carly? Carly Hughes?' he said quietly, failing to suppress his shock at the sight of her.

She may not have recognised his face as instantly as he had hers, but on hearing her name fall from his lips, she too stood still, momentarily frozen at the realisation.

Although Carly's physical appearance had barely changed, the same could not be said for Jack. He still had a cheeky handsome face and deep brown eyes, but his once thick dark hair was nowhere to be seen, it now closely shaven to a stubble equal in length to the short dark stubble around his face, the look stylishly disguising his balding head.

Carly laughed inwardly at how grown-up he looked. Although still no body builder, he no longer displayed the awkwardness of the gangly teenager she remembered. He had certainly filled out, looking broader and more chiselled, while oozing a confidence that had always been there, though in its early stages of development when they had last known one another.

'Oh God, Jack Lewis?' Carly finally managed.

'Wait, what – you two know each other?' slurred Lauren as she sat lazily in her seat with her legs spread apart, looking between the startled pair.

'Er, yes ... Once ... in a past life,' Jack said softly as he chivalrously handed the newly lit joint to Carly's friend Lauren and he and Carly continued to look at each other dumbfoundedly.

Jack stood up, his approach a little delayed, and placed his face gently next to Carly's to give her a kiss on the cheek. He took a step back and looked at her, his eyes dancing around her pretty face once again, struggling to find the freckles on her cheeks under a layer of make-up and the dark night sky.

Carly smiled widely at Jack as Lauren took a long hard pull on Jack's 'special cigarette', before tapping him on the forearm to hand it back to him.

Jack accepted the joint from Lauren and nodded towards Carly, offering it to her.

'Pah, Miss Goody Two Shoes won't touch that, mate!' scoffed Lauren, at which Jack frowned and displayed a slightly baffled smile.

Choosing to ignore both Jack and Lauren, Carly simply rolled her eyes and moved away from Jack, proceeding to walk towards the low wall in front of where Lauren had plonked herself down.

Not quite believing that Carly Hughes would refuse such an offer, Jack continued to hold out the joint, convinced that at any second the Carly he so fondly remembered would take it from him and happily take a pull.

'I'm good, thanks,' she said softly, perching on the low wall.

Jack shook his head and sat back down.

'Wow, I remember when you were fun!' he scoffed in disbelief.

'Yeah, well, I remember when you had hair,' she cheekily fired back.

'I'll issue a point for your quickness, Miss Hughes, but you score zero for originality, I'm afraid,' quipped Jack, happy to hear that she maintained her smart mouth, even if she was now displaying as a bore in other areas.

'Seriously, how do you two know each other?' asked Lauren, still awaiting an explanation.

'We used to go to school together,' Carly answered casually if a little quickly.

'School? Really? Are you sure you don't want to rephrase that?' Jack responded, shocked that Carly was so obviously downplaying their having met somewhere as prestigious as Cambridge University.

'Nope,' answered Carly.

'University. We attended university together,' Jack announced proudly, at which Lauren released a loud filthy laugh.

'Sorry, why is that so funny?' asked Jack, gently shaking his head in disbelief.

'Carly never went to uni!'

'Yes she did.'

'Mate, I'm not sure how much of that stuff you've been smoking, but Carly and me have been BFFs, work wives, for what, ten years, maybe longer? We were what, twenty when we met? And guess what, she weren't at no uni!'

Jack looked on in utter bewilderment at Carly, failing to recognise the newest version of her, and Carly could see the confusion plastered across his face. She could see, even as high as he may have been, that a thousand questions were racing through his mind as to why she would be so cagey about her past, a past that he believed she should have been proud of.

'So what brings you here tonight?' asked Carly, keen to redirect Jack's thoughts.

'Same as you, I suspect, friend's wedding.'

'No, I meant, what brings you *here*. Outside on your own?'

Jack wondered if he ought to be honest enough to tell the old girlfriend he hadn't seen in over a decade all that had led to his being here, sitting alone, getting stoned in the cold, when he should have been inside, enjoying himself and reminiscing with old friends.

'Just ... fancied a breather,' he said, keeping his response short, if a little cryptic.

Carly smiled at Jack. Although it had been many years since they had last been in each other's company, she knew him well enough to know that sitting outside alone while the party was in full swing was out of character.

'How've you been?' asked Carly, the question provoking a feeling of dread in Jack, who wanted more than anything to divert the subject away from what had been going on in his life.

'Can't complain … what about you, what are you up to these days?'

'I, well, we, work for an entertainment company.'

'Sounds exciting.' Jack nodded with approval.

'What about you, Mr Wannabe Journalist? Tell me; what fancy paper got the pleasure of your company in the end?'

Jack felt his stomach churn. He wasn't ashamed to admit that he was now marking GCSE essays rather than writing any of his own, but what it was that led him there was not a topic he wanted to touch on, not ever, and certainly not tonight.

'Oh God, Carls, I think I'm gonna be sick!' declared Lauren with great urgency, the combination of weed and alcohol taking its toll on her petite body, her sudden interruption something Jack was most grateful for.

Lauren dragged herself up from her chair and stumbled back around the corner.

'I'd better make sure she's okay,' said Carly as she got to her feet.

'Yes, yes of course,' chuckled Jack. He took another pull on his joint and stood up.

'It was nice seeing you, Jack,' said Carly with a

sweet smile.

Although disappointed their short time to-gether was over, she was grateful it hadn't been longer, possibly causing her to have to admit to Jack Lewis that she was more than happy to es-cape her present life in some way or another.

With Lauren out of sight, Carly reached for the joint in Jack's hand and gently took it from him. She glanced behind her sheepishly before turn-ing back to Jack and raising the joint to her lips. She closed her eyes and inhaled deeply, enjoying the sensation of the first joint she had smoked in years. She opened her eyes to a smiling Jack, who was happy to see the girl he had once loved so deeply and known so well was still somewhere hidden in the sensible grown-up standing before him.

'There she is,' he said comically as she handed the joint back before turning on her heels and scurrying away, disappearing into the night al-most as quickly as she had appeared, not even saying goodbye.

Jack smiled tightly to himself and shook his head.

He looked down at the joint in his hand, half wondering if his stoned mind had just imagined the whole thing, until he heard the vile sound of Lauren vomiting again. The sound was loud; but further away than it had been previously, safely confirming that the past few minutes really had happened and weren't a figment of his imagination.

Jack sat himself back down on the cold iron chair and commenced to finish his joint alone.

CHAPTER 2:

Carly was asleep; a deep, peaceful, beautiful sleep. The kind of sleep that she only ever achieved after a rare night of heavy alcohol consumption.

As she rolled onto her side, she was gradually woken by a warm sweaty hand crudely fumbling its way up her inner thigh.

'Craig, what you doing?' mumbled Carly, feeling too tired and hungover to react, even if the feel of his touch did fill her with disgust.

'What? Come on, you were out all last night,' muttered Craig, implying that she owed him one, using her absence from the house as some kind of bargaining tool.

He breathed heavily into her neck so that she smelt his morning breath, the stale unwashed smell almost making her gag as the bulge of his pot belly pressed into her back.

Carly reached under the duvet and forcibly shoved Craig's hand away.

'Craig, go away, I'm asleep.'

Unfortunately Carly was now very much awake, her beautiful sleepy state now a thing of the past, her mind focused entirely on escaping Craig's wandering hand; but he was persistent.

No sooner had she pushed him away than he was back, this time with even more force, using his hand to prise her legs apart.

Usually Carly's refusal was met by little come-back, but as she worked out the dates in her head, she realised it had been nine, maybe even ten weeks since they had last had sex, so it stood to reason that Craig was being more persistent than usual.

Ten weeks was a personal best for Carly.

It seemed her life over the past few years had solely revolved around not having to see, touch, hear or even smell Craig. She'd volunteer to work every available shift, the longer and later the better, usually returning home long after he had fallen asleep in order to avoid spending any real time with him.

'Come on, you'll enjoy it when we get going.'

Carly wouldn't, she hadn't in years.

It wasn't that she didn't like sex, she just didn't like sex with Craig, not any more.

When they first met the sex was okay – not the best; never the best – but she was happy to go along with the motions. But now, all these years later, she had no interest whatsoever. She would skilfully fake her time of the month, leaving boxes of tampons out long after her period had finished, and would fake stomach, head, tooth, leg, even toe aches, anything she could think of to put Craig off coming near her. The very sight of him made her skin crawl: she always wanted to turn the other way when he was next to her in bed so she could fantasise she was alone.

Carly finally opened her tired eyes and caught sight of the clock radio on her bedside table, the red digits reading that the time was 7.30 a.m. It was rather early to be woken on a Sunday morning, especially after such a late night, but the time was significant. They had half an hour before Craig's mum woke up, not that a session with Craig would ever last that long, but it still meant they had thirty undisturbed minutes Craig was clearly keen to cash in on.

'Okay, fine … but I'm not moving,' huffed Carly, making no effort to disguise her unwillingness, but aware Craig was too sex-starved to back down.

Carly reached under the covers and swiftly pulled her knickers down just past her knees and, still lying on her side, pushed her bottom out towards Craig. Keeping her gaze firmly on the bedside table in front of her, she could hear Craig behind her, pulling down his underwear and getting himself into position.

Foreplay having never been one of Craig's strong suits, within seconds he had forcibly entered her. Keen to get activities underway before Carly had a chance to change her mind, he heavily pounded into her from behind, not in the least bit concerned about her dryness or lack of participation.

Craig's breathing quickly became rapid, his wiry beard roughly brushing her skin as he groaned into her neck, her body muffling the sound as his warm breath spread across her skin like a virus.

Judging by his speed, Carly knew she would only have to endure Craig inside her for a few moments longer, that knowledge being the only thing that made the experience bearable. Craig made a tight grab for Carly's left breast through her T-shirt, the telltale sign that he was about to come. Carly closed her eyes just as Craig came inside her, his heavy, satisfied panting invading her personal space as she continued to lie resentfully in his hold, he as usual giving no consideration as to whether she had enjoyed herself.

Carly opened her eyes and quickly moved herself away from Craig just as the digits on the clock changed to 7.32 a.m. Feeling sore, she reached under the covers and pulled her knickers back up. Her head felt heavy and tired, but not wanting to spend a minute longer next to Craig, she forced her body to sit up and climbed out of the bed.

'We're really gonna have to go at it more, you know,' said Craig, his breathing still jagged.

Carly looked at him for the first time as he readjusted himself under the covers.

'What you on about?' she said, struggling to care.

Craig ran his pasty hand through his dark floppy hair then stroked the dark untamed beard that covered most of his round squashy face.

'If we wanna make a baby, we really need to be doing it more than once every couple of months.'

'Well you can actually only get pregnant over two or three days of the month anyway. So we really don't need to be at it like rabbits,' Carly responded curtly, turning round to pull her light blue dressing gown from the hook on the bedroom door.

She turned back to face Craig as she slipped the dressing gown on. He had a warm hopeful smile on his face, unfazed by her coldness towards him.

'Well, you never know, a baby could be making itself in you as we speak.'

Carly pursed her lips and raised her eyebrows at Craig.

'Here's hoping,' she said, holding up her hand and crossing her fingers, before turning back round and walking slowly out of the bedroom towards the bathroom.

Carly pulled up her knickers as she stood up from the toilet.

She pressed down the silver button on the back of the cistern to flush, then went to the bathroom sink. She turned on the cold tap and held her cupped hands under the running water, creating a small pool, then lowered her face to it. The cold water instantly refreshed her, eliminating any leftover sleepy state. Carly turned off the tap and took a look at her face in the mirror of the bathroom cabinet above the sink. She felt embarrassed by the sight of herself: she looked worse than she felt, with dark circles under her eyes as well as a dark smudge on one cheek, the result of not having removed last night's make-up properly. Her mind wandered to the night before and her fleeting encounter with the grown-up Jack Lewis. She wondered what on earth someone as handsome and educated as Jack Lewis must have thought of her.

If only he could see her now, hiding in the messy bathroom of a council house that wasn't even hers.

Lifting the green fluffy towel to her face, Carly realised she never did ask Jack where he was living these days. She imagined it was somewhere fancy, among the upper middle classes, he enjoying the fruits of his labour with an endless stream of leggy blondes, all with their own fancy degrees and well-paid jobs.

Placing the towel down over the bath, Carly opened the bathroom cabinet and pulled out the purple cosmetic bag that lived on the top shelf. She unzipped the bag and rifled through the make-up and tweezers to find the zip to the inside pocket. She unzipped it and pulled out a half-used foil packet of contraceptive pills, just as the sound of someone jiggling the handle to the bathroom door sounded from outside.

'Carly, unlock the door, I'm busting for a piss!' called Craig, the mere sound of his voice infuriating her.

'One sec!'

Carly snapped a pill from the pack, popped it in her mouth and swallowed it dry then hurriedly placed the packet back in the cosmetics bag and shoved it back inside the cabinet.

Carly opened the bathroom door to find Craig on the other side. Neither of them stopped to engage in any pleasantries, he brushing straight past her into the bathroom. Within seconds of his entry she could hear the sound of him peeing loudly due to his failure to close the bathroom door.

Carly cringed at the intimate sound of Craig's bodily functions and made her way down the stairs.

The staircase led straight into the open living room.

'Morning, May!' said Carly as she entered, heading straight towards the curtains and pulling them apart, allowing the light from outside to burst into the room and cast a bright glow onto the clutter, the living room now resembling more of a makeshift hospital than a family living space.

A small bedside table was laden with boxes of

pills and an adult sippy cup, a much safer alternative to a regular tea mug now that May's hold was so weak. Next to the shabby cream sofa an electric wheelchair was crammed next to a large black leather reclining armchair. The recliner was Craig's most treasured possession; but just the very sight of it annoyed Carly.

Not only did it not match the other furniture, but now there was hardly any room for it with the addition of May's bed and wheelchair, however that fact had never bothered Craig, who spent countless hours slumped on his own luxury island of comfort while Carly took refuge on a sofa that had seen better days.

'You're up early, lovey,' responded May from her horizontal position on her hospital-style bed.

As May lay in bed, she could almost be mistaken for a healthy person. Her hair was now mostly grey all over but still cut in a stylish crop that Carly made sure was maintained at least every six weeks by the mobile hairdresser. Although May never felt the need for make-up these days, she displayed the same friendly face she always had, with warm brown eyes that possessed a cheeky glint. She was still the same old May, kind and warm and understanding, but her energy and strength were weakening with every passing month.

'Yeah, well, no good will come from lying in bed all day,' Carly chirped as she bounced over towards Craig's mother and placed a loving kiss on her smooth cheek.

'You should've given yourself a lie-in, lovey, let ol' soppy bollocks get his arse into gear for a change!' said May, pressing the button on her bed control to sit herself upright.

Carly chuckled at May, her unforgiving potty mouth being just one of the many things that she loved about her.

'It's fine, May, do you want me to put you in your chair or you stopping in bed for a bit?'

'I'm fine here, lovey. How was last night? Did you have fun? How was Katie? How did she look in her dress?'

May often fired off questions like a machine gun, keen to catch up on all the goings-on of the outside world she was so disappointed to be missing out on.

'Yeah, it was a really good wedding, lots of people, lots of dancing. Katie looked stunning, oh and I bumped into an old schoolfriend outside the venue, they were a guest at the other wedding downstairs I think,' answered Carly as she meandered her way into the kitchen to boil the kettle.

'What's this?' yawned Craig as he made his way into the living room wanting to be included in the conversation.

'Carly was just saying she bumped into an old schoolfriend last night. What's she up to these days, lovey?'

'Who?' asked Carly as she wandered back into

the living room to collect up last night's used tea mugs that Craig had failed to take into the kitchen.

'Your old schoolfriend?'

'Oh, I'm not sure, the conversation didn't get that far. Lauren started being sick so I had to see to her,' answered Carly, not feeling any need to correct May's assumption that her 'friend' was a she, whilst doing an excellent job at concealing her own interest in what Jack Lewis could possibly be doing with his life these days.

'That's the problem with you, lovey. Spend too much of your time taking care of everyone else.' Carly smiled a tight smile at May before pausing by the television to straighten up the picture frame on the wall– A faded print of Bar at the Folies-Bergere by Manet. The small masterpiece depicted a young uninterested barmaid. She was pretty, wearing a tight corset and her blonde hair up, staring blankly into the abyss while in the reflection behind her a male customer could be seen making what Carly had always believed to be tedious conversation.

Carly found it darkly amusing at just how much she and the barmaid seemed to have in common.

'So breakfast, you ready for something to eat, May?' asked Carly, pulling her attention away from the picture.

'I'll have a bacon sarnie if you're making,' piped Craig, burying his hand inside the crotch of his navy-blue jogging bottoms to scratch himself whilst slumped on his recliner opposite his mother.

'Your mum and I are having porridge, Craig. if you want a bacon sarnie you can make it yourself.'

'All right, I'll have porridge too then, I'm not fussed. As long as it fills an 'ole.'

'As long as you don't have to make it, more like!' quipped May, never too proud to call her son out on his bone idleness.

As Carly carried the dirty mugs into the kitchen she could hear the whisperings of Craig and May. She figured they were probably discussing her curtness towards Craig, which she knew herself was becoming more frequent and spiteful with every passing day.

'So er, Carly,' spluttered Craig, surprising her as he appeared in the kitchen doorway. 'Since Chrissie is popping over today to see Mum, I was wondering if you fancied going out?'

'Yeah, I was planning on popping out. I was gonna try and do a big shop, saves doing it in the week,' answered Carly, as she filled the sink with water to wash the mugs.

'No, I meant, going out with me. To go and get some lunch somewhere?'

'Why?' asked Carly, looking up at Craig, genuinely baffled by such an out-of-the-blue suggestion.

'I ... just thought it would be nice.'

Carly tried to cast her mind back to the last

time she and Craig had done anything remotely romantic together. She could recall the odd trip to the cinema in the early stages of their relationship, but that was about the extent of it and that was years ago, and certainly in the days before May got too sick to be left on her own for long. Craig's suggestion ignited a feeling of guilt in Carly at how cold she had been towards him over the past few months.

After all, he wasn't a bad guy, he worked hard and he was loyal. When they first met, there was a kind of ease, a security and sense of comfort that came from their being together, but over the years comfort and ease had gradually been replaced by resentment and disdain, with neither of them willing to put in the effort to change things. It bothered Carly that the very sight and sound of Craig irritated her, and she wished she could feel differently, the way she once had. But it seemed the deeper she dug inside herself, the more resentment she unearthed, so much so that she often struggled to keep a lid on her moods. She wondered if the idea of a lunch date was Craig's way of trying to make amends, his own way of trying to do something nice, so she felt it only fair to throw him a bone.

'Sorry, yeah, you know what, that sounds good.'

'Okay, we'll grab some lunch, somewhere nice. You like Pizza Express, right?'

'Yeah, okay, that'll be really nice,' smiled Carly,

willing herself to feel some excitement at the idea.

Craig leaned in and gave Carly a kiss on the cheek, a loving gesture that again was very out of character. The feel of his rough beard on her face made her want to recoil, but she suppressed the urge and allowed Craig to show her some affection.

Craig flashed a smile as he left the kitchen, leaving Carly to tidy up and make breakfast for everyone.

Jack's mouth was so dry that it caused the back of his throat to feel sore. He opened his gritty eyes, rubbing the back of his hand over them to remove the sleep that had built up over the hours.

He prised his head from his flat pillow and sat himself up in his narrow single bed, resting his weight on his elbows. The curtains were still drawn over the large window next to his bed, but they were thin enough to allow in the daylight and it was clear the early morning had passed.

Jack's head still felt fuzzy, but he felt well rested, having achieved what he felt to be the best night's sleep he'd had in years. He swung his legs out of the bed, rubbed his hand over his balding head and cast his mind back to the events of last night, the first memory to come to mind that of Carly Hughes.

Jack still couldn't believe how stunning she'd looked: for the rest of the evening he hadn't been able to get her image out of his mind. He felt regretful that he didn't get more time to speak with her about what she had been up to over the past decade and he wondered how she must be spending her morning.

Carly certainly didn't resemble a woman bogged down by a bunch of kids or a dead-end job; regretting every shitty life choice she'd made. No, he was sure she was living her best life. Waking up in the arms of some successful entertainment executive whilst pondering over the destination of their next exotic holiday.

Jack let out a deep sigh and deciding that it was time to stop torturing himself and join the land of the living, lifting himself from the bed wearing nothing more than a pair of black boxer shorts.

The hallway belonging to Jack's grandmother was somewhat reminiscent of a teenager's bedroom, the long walls either side covered with the evidence of her idols; if of course teenagers' idols were Van Gogh, Rembrandt and Lowry. Where most grandmothers would have displayed proud photos of their awkward-looking grandchildren, Grandma Barb displayed the works of her favourite artists. Postcard-sized prints of their masterpieces hung in pound shop glass frames all along the green hallway that led to the kitchen.

Jack tuned his hearing in to the sound of Grandma Barb, who he could hear faffing around in the living room to the background noise of Radio 4.

'Want some breakfast, Gran?' Jack called out from the kitchen doorway, and turned to the fridge, stuck with souvenir magnets purchased from every corner of the globe, scrappy shopping lists and social invitations. He opened the fridge door and peered inside, waiting for inspiration.

'You mean lunch, darling. It's 12.30!' Grandma Barb called back.

Jack could hear her coming into the kitchen, but couldn't be bothered to turn and look, keeping his gaze on the eggs on the second shelf.

'Okay, lunch then?'

'No thank you, I'm off out and I'm already running late. I told you, today is the AGM at the cinema-organ society, then I'm going for drinks with Trevor and Gloria, so don't wait up for me!'

'Let it not be said that the cinema-organ enthusiasts of London don't know how to have fun!' said Jack, pulling himself up from the fridge and letting the door close behind him before finally turning to look at his grandmother.

She was dressed ready to go out, wearing a heavy burgundy coat over smart grey trousers which she'd matched with her favourite candy-pink cashmere jumper. She resembled a woman much younger than her eighty-six years, standing short but proud with her blonde curly hair sitting a little wild on her head and her freshly manicured hands clutching a green handbag.

'Ha, you're not wrong, darling! There's a four-hour-old bacon sandwich there if you want it!' she said, pointing towards the counter next to the fridge, not in the least bit fazed by Jack's lack of clothing.

Jack turned, picked up the white-bread sandwich and devoured it, not bothered in the slightest that the bread was now stale and the bacon stone cold.

'You know you should join us later for drinks,' suggested Grandma Barb as she placed her handbag down on the counter. Digging into her bag she pulled out her pink lipstick, applying it to her thin lips without the use of a mirror. 'Gloria has a granddaughter that's single ... she was recently jilted. She's an accountant for an abortion clinic, one of the big ones—'

'A jilted baby killer, *and* she's single! I tell you, Gran! What. Are. The. Chances?'

'She doesn't kill babies, she merely funds the process. She's not Jewish though, but then again that never has bothered you,' she said with a sideways glance and her usual heaped spoonful of Jewish guilt as she tossed her lipstick back into her bag.

'Says the bacon fryer!'

'It's grilled. I'm watching our cholesterol ... So?'

'So what?'

'So will you be joining us, later, for drinks?'

'I'll pass, Gran. I've got a ton of marking to do and lesson prep. Maybe next time?' answered Jack, feeling resentful that drinks with three pensioners was indeed going to be the best offer of a social engagement he would get today.

'Hmm, suit yourself. Right, I'm off!' announced Grandma Barb, drawing closer to Jack, who towered over her petite frame. Taking a firm hold of his chin, she yanked his face down to hers and planted a sloppy kiss, transferring her fresh lipstick onto Jack's cheek. 'And if at any point today you do feel the urge to tackle your own washing, don't fight it!' she said, playfully slapping the side of his face before releasing him.

'Right you are!' replied Jack, as Grandma Barb made her way out of the flat.

Jack looked over at the small table tucked into the corner of the kitchen. It was laden with students' exercise books, his brown leather work satchel and laptop. His gaze drifted away and fell to the nearby washing machine, in front of which rested a blue plastic basket containing a large pile of his dirty washing.

About to tackle it, Jack caught sight of his grandmother's special biscuit barrel that was in the shape of a free-standing gingerbread man. He lifted off the gingerbread man's head and delved inside the barrel, pulling out a large handful of chocolate digestives. He wandered out of the kitchen, abandoning any productive plans for the day, and headed back to bed, armed with nothing more than a handful of biscuits and a fuzzy head.

Carly and Craig sat opposite each other at a small round table in the centre of a busy Pizza Express restaurant.

The young, floppy-haired waiter noted down their dessert order on an electric notepad and seemed to grimace at Craig, who had strings of cheese in his beard, along with a sprinkling of white crumbs. Carly found it so hard to care about Craig that she couldn't muster the strength to alert him to the state of his face, instead continuing to stare blankly at him whilst he waffled on about how much Tim at work had pissed him off that week.

'He's such a prick, I can't be arsed to talk about him any more! Anyway, have you had fun?'

'Yeah, it's been nice,' Carly answered with as much sincerity as she could.

'Good, 'cause I, er, I've noticed you've not really been yourself lately.'

Carly felt uneasy. She knew her recent shortness with Craig hadn't gone unnoticed, and she felt nervous at the idea of addressing her feelings, unsure as to where such a conversation could lead.

'Yeah, I ... I dunno, Craig, I just think, maybe ... maybe something needs to change,' she said, willing to discuss the elephant in the room, but making her discomfort clear as she squirmed in her seat.

'I agree, I think a change would be good for us.'

Carly felt herself light up inside, surprised they were both finally landing on the same page.

'I mean, maybe we should just try doing more things together,' she suggested with building enthusiasm, impressed that Craig was brave enough to approach what she had deemed to be too uncomfortable a subject.

'Er, yeah, I was—'

'I saw the other day that a Picasso exhibition is coming to the Tate next month. We could get tickets? Maybe make a day of it? We could get someone to check in on May—'

'I'm not going to an art gallery, Carly,' scowled Craig.

'Why not? You just—' began Carly, insulted by his shooting down her idea so quickly.

''Cause I don't need to spend my day looking at pictures of sodding sunflowers!'

'Van Gogh.'

'What?'

'Van Gogh. Van Gogh painted the sun-flowers, Craig!' snapped Carly, impatient with Craig's ignorance, his small-mindedness being one of the many qualities she despised.

Craig grimaced, frustrated by Carly's effort to outsmart him.

'Carly, we're digressing. What I was actually thinking was that maybe it's time we, made a change and took a step forward, and ... and maybe before a baby gets made... maybe we should finally make it official?'

Craig's nervous spluttering baffled Carly; having lost interest in what he was trying to say.

Craig beckoned over their waiter who ap-proached in what seemed like slow motion. Armed with a black slate plate, he placed down a chocolate brownie and a mound of vanilla ice cream. Spiked through the ice cream, a metal sparkler was furiously flash-ing, its bright fiery light causing the entire res-taurant to turn their attention to their table.

To one side of the dessert the word *Con-gratulations* was spelt out in white chocolate. As Carly's eyes wandered over the plate she saw, poking out of the mountain of ice cream, a gleaming diamond ring.

Craig got up from his chair and kneeled down on the floor next to Carly, unaware he was resting his knee on a discarded napkin encasing pizza crust, and took her hands in his.

'Carly Annette Hughes, will you marry me?'

Carly's eyes widened at the car crash unfolding before her very eyes. She felt her jaw drop and her mouth dry out as she sat and stared at Craig in a deafening silence; everyone in the restaurant looking on excitedly, eagerly awaiting her answer.

'You're surprised, aren't you?' Craig laughed nervously, mistaking Carly's pained silence for elated disbelief.

'Er, yeah,' Carly said quietly, desperately wanting to escape the invasive stares of excited strangers, baffled as to how her and Craig's strained conversation had suddenly turned into a proposal.

'Yes? She said yes!' Craig declared, his announcement met by rapturous applause, which added a heavy dose of humiliation to Carly's horror at his misunderstanding.

Craig reached over towards the plate of dessert on the table and dug his stubby fingers into the ice cream. He pulled the ring out and placed it in his mouth, licking the ice cream residue from it, before slipping the saliva-soaked ring onto Carly's finger.

Carly sat frozen in her seat as Craig put his hands either side of her face and kissed her hard on the lips, the pizza crumbs trapped in his beard scratching her chin.

'I love you, Carly,' whispered Craig as he pulled his lips away, looking back at her with a wide smile of pure joy.

Still in a state of utter shock, Carly was unable to respond. She looked into Craig's hopeful happy face and, knowing she simply couldn't match the depth of his feelings, felt a deep stab of sadness.

'Mum is gonna be over the moon!' beamed Craig as he finally hauled himself up from the floor and sat back down in his seat opposite Carly.

At the very thought of May, Carly felt her eyes well with tears. May had shown her nothing but kindness, from the moment she who took her in to the safety and warmth of her family when she had nowhere else to go, and May had never asked for a single thing in return.

Carly loved May almost as much as she had loved her own mother, and although she could be cold towards Craig, it was May whose heart she kept tight hold of, and she knew it was May she could never abandon.

Carly looked down at the diamond ring on her finger as sadness overcame her and tears rolled down her cheeks. She looked up at Craig, still beaming with joy and pride, and she was unable to remember the last time she had seen him look so stupidly happy.

She couldn't be so cruel as to say nothing, so she dug deep inside herself for the kindest, most loving words she could find.

'I ... I ... thanks, Craig. Thanks ...' she said finally, her voice breaking.

CHAPTER 3:

All staff on shift at Pinky Bingo had been called into work early ahead of an emergency meeting. As they waited for the meeting to start, Lauren and Carly stood together over a pink branded mug of milky tea in the staff canteen, both in their matching bright pink Pinky Bingo polo-neck T-shirts, which displayed the company's winking bingo ball logo on the right breast pocket.

Lauren couldn't help noticing Carly's newest piece of jewellery. She took Carly's left hand in hers for a closer look.

Although Carly was without a trained eye, she was sure the diamond in her ring couldn't possibly be real. The stones clarity was rather cloudy and certainly far too big to be within Craig's budget, but Carly couldn't be sure, and thought it mean to question.

'Wow, well, it's a beaut, Carls, congrats, babe!' said Lauren, her voice lacking the enthusiasm one would expect in response to a best friend's engagement.

Carly smiled tightly at her friend and remained silent as her eyes slowly filled with tears she couldn't control. Trying to compose herself, she took a deep breath, as Lauren worriedly searched her face.

'You know, Carly, it doesn't have to be like this. You could always—'

'What? Leave? Abandon May? I ... it's not like he's a woman beater ...' Carly looked up at the ceiling, wishing she could push her tears back into her eyes.

'No, I know, he's a decent enough bloke, but, Carls ... you don't love him!' Lauren said quietly, as if reminding Carly of something she had forgotten.

'People get married for all sorts of reasons, Lauren ...'

Lauren nodded, at a loss as to what to say, feeling bad that she had no profound words of advice or wisdom to offer her friend.

'Okay, can everyone take a seat! Meeting's about to start ... Can we get a move on, please, I haven't got all day!' bellowed Stuart, Pinky Bingo's regional manager.

Stuart Childs was the definition of loser.

A tall lanky man with greasy mousy brown hair, Stuart had a love–hate relationship with his staff, in which they loved to hate him. It wasn't the most positive of mind sets, but oddly, their shared mutual hatred was what united his staff.

Stuart had begun working at Bingo Pinky some ten years ago, around the same time as Carly and

Lauren. Pinky Bingo was Stuart's life. Originally a part-time job waiter, he had gradually climbed up the bingo career ladder to become the Dagenham branch's regional manager.

At thirty-two years old, Stuart still lived at home with his parents and displayed every characteristic of an adult virgin. He lacked any sense of charisma or style, it not going unnoticed that he'd worn the same tired black shoes for ten whole years. The female staff intimidated Stuart greatly; he would flush bright crimson whenever he had to engage with any of them.

Unfortunately for Stuart, awkward squirming men were Lauren's speciality. Ever since Stuart had made a very ill-conceived pass at her at the Christmas Party three years ago, she had held no mercy, often getting her kicks making smutty lewd comments that Stuart had no idea how to handle.

'Calm down, Stu, we wouldn't want to see you blow your load all over this clean floor!' Lauren said. This was met by a cackle of laughter as the other twenty members of staff took their seats around the large canteen table.

Stuart stood at the head of the room, his reddening face doing little to hide his level of discomfort. Shrugging off his embarrassment, he cleared his throat loudly, nervously pulling at his ill-fitting black trousers.

'Right, I'm sure you've all seen the articles in the press about Pinky Bingo shutting ten of its halls in the next few months. Now I don't want any of you to panic. I've been in meetings with head office over the past couple of weeks, and it seems that this hall has no plans for closure at this time—' Claps and small cheers sounded from the workforce, all relieved by news.

'However...' Stuart continued, eager to deliver his news as quickly as possible as white blots of saliva developed in the corners of his mouth. 'It's no secret that business has not been what it once was. I made it clear I am not willing to make any of my staff redundant, but, in the interests of saving money, we are going to have to cut back on everyone's hours.'

Relieved claps and cheers quickly morphed into gasps of outrage and groans of dismay, Carly and Lauren looking at each other in wide-eyed shock.

'Everyone's hours? Does that include your hours, Stuart?' bellowed Lauren, sure that Mr Adult Virgin wouldn't have to suffer the same financial injustice.

'I know this isn't ideal, not for any of us, but I assure you, it's the only way forward right now that doesn't involve any casualties.'

'Answer the question, Stuart! Does that include your hours?'

Stuart nervously readjusted his trousers again, his silence and inability to look at anyone in particular telling his staff all they needed to know.

'This is bullshit, Stuart, and you know it! You

can't cut back the hours of people that are already earning piss all!' shouted Lauren, banging her hand down on the table with such force her mug of tea shook.

Stuart looked on the verge of tears, possibly out of fear, or guilt, knowing he couldn't offer his staff the kind of reassurance they deserved. Standing helplessly before them, he made the cowardly decision to remain silent, allowing them to rant amongst themselves.

'This is bullshit!'

'I know, I know!' Carly responded, rubbing her head as her own sense of panic set in; not because of the loss of money, but because of the extra hours she would now have to spend at home.

'I'm gonna have to get a second job,' ranted Lauren.

'I could always get you a shift at the hospital with me,' suggested Carly.

'The hospital? I thought that was voluntary?'

'Yeah it is, but it'll get you out the house.'

'We're not all desperate to escape our loved ones, Carly,' snapped Lauren, pushing back her chair and storming off, annoyed at her friend's unhelpfulness, and leaving Carly to process her worries alone.

Jack sat casually in the green visitor's chair next to the draughty window on Violet Ward.
A strong scent of urine and disinfectant hung in

the air of the all-male ward as old and middle-aged men lay in their hospital beds; their common ground their 'waterworks' issues.

After a long week at school the last thing Jack wanted to do on a Friday night was spend the evening at his father's bedside in an NHS hospital ward, but seeing as Maxwell Lewis had been in hospital for a whole week already, Jack felt; after receiving an aggravated text message from his Mother ordering him to, it was maybe time he paid him a visit.

Maxwell didn't look sick. If anything, he seemed to be enjoying the attention being in hospital was bringing; surrounded by Get Well cards from family and friends. A multicoloured Get Well balloon was tied to the foot of the bed, a gesture that, Jack knew, could only have come from his sister and her daughters. Louisa was for sure a much better offspring than he was, having arrived empty-handed and miserable.

Jack had inherited many qualities from his father, including his hair loss. Maxwell liked to let his hair grow around the sides of his head: fine, white, barely-there hair surrounding a shiny dome of skin on the crown. Wrapped in a smart navy-blue robe, Maxwell sat assertively in his bed, enjoying the belated visit from his only son.

'The doctor said my prostate was so swollen it was blocking the way for urination. Almost a full litre of urine. That was how much urine I had in my bladder. He said he'd never seen a bladder so full. It was a miracle it didn't burst open!' Maxwell recalled proudly with some exaggerated hand movements.

'Really? Well, *many* congratulations on that, Dad!'

'Anyway, they said there's an operation they can carry out, but it can leave me in potent.'

'In potent?' repeated Jack, failing to understand.

'Yes, yes, in potent, you know what in potent means!' shouted Maxwell, angrily pointing towards his nether regions under his green hospital blanket.

'Honest to God! Impotent, Dad, it's pronounced impotent!' said Jack, correcting Maxwell in his usual patronising manner, another quality Jack had inherited from his father.

Choosing to ignore his son's tone, Maxwell continued with his medical updates.

'It's really something I'm going to have to discuss with your mother, as we're both still quite partial to a little—'

'Dad, Dad, I'll projectile vomit if you don't change the subject,' interrupted Jack, holding up his hand, willing his father to stop.

'What? You think *you* invented sex?'

'Please, Dad, can we just talk about something, *anything,* else?'

'Fine …' said Maxwell, frustrated that Jack was still not grown-up enough to engage in such a conversation with him.

'I spoke to Philip Cohen last week. He said his son had just started at the *Independent*. Said there might be an opening if you were interested ...'

'Well, when you speak to him next you can tell him I'm not,' answered Jack, eager as ever to shut down any of his father's interference when it came to his career choices.

'So that's it? You're just going to throw away your degree because one bad thing happened?'

'I'm not throwing it away, Dad. I'm teaching, and look, this month I start teaching an adult creative writing course,' said Jack, burying his hand in his brown work satchel that was resting on his lap and pulling out one of his leaflets advertising the class.

Trying to seek his father's approval in some small measure, Jack placed the small blue flyer down on the wooden bed table beside a plastic container of white grapes and a copy of *The Tattooist of Auschwitz*.

'But you were a journalist at a national newspaper!' Maxwell ranted, angrily picking up the flyer to scan over it, unable to bury his frustration.

'And once you had private healthcare! Things change, Dad!'

'I still have private healthcare! It was your mother that made me go to A & E! It's not my fault they won't let me leave!'

Whilst Maxwell continued to rant, Jack felt

the vibration of his mobile phone ringing in his trouser pocket, the buzzing sound causing further frustration to Maxwell, but much in the way of relief to Jack.

Still sitting in his chair, Jack reached his hand into the pocket of his smart work trousers and dug out his mobile phone. He looked down at the screen and felt his heart miss a beat when he saw the name *Jess* displayed across the screen. It had been the best part of a month since they had had any form of contact. Although unsure as to why Jess should be calling him, Jack was secretly relieved to be finally hearing from her.

'Sorry, Dad, it's Jess. I should really take this,' said Jack, springing up from his chair and leaving the bay before his father had a chance to ask any prying questions.

Standing outside the entrance to his father's ward Jack inhaled a deep breath, preparing himself for his conversation with Jess. He knew that it was important to play it cool, he mustn't come across as too needy or desperate. However, if she was calling to tell Jack how much she missed him, then he wasn't too proud to offer a grovelling apology.

Jack swiped the screen to answer, lifted the phone to his ear and began to pace down the long corridor.

'Hello …'

'You need to get over here now!' Jess barked.

Although Jess had said what Jack had hoped to hear, her tone wasn't exactly loving.

'Is everything okay?' he asked hesitantly.

'No, Jack, everything is not okay. Your idiot friend Simon has just left!'

Simon – journalist for a national newspaper, good friend and former colleague of Jack's, his work taking him all over the world, but mainly the Middle East. Simon was the proud owner of a black miniature poodle that went by the name of Betsy. Betsy was quite possibly the oldest living dog known to man. With a skeletal frame, few teeth and little hearing, she also possessed an odd smell that was not too dissimilar to that of excrement, but Simon loved Betsy, and often left her in the care of Jack when he went away on working trips abroad.

'Oh shit, sorry, Jess, I forgot—'

'How could you not tell him you'd moved out!'

'I'm sorry, it slipped my mind. You should've just given him my gran's address.'

'I did, he said he didn't have time, he dropped her off en route to the airport. You need to get over here now, Jack and take this dog—'

'Okay, okay ... I'm at the hospital right now, but I'll get there as soon as I can.' Jack held his breath, wondering if telling Jess he was at the hospital might alarm her into some concern or sympathy.

'JACK, I DON'T CARE WHERE YOU ARE, YOU NEED TO GET OVER HERE NOW!' screamed Jess, making it clear that she was unwilling to engage in any kind of mind games, before hanging up the phone.

'Jess …? Jess …?'

Carly pushed the heavy book trolley along Violet Ward's corridor. She had been volunteering as a member of the hospital's Books for Bed team ever since the passing of her mother. Wanting to give something back to the hospital for all they had done, but with no money to spare, Carly took on the role of volunteering. Every week she would stroll the hospital wards with a trolley full of books, selling them on to patients at rock-bottom prices.

Carly loved working at the hospital. The surroundings made her feel close to her mother somehow and she enjoyed the interaction with the patients. She also enjoyed the easy access to the many, many books that were donated to the hospital, and above all she loved being away from Craig.

Carly was usually joined by one of the other volunteers, but tonight she found herself on her own. As she struggled along with the heavy book trolley, she turned into Bay C and caught the attention of Maxwell Lewis, who was sitting up in his bed waiting for his son's return. Maxwell remembered Carly fondly from a few days previously and lit up at the sight of her.

'Hello, Carly. How lovely to see you again. How are you?'

'Hiya, Max. I'm well, thanks. How you getting on with *The Tattooist*?' asked Carly, pointing at the book on Max's table.

'Nothing more than a poorly written biography, I'm afraid!'

'What!' exclaimed Carly, sitting herself down on the vacant visitor's chair next to Maxwell's bed, picking up the book and looking down at it. 'I really enjoyed it. Were you not just a little bit moved by the love story of Lale and Gita?'

'No, I can't say I was. All a bit too soft and fluffy for my liking. I think it was more aimed at the young-adult market.'

'Hmm, can Holocaust love stories ever be too fluffy?' questioned Carly, before placing the book back down on the table.

Maxwell laughed lightly at Carly's response, enjoying her easy company.

'Have you got anything with a bit more of a punch?' he asked.

Carly raised herself from the chair, careful to give a wide birth to Maxwell's catheter tube dangling over the side of the bed, and walked back over to her book trolley.

'Er, well, if World Wars are your thing we just got a copy of *Birdsong* donated today?'

'No, read it … what else?'

Silence fell for a moment as Carly turned her back on Maxwell and bent to inspect the trolley.

'*Bravo Two Zero*?'

'I think I've endured enough torture already this week!' joked Maxwell, pointing towards the full bag of urine attached to the side of his bed.

'Ha, that's a shame, otherwise I would have suggested *Fifty Shades of Grey*. We have about five copies lying about!' joked Carly, lifting one of them.

'You know, I've never read it! Does it live up to the hype?'

'Well it sold over 90 million copies. Why don't you give it a try? Allow your horizons to be broadened in a whole new way!' said Carly through a cheeky giggle.

'And how much will the broadening of one's horizons set me back?'

'For you, Max, let's call it 50p.'

'Go on then. Although I'm not sure what my son will say!' replied Maxwell with a coy smile.

Carly laughed softly as she approached Maxwell's bed with the book. She waited as he sorted through the loose change on his bed table and counted out 50p to hand over to her.

'I see you fancy yourself as the next best-seller yourself there, Max,' said Carly, pointing towards the blue flyer promoting Jack's creative writing class.

'Oh goodness, no. My son, he's teaching the course.'

'Well, he sounds like a smart cookie!' said Carly, at which Maxwell displayed a pleased smile. Although his son's recent career choices frustrated him, he was proud of Jack's intelligence and achievements.

'Here, you should take it. You're clearly well read, you might well enjoy it!' suggested Maxwell, handing the flyer to Carly, doing his bit in the way of recruiting students.

Carly accepted the small flyer from Maxwell and looked over it.

Indeed Maxwell was right, Carly was well read and writing did interest her greatly, for she could write. So well in fact that her talent had once won her a place to read English at Cambridge University. But Carly hadn't written anything for a while, some ten years in fact. It wasn't that she ever fell out of love with writing, but as the years ticked by, she struggled to find inspiration as well as the time.

Creative Writing for Adults – Every Monday, Wanstead House, 7.30 p.m. – 9.30 p.m.

Now that Pinky Bingo had cut back her hours, Carly was free on Monday evenings. Though so far she hadn't informed Craig and May ... Well, now the class would give her an easy excuse to be away from the house.

'Thanks, Max .... Enjoy your book,' said Carly, keeping her eyes on the leaflet in her hand as she veered back towards the book trolley.

'See you soon, Carly.'

Carly folded the leaflet and slipped it into the back pocket of her jeans. She flashed Maxwell a sweet grateful smile and made her way out of the bay, turning right.

Seconds later, Jack entered from the left, fresh off the phone from Jess. Feeling anxious, he hurried towards his father's bed.

'Sorry, Dad, I've got to head off,' he said, bending down to the floor to reach for his work satchel.

'But you've only just got here!' protested Maxwell, disappointed that Jack couldn't bring himself to spend more than fifteen minutes in his company before finding an excuse to leave.

'I know, I know. I'm sorry, but there's something I need to go and take care of.'

Jack threw his satchel over his shoulder and leaned forward to give his father a kiss on the top of his bald head, but before his lips made contact, he caught sight of the copy of *Fifty Shades of Grey* on his father's table.

'Seriously, Dad?' Jack picked up the book in disbelief and faint disgust.

'What? It sold 90 million copies, you know!' replied Maxwell.

'Hmm, well, you can keep your findings to yourself on that one,' said Jack as he put the book down. 'See you soon, Dad.' He scurried out of the ward, not looking back or even waiting for his father to respond.

It was nine o'clock by the time Jack arrived at what was once his home, now solely occupied by his former fiancée, Jess. He pulled his black Mini Cooper into what was once his designated parking spot outside the ground-floor flat and could see that the living-room light was on. He sat with the engine running for a moment as he willed himself to get out of the car.

He knew from Jess's tone that he was unlikely to be welcomed in for a glass of wine and a flirty conversation, but he figured if he could exude just the right amount of charm and remorse, he might be able to wriggle himself in past the front door, and thus, back into Jess's affections.

Jack took one last deep breath, turned off the car's ignition and climbed out.

Standing in front of the small block of flats he felt nervous. Reaching to press the number 7 on the metal keypad in front of him, he noticed that his hand was shaking, which wasn't like him. He soon heard the sound of the heavy metal door unlocking.

Jack pushed the door open and strode inside into the dimly lit corridor trying to fool himself into oozing confidence. Before he had reached the brown front door of the flat, he heard it open, then heard the sound of Jess's voice.

'Hiya!' she called down the corridor as Jack approached.

When he got to the flat's front door Jess had disappeared.

Jack stood in the familiar doorway of what had once been his home, next to a large yellow bag of dog biscuits and a red and cream fluffy dog bed.

The smell of floral-scented candles filled his nostrils, a smell he had once found nauseating, it now the comforting smell of a home where he was no longer welcome.

'Actually, it's good that you're here,' said Jess, appearing in the hallway, her tone decidedly softer than it had been only an hour ago, flooding Jack with a sense of hope.

'Oh really? Me too, actually. How've you ...' Enchanted by the sight of Jess, Jack trailed off. It was the first time he had laid eyes on her in almost a month and he had forgotten how beautiful she was.

She was dressed in her usual lilac silk kimono, tied tightly around her small waist. She was in her relaxed, just-got-home-from-work state. It was a routine Jack knew well: Jess undressing the moment she stepped through the door, slipping into her kimono, getting comfy to eat her dinner and watch TV. Jack smiled to himself, relishing the fact that she obviously still felt comfortable enough in his presence for him to see her like that. Her dark wavy hair framed her round face perfectly, her make-up highlighting her delicate features.   Jack's gaze fell to the large brown cardboard box she was holding.

'Here,' she said, thrusting the box at him, her brashness snapping him out of his trance.

Jack took hold of the box, surprised by its

weight.

'What is this?' he asked, tilting his head to peer inside.

'Just the last of your stuff,' Jess replied casually, her words cutting through Jack as he held in his arms the symbol of their dissolved relationship.

He stood and stared into Jess's large, doe-like brown eyes, searching for the kindness and softness he had once known and finding only hardness.

'Wait there, I'll get the dog,' said Jess, just as the clink of what sounded like a glass came from the kitchen at the end of the hallway.

'Have you got someone here?' asked Jack, his feet moving forward of their own will, directing him straight to the kitchen.

'Jack, wait there!' Jess ordered, willing him to stay put; but Jack chose to ignore her, forcibly pushing open the kitchen door and freezing at the sight of Elliott Adams.

Elliott Adams, wrapped in a black fluffy bathrobe, stood broad and proud at the kitchen counter.

Jess had worked as Elliott's paralegal for the past five years. There had always been an undeniable chemistry between the pair, with Jess often working late and engaging in long lunches with the 'hilarious' Elliot. Jack had often wondered if they were more than just colleagues, but because his own behaviour was anything but faithful he'd felt it would be hypocritical to accuse Jess of infidelity, even if he did have his suspicions.

Elliott Adams was sickeningly handsome. It bothered Jack immensely that Elliott, at forty-one, had maintained a full head of curly blond hair. The only flaw on his perfectly chiselled face was a long vertical scar on the left side of his forehead, the result of an old rugby injury, or at least that was the tale Elliot had enjoyed telling Jack; when he had last had the displeasure of Elliott's company at his firm's summer barbecue.

 Boot studs had trampled over Elliott's face, or so the story went, ripping apart the skin on his forehead. There'd been a lot of blood, agonising pain, and then, mustering all his courage, Elliott had got back on his feet, his legs trembling as he steered forward, speedily enough to score the winning try of the match.

Jack remembered Jess's face that day, awestruck at Elliot's inspirational story, it leaving Jack a tad emasculated, his contempt for Elliott and his detestation of all things athletic rising to a nauseating level.

'Hiya, Jack mate!' said Elliott, greeting him as if he were an old friend he was so pleased to see and brazenly pouring himself a large glass of white wine.

Having followed Jack into the kitchen, Jess now stood beside him, in her hand Betsy's bright pink dog lead, Betsy at her feet. Jack looked at

Jess in shock and disbelief.

'Is this why you wanted me to come by? So you could parade *him* – *this* in front of me!' he yelled.

'Seriously, Jack, don't be under any illusion that I would *ever* want you here!'

'Come on, Jack mate, really there's no need to get upset,' said Elliott in what Jack felt to be a condescending manner, leaving him unsure as to whether Elliot was trying to pacify or anger him.

'Upset! Oh no, I'm not upset, Elliott—'

'Sorry, what did you think was going to happen, Jack? That I was going to invite you in for dinner? What? Open a bottle of wine while we mull over old times?' interrupted Jess.

Jack turned back to Elliott and scanned him from top to bottom. He could see thick fair chest hair escaping from Elliot's robe, the glimpse of his naked body causing a vile sick feeling in Jack's stomach. Elliott's long supple fingers stroked the stem of his wine glass; with that casual gesture he was showing no sign of discomfort.

At the sight of Elliott's feet Jack was angered even further. Each foot rested inside a large yellow Homer Simpson head-shaped slipper. The slippers belonged to Jack, a recent birthday gift from Grandma Barb, the left one displaying a small faded tomato ketchup stain at the front, confirming that they were indeed his.

'Well I didn't think I was going to walk in

on your boss wearing my slippers! Yes, my slippers! I mean, what the hell! I've been looking for those. Funny how you forgot to box them up! I mean really? What kind of monster just gives away another man's slippers!' Jack shouted, and noticed that Betsy was cowering.

'Oh I don't know, Jack, maybe the kind of monster that's had it up to here with you!' Jess yelled back, unable to keep her composure any longer.

'Oh right, because living with me was such a chore for you!'

'Well, now you mention it, Jack, finding a pair of knickers belonging to whatever fucking whore you brought into our home wasn't exactly the stuff of fairy tales!' screamed Jess, her explicit language shocking Jack.

Jess seldom swore, usually opting for a more eloquent way of expressing her anger. Jack watched as her cheeks flushed a light shade of pink; she was clearly embarrassed at not being able to keep a tighter lid on her emotions in front of her new love interest.

'Come on, Jack mate, I think it's time you left, don't you?' interjected Elliott, slowly manoeuvring himself closer to Jack, his mere presence infuriating Jack even more.

'I will leave when I am ready, Elliott, and I'll tell you another thing, I will not be leaving without my slippers!'

A silence fell in the kitchen as Jack stood and stared Elliott hard in the eye, tacitly ordering him to remove the slippers from his feet.

Elliott knew that, although he might be losing this particular battle, he was the one winning the war, and, maybe, the very least he could do for the lesser mortal in front of him was to give him back his slippers.

He slid them off his feet, slowly bent to the floor and picked them up, placing them inside the cardboard box held in Jack's arms.

Elliott nodded at Jack in a silent truce, signalling that he now owed him no more.

Jack turned back to Jess and untucked a hand from under his box to gently take the dog lead from her hand.

'Come on, Betsy, let us leave the flat of ill repute!' said Jack with great outward confidence, looking Jess in the eye.

Jess looked away sheepishly, unable to hide her discomfort as Jack walked away with his slippers, and Betsy in tow.

CHAPTER 4:

Carly tucked her pink work T-shirt into her snug black trousers. She took a look at herself in her full-length bedroom mirror and tugged gently at her high ponytail, making sure it sat securely where she wanted it.

Satisfied with her appearance, she lifted her small black handbag from the edge of the bed and carefully pulled out the small blue flyer that had been given to her at the hospital by Maxwell. She scanned the flyer and glanced at her watch. It was 6.30 p.m. She would usually leave for work about now, but tonight it wasn't Pinky Bingo she was heading to.

Carly heard the front door bang shut and the murmur of conversation: sounds that signalled Craig's return home after a long day's work. Normally she would leave the house the moment he was back. They told themselves it was all a matter of convenience. Carly would spend much of the day at home tending to May and whatever other jobs needed doing, while Craig went to work. Then when he was back he would take over. She would head out, knowing that May was not alone, and without having to make small talk with a man she no longer felt any affection for, often returning long after Craig had fallen asleep.

Although her urge to flee from the house was strong, Carly still felt a strong sense of guilt.
They were a family, the three of them, they had been for a long time, and she was worried something was fundamentally wrong with her.

Of course, the cut in her hours would create a dent in the family's finances, but if she was a normal person she would see that it had its advantages, namely the extra time she was gaining with her fiancé. Carly knew she needed to change her attitude towards Craig for the sake of her sanity and happiness.

She exhaled a large sigh and tugged at her T-shirt, lifting it up over her head. She figured she could tell Craig and May that her shift had been cancelled today, maybe a mix-up with the rota or something?

Carly tossed her T-shirt onto the bed just as the bedroom door swung open.

Craig walked in, one hand fondling his stomach under his grubby work T-shirt.

'All right, you off?' he said, not bothering to make eye contact with Carly, instead lifting his T-shirt and extracting a large piece of blue fluff from his belly button. Craig held the fluff between his fingers and brought it up close to his face. After inspecting it for a few seconds he sniffed it before flicking it to the floor.

Carly looked on with her usual silent disgust. Not feeling the need to doubt her decision any longer she retrieved her work T-shirt from the bed.

'Yeah, I'm going now,' she answered, slipping on her T-shirt. 'There's some dinner in the oven for you whenever you're ready.'

Craig lay down on the bed fully clothed and dug his finger into his ear, wiggling it around inside. Carly watched as he pulled out a large golden lump of wax and peered at it in wonder with his small eyes.

'Craig!' she snapped as she tucked her T-shirt back into her trousers.

'What?'

'I said—'

'Yeah, yeah, dinner in the oven. What time you back tonight?' asked Craig, still inspecting the large lump of ear wax held between his fingers.

'Usual time ...' answered Carly, looking away from Craig, worried he might be able to see through her dishonesty.

Carly wished she could miss Craig when they were apart, or feel the urge to hurry home in the hope of spending a few precious minutes with him before they drifted off to sleep and their days began all over again, but it seemed that no matter how hard Carly pushed herself, nothing came.

'Okay, well I'm off then,' said Carly, grabbing her handbag, her voice downcast.

Craig flicked his ear wax onto the bedroom floor and looked up at Carly.

'Bye.'

'See ya,' said Carly, scurrying out of the room.

Jack felt a little woozy.

The heating was on very high in the empty carpeted bar area of Wanstead House. Jack could feel himself burning up under his thin grey jumper and shirt combo as he struggled to take in the relentless drivel of Beryl, Wanstead House's resident busybody.

Beryl was a mere five foot two tall and had a long pointed nose and thin, pink-painted lips. Her grey hair was styled cleverly in short ruffled spikes in an effort to disguise her scalp: this the first time Jack had come across a woman with hair so thin it was practically see-through.

'Now there's a first-aid box behind the bar should you need it but our current first-aider only works until 5 p.m. so in the event of a medical emergency you may need to perform your own first aid. Are you a registered first-aider, Jack?' Beryl turned her face sharply towards Jack. She had the distinct feeling he was no longer paying attention.

'Um no, no, I'm afraid not,' he answered, jolted into alertness by her sudden question.

'Oh dear,' said Beryl, bringing a hand up to cover her mouth as a look of deep anguish swept over her.

'I shouldn't worry, Beryl, it's creative writing, not flame-throwing for beginners. Now if there's nothing else, I should really start setting up now …'

'Hmm. Do you need me to go over the fire-assembly points again?'

'No, no, that won't be necessary!' Jack replied sharply, walking away from Beryl, so desperate to escape he no longer cared about being polite.

He reached his classroom and pushing the door shut on ajar looked around him. There was a large window on one side, but unlike his classroom at school there were no colourful displays of pupils' work decorating the walls, which were bare, except for a small white board. As he gazed out at the long rectangular table and its plastic chairs he felt irate and his mind cast itself back to the bygone era when evenings after work were spent drinking in fancy London bars or overpriced pubs with colleagues who went out there into the world and experienced war and political conflict. Now here he was, alone in an empty council-run building, about to help others to be creative while he sat back and observed.

Jack missed the excitement of the news desk, the adrenalin rush of never quite knowing what the day would bring. But whenever he thought of the news desk, he couldn't help thinking of Peter. His friend's image would often come into his mind, filling him with such sadness that he'd become an expert at banishing the image. Jack tried to banish it now, but there wasn't much to distract him in the empty room. He looked up at the clock and seeing that he still had a full half an hour before the class was scheduled to begin decided to focus on preparing himself, having so far failed to even look through the register to familiarise himself with his students' names.

Jack sat down at the table and reaching into his brown satchel pulled out a green cardboard folder of papers and began to go through them.

'Come on through,' he heard Beryl say through the partly closed door.

Jack sat perfectly still in the vain hope that it wasn't his classroom she was about to invade. He tuned his hearing in to the sound of footsteps and willed the sound to fade away.

The door creaked open and he looked up in dismay as a short, tubby African lady, displaying all the obvious signs of Down's syndrome, walked in. She looked middle-aged, but was dressed in a rather childlike manner in a bright pink Puffa jacket, her hair tied in high bunches. Her large dark brown eyes beamed towards Jack through her thick square glasses.

Certain she'd made a mistake and would soon be gone, Jack felt a rush of relief.

'Oh sorry, the basic adult literacy is being held upstairs,' he said, helpfully pointing towards the stairs.

'Oh no, Jack, this is Mandy, she signs up every term,' piped Beryl, following close behind her.

'For creative writing?' blinked Jack, slightly bemused.

'Yes, Jack, read your register. Now, Mandy, do you want to sit here at the end next to Jack? He'll take very good care of you, won't you, Jack?'

Jack frantically searched through the few names on his register until he spotted Mandy's. Next to it were the letters *SEN*, not something Jack would have expected outside his school setting. Mandy had Special Educational Needs.

'Er … yes, yes of course, please, Mandy, do take a seat,' he said. As Mandy made herself comfortable Beryl left the room.

'Where's Janine?' asked Mandy resentfully.

'My sources tell me she's retired to a French chateau, so you're stuck with me this term, I'm afraid.' Replied Jack, trying his best to ease Mandy's concerns.

Mandy gave him a withering look, displeased with Janine's replacement.

'So, Mandy. You're rather early …' said Jack, making his best effort at small talk.

'My dad dropped me off. He doesn't like me to be late.'

'Quite. Well seeing as you're so very early, Mandy, how would you like me to issue you a job?'

Mandy nodded her head, seemingly happy

to be handed such responsibility by her new teacher.

'Right, I have some papers here, Mandy. If you could go round and put one down at every place I'd be ever so grateful,' said Jack with great kindness, a quality he often kept well hidden from public view.

By 7.35 p.m. there were only seven people from the list of ten in attendance but Jack decided to get things underway.

'Okay, well now is probably a good time to start,' Jack announced to his class in the confident, proud manner he was always able to exude when addressing his pupils. 'So my name is Jack and let me start by welcoming you all to our first session of creative writing!'
Despite the deathly silence and the gormless stares he continued. 'Okay, so I'm afraid before we have the chance to get into the good stuff I just need to run through a few housekeeping rules. Can I ask, has anybody attended a course at Wanstead House before?'

Mandy shot up her hand enthusiastically and Jack, grateful that somebody was willing to interact with him, smiled at her.

He heard the creak of the door.

'Sorry to interrupt, Jack ...' said Beryl. 'You've got a latecomer.'

Jack turned to Beryl and at the sight of the student beside her froze.

It was Carly Hughes.

Their eyes locked as they both absorbed the surprise.

'Carly?' uttered Jack in disbelief.

Dressed casually in a black jacket, Carly might not have looked as glamorous as she had the last time they had met, but she still looked effortlessly beautiful, if a little flustered, her pink cheeks bright against her pale skin, the result of rushing in from the cold into the well- heated building.

Carly looked around the room of strange faces. As if she wasn't already nervous about turning up to such a group, now there was the embarrassment of facing Jack Lewis. Carly couldn't understand what he was doing here; on a Monday evening, in a run-down council building, teaching the basics of his craft to a bunch of nobodies.

A week had barely passed since they had last laid eyes on each other, and now here they were again, in the most unexpected of places.

'I, er … I don't remember seeing your name on here, Carly …' spluttered Jack, picking up the register and frantically looking up and down it, not believing for one second that he would have missed Carly's name, had it been there.

'No, it won't be. We've been over this, Jack. Carly's the lady that only signed up for the class this morning,' Beryl said curtly, convinced now that Jack hadn't been listening to a word she had said earlier.

Close to her chest, in her left hand, Carly was clutching a mint-green notepad. The hand sparkled with a large diamond ring. The sight of it knocked the wind out of Jack: he didn't recall seeing that statement on Carly's hand the last time they had met, but then again he was stoned, so maybe it had passed him by.

'I, er, I'm not sure I'm in the right place ...' said Carly, turning to Beryl in desperation, wanting nothing more than to run out of the building and as far away from Jack as possible.

'No, no, you're in the right place. Creative writing, this is it,' said Beryl in a reassuring tone.

'Yes, yes, you're in the right place. Exactly the right place,' said Jack as he looked into Carly's glittering grey-blue eyes, silently willing her to stay.

Carly smiled tightly at Jack and looked away, spotting a vacant chair at a far corner of the table. She hurried towards it as the thin middle-aged black lady in the next seat gave her a welcoming smile. She slid the notepad onto the table then reluctantly removed her jacket, placing it on the back of her chair before finally sitting herself down.

Carly kept her gaze glued to the notepad in front of her as Jack took note of her attire.
He could see she was dressed for work, but not in a smart, tailored work shirt. He couldn't quite make out what the logo on her pink T-shirt read,

but he could tell that it was the kind of uniform given out by a large company, the type that thrived on the cheap labour of loyal staff.

'Um, right, okay … so now it seems we're all here, if you want to take a look at the leaflet in front of you it should give you all the information you'll need in the unfortunate event of a fire or a fatal paper cut,' Jack announced, trying to suppress his feelings of shock.

Jack's classroom was the quietest it had been for a while, with all eight of his students sitting with their heads down as they scratched frantically in their notebooks. After an hour and a half of housekeeping rules, a rundown of the course syllabus and meek introductions, it had finally been time for Jack to put his students to work and have them do some writing. The assignment was simple enough. In the centre of the large rectangular table Jack had placed down a small, half-empty bottle of Jim Beam whisky, the task: Write about the bottle. Jack had already provided the class with an example, a mediocre poem he had penned earlier in the day on his lunchbreak.

Jack peered over at Carly.

She'd barely looked up at him, even when introducing herself to the class. She'd kept it brief, giving little away about herself, much to the frustration of Jack, who was desperate to know more about her.

The only notable noise in the room was that of Kevin's heavy breathing. Kevin was in the later stages of middle age and about two stone heavier than he ought to be, the extra weight no doubt contributing to the loud heavy breathing that was driving Jack silently insane.

With only fifteen minutes of the class left to go, Jack was prompted back into action.

'Okay, we only have about a quarter of an hour, so would anyone like to read what they've —'

Mandy shot her hand up in the air. Although Jack wasn't that curious about what Mandy had managed her enthusiasm was welcome, just as it had been earlier.

'Yes, of course, please go ahead, Mandy,' he said.

Mandy pushed back her chair and climbed to her feet, standing proudly at the front of the class, displaying zero signs of discomfort or nerves, a quality Jack couldn't help but envy.

'"Oh I love this bottle,"' announced Mandy with great deliberation as she stared intently down at the paper in her hands. '"It is glass and it is shiny and holds my drink on hot days. Oh, how I love the bottle,"' Mandy finished with a huge beaming smile, proud of the few words she had managed to piece together.

Worried her reading would be met with silence, Jack brought his hands together to clap, at which the rest of the class joined in.

SAMANTHA KAY

'That's lovely, Mandy, very well done ... very ... descriptive. Yes, shiny, and ... glass, yes, very good!' said Jack over the dying sound of applause, doing his very best to give Mandy some positive feedback on her carefully constructed sentences.

'Good, would anyone else like to read what they've written?' said Jack, purposely looking over towards Carly who was still keeping her gaze fixed firmly on her notebook as she nervously bit down on the cheap biro held in her hand.

'I don't mind reading,' said the black lady next to Carly, much to her relief.

'Yes, great, go ahead, Margery,' said Jack, doing an excellent job of hiding his disappointment at Carly's reluctance to volunteer.

'"What to say about a bottle ..."' began Margery, raising her open hand with its unusually long fingers to the bottle in front of her. '"Here it sits, in the middle of the table, as we all search our heads for what to say. I'm not really much of a whisky drinker myself, opting more for gin. But I like its size, just small enough that I could pop it in my handbag without it being too heavy ...." That's all I've got.'

Once more Jack brought his hands together, using the applause to give him time to decide on what feedback to give a truly dire effort at creativity.

'Great, you're on the money there, Margie, just

78

big enough for the handbag! I like your think-ing!' said Jack, genuinely struggling to think of anything more positive to say as Margery smiled proudly to herself.

Jack looked back at the clock. With only five more minutes of class left, he knew there was only enough time for one more reading, and he knew exactly whose he wanted it to be.

'I think we have time for one more—'

Clive raised his arm and opened his mouth to speak. Although it was only the first lesson, Jack had already decided that he didn't like Clive, the self-proclaimed inventor of the written word. Clive had used his introduction to brag about the historical novel he was

writing, whilst continually brushing his hand through his thick mane of floppy white hair. Clive had also felt the need to inform everyone that he was in possession of a PhD, a fact that Jack honestly couldn't have cared any less about if he'd tried.

Before Clive had a chance to volunteer himself Jack cut in.

'Carly? Would you like to read?'

Believing she had succeeded in making her-self invisible, Carly was caught off guard. She looked up at Jack, her pale cheeks turning pink, her mouth open in shock.

'Er, I dunno if I should. I think I may have mis-understood the task, if I'm honest,' said Carly, her voice small and nervous, on the point of breaking.

'That's okay, even if you have, it doesn't mat-ter,' said Jack, keeping his tone uncharacteristic-ally soft.

Carly inhaled a deep breath and looked down at her scrawly handwriting. It had been so long since she had written anything of creative value and even longer since she had been willing to share it with anybody.

Carly began tapping her foot, the sign of her obvious discomfort making Jack feel guilty for putting her on the spot.

'Okay,' mumbled Carly, before clearing her throat nervously.

'"The room was dark, with only the dim light and hum of noise coming from the television in the corner of the living room. She wasn't aware of the time, unable to remember when she had last stopped to check. Nor could she remem-ber when she had last showered or changed her clothes as she struggled to recall when last she had even cared.

'"She stared blankly into the distance as tears poured from her eyes and she replayed the whole sorry saga in her head for the one thousandth time. It was seconds, mere seconds she had left her for. Just a few short spurts of time: how could so much have happened, how could so much have changed? She reached for the half-drunk bottle that lay next to her on the couch and stroked its glass as she wailed aloud, all alone. She unscrewed the cap and lifted the rim to her mouth, taking a large gulp, the liquid filling her with a familiar warmth and comfort, flooding a deep unbearable void."'

Relieved that the agony she had just endured was over, Carly relaxed and looked past the baffled faces and up at Jack. There was a huge grin on his face.

Jack was already aware of how talented Carly was and he felt reassured by the reminder that Carly's talent was still burning somewhere deep inside her, even if it did pain her to light the match.

'It's not really about the bottle though, is it?' said Kevin, unable to comprehend what he had just heard.

'Well, no, not in a physical sense. It's about the role that I guess the contents of the bottle are playing in the midst of this person's tragedy. The whisky offering a form of comfort in some small measure, but like I said, I may not have understood what you were looking for exactly,' explained Carly, darting an anxious glance at Jack, who was surprised by her lack of confidence: it a quality he failed to recognise.

'I thought it was brilliant. It sounded like the opening to a novel. You should carry on with it, see where it leads?' Jack said reassuringly.

'Thank you,' said Carly, so quietly it was almost said in mime, her eyes shyly darting back to her notebook.

Carly sat in her silver Ford Fiesta, parked just round the corner from Wanstead House, doing her best to wind down after the last two hours.

She leaned her head back on the headrest and let out a loud groan of frustration, her mind unable to concentrate on anything other than Jack Lewis. The last Carly heard, albeit some ten years ago, Jack had secured a job at one of the national newspapers, his ultimate dream. Carly knew that, if she had managed to get herself the fancy Cambridge degree she had so desired, there was no way she would be spending her evenings teaching a class of nobodies.

She couldn't shift her embarrassment at being seen by Jack in her work attire, and she wondered if his presence at the class was the universe's way of playing some sick joke on her, confronting her with Jack as payback for lying to Craig and May about her whereabouts.

Carly glanced down at the time on the phone in her hand: 9.45 p.m.

Usually when she worked a late shift she wouldn't return home until around 12.30 a.m. and she was eager to keep up the pretence that tonight was just another ordinary night at work. Of course she could just return home early if she wanted to; tell May and Craig that the bingo hall was quiet tonight and she'd been allowed to leave early, but that would mean spending extra time with Craig; an option Carly wasn't willing to consider.

The evening was a rather chilly one and Carly could feel her feet, stationary in the foot-well of her car, becoming cold. With no plan for how to kill the next couple of hours, Carly closed her eyes and let out another groan of frustration.

How is this my life? she thought. Hiding in a car on a dark cold night being better than returning home?

It was then that Carly's thoughts were interrupted by a sudden tap on her driver's window. She jumped, startled by the unexpected sound, and turned her head to see Jack peering through the window.

'What are you doing?' he asked, the pane of glass between them muffling his voice as his face displayed a look of confusion.

Carly turned on the car's ignition and pressed the button next to her to lower the window.

'Haven't you got a home to go to?'

'I was just ... killing some time ... I er, I heard that there was traffic. Just thought I'd wait out here for a bit.'

'Okay, well if you're not in a rush to get home, there's a pub just down the road.'

'Yeah, okay, thanks ... I'll give it a try,' replied Carly, her finger on the window button, ready to close it again.

'Sorry, I think you've misunderstood me, Miss Hughes. That was me asking you to join me for a drink, as long as it doesn't interfere with your

plans to sleep in your car, of course?' said Jack before Carly had a chance to close the window on
him.

Carly could feel herself squirming. She wasn't
against the idea of having a drink with Jack;
if anything, she was glad of the chance to find
out why he'd ended up teaching a creative writing class. However, an intimate drink with the
old boyfriend who had once known her so well
would surely mean her having to divulge all, or
at least something about her current life, a conversation Carly wasn't so willing to have.

'Aren't there rules about teachers fraternising
with their students?' said Carly, trying to wriggle out of going for a drink.

'Yes, yes, I'm sure there are … So, are you
ready?' Jack said assertively, unwilling to accept
no for an answer.

The George pub sat on the corner of Wanstead
High Road and was rather busy for a chilly Monday evening. Carly sat waiting for Jack at a small
square table in the corner. At the next table an
elderly man in a flat cap and thick jumper sat
alone nursing a lonely pint.

The man flashed Carly a tight smile which she
matched. Usually she would have engaged in
small talk, but not tonight. Right now she was
feeling far too nervous to engage in anything
other than her own feelings of anxiety.

'I couldn't remember what you wanted, so I

just went with old faithful,' said Jack as he appeared in front of her and placed down two bottles of apple cider with pint glasses turned upside down on top.

'I asked for a soda and lime. I can't drink that, I'm driving.'

'Really? From what I remember it would take more than one cider to push Miss Hughes over the edge,' said Jack as he dropped his satchel to the floor and began to pour his own drink.

'Yeah, well that was a long time ago,' huffed Carly as she took hold of the glass and poured her cider into it.

'I can get you another drink, if you like,' offered Jack, secretly having remembered Carly's choice but taking it upon himself to order her something a little more interesting.

'It's fine,' said Carly, making her annoyance known as she took a large gulp of her drink.

'So ...' said Jack, not quite sure where to take the conversation. 'It's been a while ...'

'Indeed, it's been what, nine days?' said Carly, taking another sip from her drink.

Jack laughed inwardly and nodded his head, for in actual fact it really hadn't been all that long at all.

'You know what I mean. It's been what, eleven, maybe twelve years now?' he said, narrowing his eyes slightly, counting back the years in his head.

Carly looked down at the table, nodded her

head gently and began nervously tapping her glass with her index finger.

'So … is that the entertainment company you mentioned? The one you work for?' asked Jack, glancing at the Pinky Bingo logo on Carly's T-shirt and trying not to use his default judgemental tone.

Carly gave a nod and a thin smile, feeling pure humiliation.

'So you work at a bingo hall, and you write like that?'

'All right, Simon Cowell! How I write shouldn't come as any great surprise to you.'

Carly was right. The skill with which she had written hadn't come as a great surprise to Jack. He was fully aware of how talented a writer she was, but what intrigued him was what she was doing working at a bingo hall.

'Do you enjoy it? Working there?' he asked, unable to fire back a quick witticism of his own, yearning to find out more.

'It's okay. What about you? Are you still at the paper or do you teach full-time?' asked Carly, equally curious.

Carly's question hung in the atmosphere between them, she blissfully unaware that such a simple question had ignited a flame of horror and sadness inside Jack. Fortunately, these days he had become a seasoned pro at pushing his feelings deep down under the surface, squashing and cramping them tightly into a compartment of his being where nobody but him could see how much pain he was suffering.

'No, no, Miss Hughes, no diverting away from the subject. I want to hear all about this Bingo company you work for,' replied Jack, outwardly so relaxed that Carly had no reason to believe he was feeling anything other than deep interest in his one-time teenage sweetheart.

'There's really not that much to tell. I just work there a few evenings a week.'

'What do you do in-between?'

'I care for my soon-to-be mother-in-law. She has MS. Her son—'

'Your ... intended?' Jack asked, nodding towards Carly's left hand, wanting confirmation of the obvious blinding fact that it was her engagement ring.

Carly nodded and took a fleeting glance at her ring, choosing to ignore the feelings of entrapment her newest piece of jewellery brought her.

'We care for her between us and we have district nurses coming to the house. So I gave up working full-time last year to be at home more.'

As Carly spoke, Jack could sense the sad undertone. No one knew more than he did what a brilliant mind Carly had. He thought back to the fiercely intelligent girl who had a whole world of opportunity before her, and failed to recognise the woman now living only a fraction of the kind of life she deserved.

'So what were you doing before you went part-time?'

'Christ, what do you want? A copy of my CV!' said Carly, feeling defensive at what felt like a barrage of personal questions being fired at her.

'What can I say! I'm a seasoned journalist. It's in my nature to take a healthy interest in people,' chuckled Jack, not in the slightest bit put off by Carly's discomfort as he took a casual sip from his drink.

'I did lots of things. I did a lot of telesales work, double glazing, photocopiers and fax machines, phones. Then I was a receptionist for a building company, then I did a short stint selling advertising space online, which didn't last all that long. Then I got a job doing admin for a recruitment company. Then I took a bizarre leap of faith and decided to become a florist for a couple of years.'

'Florist? Creative? Sounds fun …'

'Trust me, it wasn't. Long hours, crap money, freezing cold, on your feet all day. So I packed it in after a while and then got a job just doing admin for children's social services.'

'Ah the public sector. It's a laugh a minute, isn't it?' said Jack with a chuckle, referring to his own recent experiences of working in such an environment.

'It was really interesting. I learnt a lot, made some really good friends. But then it all got a bit political when they started threatening us with redundancies. So I started looking for something else and I landed this job at a media company in town.'

'Which one?' asked Jack, his interest piqued at the idea of their career paths suddenly making a crossover.

'Bloomberg.'

'Wow, one of the big boys!' said Jack, impressed, but by no means surprised, that Carly had managed to secure a job at such a prestigious company.

'Yeah. It was only working on the reception desk, but I was really excited about working there. It was amazing. State of the art offices, fish tanks on every floor, free food and drink all day. Good-looking men in sharp suits ...'

As Carly spoke with such enthusiasm about working in the City of London, Jack was reminded of his own time working there. He could relate to her excitement, the feeling of being a part of something so much bigger than yourself, something important and fast-paced, where the people worked hard and partied even harder. A world that he once slotted into so easily, at a time in his life that now felt so long ago it might have been someone else's life.

'... I worked there for a grand total of sixteen weeks. Then, my soon-to-be mother-in-law, she took a turn and well ... the rest as they say is history,' said Carly, the disappointment in her voice clear.

'That must have been tough.'

'Yeah, well, you do for family, right?'

Jack nodded his head gently in agreement, although he wasn't so sure he would be capable of such a selfless act.

'And the bingo stuff ... where did all that fit in?'

'I've worked there part-time on and off for years. I've also been an Avon lady and I was an Ann Summer's party rep for a while,' admitted Carly with a mischievous smile.

'Ha, those women that go door to door selling naughty knickers!' laughed Jack, pleased to hear that she still possessed the naughtier part of herself.

'Amongst other things ... and I do volunteer work at Queen's Hospital. That was the hospital my mum was at. I've volunteered there ever since she passed away.'

Carly had finally confirmed what Jack had suspected all along, but with such limited contact since her departure from Cambridge he hadn't had the chance to find out for sure, making his condolences well overdue.

'I er, I'm sorry ... about your mum,' Jack said sincerely, and took a sip from his cider.

Carly's mood darkened, not because of the obvious sadness that was the death of her mother, but because she'd been reminded of the love that had let her down.

'Better late than never, I suppose,' she said, pursing her lips and frowning as she stared daggers at Jack.

'Excuse me. What's that supposed to mean?' asked Jack, making it clear just how offended he was by Carly's sudden change of mood.

'You know exactly what that means,' Carly barked, taking another swig of her drink, then thudding her glass down on the table.

'Actually, no, no I don't!' said Jack, his voice high-pitched in shock at Carly's cutting reaction to his condolences. 'You left! You left one day and I never heard from you again! It was like you'd fallen off the edge of the earth or something!' he protested defensively, remembering all too well his own feelings of hurt and utter confusion at being ignored by the girlfriend he once loved so much.

'Well, apologies for that, Jack, I was a little preoccupied dealing with my dying mother if I recall! But from what I heard, it didn't take you long to find somewhere else to store your anatomy!'

Jack's mouth dropped open at the uncomfortable realisation that Carly had known all along, and he'd been wrong to assume that just because he had so quickly fallen out of touch with her, others had as well.

'That's not fair, I had no idea if you were ever coming back!' said Jack, defending the behaviour of his nineteen-year-old self while desperately trying to keep his voice down.

'I know I went quiet, I know that, but I just needed some time to deal with my situation.

I mean, we were never just fooling around, we were inseparable! I'd have thought it would have taken you longer than a week of my absence before you said yes to a blowjob from Amy bloody Shepherd!' hissed Carly, her voice a little too raised for Jack's liking, her aggressive tone causing the elderly man next to them to turn his head and face them, making no secret of his eavesdropping.

'How do you know about that?' asked Jack, wanting confirmation of the fact that Carly had known for all these years about his indiscretion with Amy Shepherd.

'It doesn't matter how I know.'

'Yes it does. Who told you?' said Jack, refusing to be fobbed off.

'Daniel Buckmaster. He messaged me.'

'Daniel Buckmaster? Daniel Buckmaster! That dweeb who had more craters in his face than the surface of the moon! So you spoke to crater-face but ignored all of my messages?' said Jack, reeling at the information he was being given.

'I never spoke to him. I never spoke to anyone. He sent me a message and I ignored it. Don't you get it? I had too much to deal with to worry about what you were getting up to!' snapped Carly, angry that Jack still failed to understand what she had had to go through.

'Do you have any idea what that time was like for me? Do you have any idea how alone I felt?' said Carly, emotion filling her voice as she reflected on an experience that had brought her such pain.

Jack sat silently, uncomfortable with Carly's heighted emotions and too ashamed to look at her.

Jack had often regrettably wondered after Carly's departure from university if he had he done enough to reach out to her. Of course, now, all these years later, as they sat across from one another, the pain in her eyes all too clear, it was obvious that he hadn't; but aside from leaving Cambridge and abandoning his own studies, what more could he have possibly had done?

Jack remained silent and fixed his gaze on the bar area behind Carly.

'I thought not,' Carly said quietly as she pushed back on her chair and climbed to her feet.

A look of panic showed on Jack's face as he helplessly watched Carly preparing to leave.

'Carly, Carly, come on, it was a long time ago. We're both different people now,' pleaded Jack, desperate for her to stay.

'Yes. Yes, we are,' replied Carly, struck by just how utterly separate their worlds had become.

'Carly, Carly!' Jack called as she hurried away from him.

He let out a loud sigh and turned to the elderly man at the next table.

'Don't worry, son. Plenty more fish in the sea,' he said with a raspy Irish accent.

Not wanting to show how devastated, not to mention embarrassed he was by Carly's exit, Jack swallowed hard and painted on a less than convincing smile for the stranger beside him.

'What are you drinking, my friend?' he asked, climbing to his feet, ready to head back to the bar.

CHAPTER 5:

Carly was in the kitchen preparing dinner while May was sound asleep next door in the living room. It was early Friday evening, and Craig was usually home from work by now. Any other girl might have been concerned about her fiancé's late return home, but rather than being worried Carly was relishing the unexpected 'Craig-free time'.

She stood over the pan of pasta boiling on the stove and secretly fantasised that something had happened to Craig; not something terrible like a death-defying car accident, but maybe he'd tripped on a pothole in the pavement and sprained his ankle just badly enough to have to spend a night, or even two, away in hospital ... Carly's mind wandered to the upcoming Monday night and how she was going to spend the time, now that the creative writing class was a no-go. The thought of Jack Lewis came back to plague her and she felt another pang of regret that she'd walked away from him. Who knew how the situation could have played out if she hadn't been so quick to fly off the handle—

She heard the hiss of sizzling water and looked down at the stove to see that the pan was over-flowing, frothy water spilling onto the electric ring and filling the air with the stench of burning.

As Carly turned down the heat, she heard the familiar sound of the front door closing and felt her heart sink with the knowledge that Craig was home. She could hear from their voices that the noise had woken May.

'Carly!' bellowed Craig from the living room.

'I'm in the kitchen!' Carly called back as she moved the overflowing pan from the stove over to the sink's draining board.

'Carly, come here, I've got news!'

Carly could hear the bubbling excitement in Craig's voice, a tone he rarely adopted. Intrigued as to what his news could be, she picked up the tea towel and wiping her hands with it went into the living room.

Craig was standing at May's bedside, still wearing his mucky work boots, his failure to re-move them before entering the house a habit that had always aggravated Carly.

'Craig, boots!' she snapped, flapping the tea towel in their general direction.

Craig bent down to untie his laces, his mood not deflated by his telling off.

'So come on then, what's this big news?' asked May, wide awake and sitting up in her bed, a smile plastered across her face, and as impatient as Carly to hear what Craig was so excited about.

'So I was at work, and I finally managed to catch Rev Thomas, and I started speaking to him about the wedding.'

Craig worked for the local council as a grave-digger, an unskilled occupation that didn't pay particularly well. Although neither Craig, Carly nor May ever attended church outside of rou-tine hatches, matches and dispatches, Craig's job gave him an odd circle of connections in the form of local reverends, connections Craig was eager to tap into, now he had a wedding to plan.

'Right ...' said Carly, beginning to suspect where Craig's story was headed.

'So I went down to meet him at St Peter's after I finished work, and I told him that we'd like to book the church for June.'

'Ah lovely ... so is it booked then, for June?' asked May, her eyes alight at the thought of her son's pending summer nuptials.

'Well it turns out if we want June they have nothing available, not until the following year, which is almost two years away.'

So relieved as to feel a little light-headed, Carly took a seat on the sofa.

'Well, that's okay ... it'll give us plenty of time to save. So what's the date in June?' she asked, happy to postpone the day she was reluctant to partake in.

'Well ...' said Craig. He picked up his work boots, dumped them by the front door with a low thud and made his way over to the sofa, sitting himself down next to Carly.

'… it turns out they had a cancellation, for a much sooner date … so I booked it, paid the deposit and everything!'

'How much sooner?' asked May, stealing the words from Carly's mouth.

'The 2nd of January!'

'January!' Carly and May both exclaimed, their tones decidedly different, May expressing sheer joy while Carly sounded a lot less enthusiastic.

Craig leaned back in his seat, picked up the TV remote from the arm of the sofa and turned on the television, looking very proud of himself for having secured what he felt to be an ideal date.

'But, Craig, we agreed on June. June was what we both agreed on!' said Carly, unable to fathom why Craig would deem it okay to go against what they had agreed.

Craig, having now shared his big news, was done with the conversation and ready to devote his attention to the TV in front of him.

'Craig!' snapped Carly, snatching the remote from his hand and turning off the TV.

'What?' said Craig, more concerned about missing the repeat episode of *Top Gear* than attending to her upset.

'We agreed on June!'

'I know. And I told you. It was fully booked,' answered Craig in a patronising manner, snatching the remote from Carly's grip and turning the

TV back on.

Too angry for the conversation to come to an end, Carly snatched back the remote and turned off the TV again.

'I don't want to get married in January. It's barely four months away!'

'What's your problem?' snapped Craig, unable to understand why Carly was so upset.

'I know it wasn't what you had in mind, lovey, but the June after next is an awfully long time to wait,' said May, trying her best to calm the atmosphere between Carly and Craig, but misunderstanding the reason for Carly's upset.

'I thought you'd be happy, it means we don't have to wait so long!' said Craig, raising his voice in annoyance.

'Whatever … it's only my wedding day after all! God forbid I should get any say in it!' yelled Carly, throwing the TV remote down on the sofa cushion and storming back out into the kitchen, where she slammed the door behind her and stood with her back to it. Through her panic she could hear the low murmur of Craig and May's voices, but all she could think of was the prospect of having to marry Craig in less than four months' time.

Carly leaned her head against the kitchen door as tears flooded into her eyes. She stared up at the ceiling, forcing the tears to roll back, and felt a stab of annoyance when the image of Jack Lewis came back into her mind. Jack Lewis, who had the leading role in the story she constantly played out in her head, the story of how different her life could have been.

It was Monday evening, and Jack found himself staring at the small clock on the wall at the back of his creative writing classroom. It had been a whole week since his heated exchange with Carly in the pub and she hadn't left his mind.

Jack couldn't shift the feelings of guilt that speaking with Carly had brought on. She had got to him: he'd spent all week questioning how much he'd really changed over the past decade. At thirty-one years old, he still, when times were hard or life got scary, found himself burying his anatomy somewhere he shouldn't. That very coping mechanism marking the end of many a relationship, including his relationship with Jess.

After all that had been said and done, Jack wasn't expecting Carly to show tonight, but that hadn't stopped him giving up hope, until now. It was 7.40 p.m.

He looked around the classroom and felt deflated at the drop in attendance. It was only the second class of the term. Mandy was sitting next to him again, only this week she was joined by her very own special needs assistant, a Jesus-like young man, with long, mousy brown hair and a short goatee beard who went by the name of Connor.

While Connor and Mandy made friendly small talk, the only other sound in the room was that of Kevin's heavy breathing, annoying Jack just as much as it had the previous Monday.

Along from Kevin sat Andrew, a middle-aged man who wore the ironic hairstyle of bald head and long hair. Andrew possessed a crow-like quality with his long nose and small round glasses, his long scraggy ponytail at the back of his head like a tail feather.

On the opposite side of the large table sat Clive, who was already scribbling something in his notebook, which even a professional of Jack's stature found peculiar, seeing as he hadn't set his students a task yet.

'Okay, it seems we're a bit thin on the ground this week, but shall we get started?' suggested Jack, climbing to his feet.

'Oh so is this it?' asked Margery, who was sitting at the back of the class, seemingly just as concerned as Jack by the drop in attendance.

'So it seems!' quipped Jack, shrugging his shoulders jovially, trying to be upbeat in front of his students.

'I believe Kevin has bravely volunteered to be the first to open tonight's class with a reading.'

Kevin nodded his head at Jack and shuffled a little in his chair, sitting himself upright to prepare himself.

'Great, and once we've heard from Kevin, we are going to be looking at monologues, and the difference between a monologue and a soliloquy.'

Just as Jack finished speaking, he heard his classroom door creak open and his heart missed a beat. He turned his head sharply, hoping above hope that Carly had changed her mind, and was disappointed by the sight of Melody and her friend Jenni.

'So sorry we're late,' said Melody, whose well-spoken voice had the unmistakable tone of a woman who had enjoyed the privilege of a private education. She was wearing an oversized grey patterned jumper with a large hole in the elbow, her pretty face free of make-up, and framed by shiny thick blonde hair. Like Jenni she was in her early thirties; they were both primary school teachers at the same school.

'Yeah, sorry, we were driving about for ages looking for parking,' said Jenni in a strong Yorkshire accent, her presence warmer and softer than her friend's. Jenni also possessed long blonde locks, but unlike Melody had a large nose and the figure of a woman that 'ate her feelings', her overweight body resting heavily on her short frame.

'Not at all, happy you both made it,' said Jack as he watched the two friends take a seat at the end of the table. 'So, Kevin, whenever you're ready,' he continued, expertly hiding his devastation that Carly hadn't shown.

Carly sat alone in her parked car, her arms crossed tightly across her body and wrapped warmly in her black jacket. On the passenger seat beside her lay her notepad. She pulled the car keys from the ignition and fidgeted with them. Through the windscreen straight ahead of her she could see Wanstead House, bright fluorescent light pouring from its large windows. All she could think about was Jack. She desperately wanted to see him, although she wasn't sure why. Now that she was so close to his presence, she felt sick with nerves. Still clutching her keys she reached for the door handle, but as if it had a mind of its own her hand found its way back to the car's ignition. Carly inserted the key and started the engine and urgently steered herself out of her parking space.

Within seconds she was driving down the road once again with no destination in mind and no plan for how to waste the next few hours.

CHAPTER 6:

'Honey, I'm home!' announced Grandma Barb as she stumbled through the front door of her flat. Grandma Barb always announced her return home in the same exaggerated manner now Jack was staying with her, her greeting invariably followed by cackling laughter at her own bad joke.

It was early Saturday evening and Grandma Barb had been out most of the day, her hectic social schedule involving a trip to the Barbican Library to return her library books, a visit to the Barbican Centre with her friend Maureen to check out the free exhibition, and a late lunch and drinks.

Jack sat at Grandma Barb's kitchen table with Betsy balanced on his knees and his laptop open. He could tell by his gran's voice that she had enjoyed more than a couple of drinks, the fact that his eighty-six-year-old grandmother had a much better social life than he did sitting a little resentfully with him.

'Hello, my darling!' exclaimed Grandma Barb at the kitchen door, opening her arms to her grandson, as Jack looked up from his laptop and smiled, his own welcome a much less elaborate one.

Undeterred, Grandma Barb staggered into the room and planted a wet sloppy kiss on Jack's cheek, her close contact giving Jack a healthy waft of Grandma Barb's breath, heavily laced with the smell of gin and garlic.

'God, that dog stinks!'

'You're one to talk! Did you have any chicken with your garlic?' said Jack, jerking his face away from Grandma Barb and stroking Betsy's head.

Grandma Barb dumped her green handbag on the kitchen counter and lifting an empty glass from the draining board turned on the sink tap to fill it.

'Have you had a good day, darling?' asked Grandma Barb before gulping down her glass of water.

'So so,' replied Jack.

Jack's day had involved little more than sleeping, masturbating and eating. He did eventually summon enough energy to put on some clothes and take Betsy for a walk down Stoke Newington High Street before returning home and firing up his laptop. His original plan was to catch up on some work, but instead he had spent the past forty minutes looking up the entertainment giant that was Pinky Bingo. Still secretly devastated that Carly had failed to show up to his class on Monday, Jack wondered if it was time to take matters into his own hands. He knew he could easily obtain her personal details if he really wanted to, using his charm on Beryl to persuade her into handing over Carly's phone number or even her address. He wasn't sure he was willing to travel down that route, though, because of the risk of having the phone put down on him, or worse, getting himself reported. However, there was nothing to stop him from turning up for a friendly game of bingo ... There weren't many Pinky Bingo halls left in the UK, and there was another mass closure on the horizon, but there was a hall not all that far away in deepest darkest Dagenham. Of course there was no certainty that Carly worked at the Dagenham branch, let alone that she'd be working there tonight, but seeing as the only item on Jack's agenda was falling asleep in front of his grandmother's television, he figured it was worth a try.

'Gran, have you got any plans for this evening?' asked Jack.

'Yes, yes, I have. There's half a bottle of Pinot that needs my undivided attention, and I need to finish off yesterday's *Guardian* crossword.'

'How do you fancy a night out with your favourite grandson?' he asked, using a heavy dose of his effortless charm and closing his laptop.

Jack and Grandma Barb sat opposite each other at a square four-seater table in the busy main hall of Dagenham's Pinky Bingo and were lucky to have found a table. The hall was packed, mainly with middle-aged and elderly women, the few men displaying serious expressions and blurry tattoos on their arms.

Jack was feeling anxious, on constant lookout for a pretty lady with light ginger hair.

'Jack, Jack, that woman has a tattoo on her neck. Look, look, you're not looking!' said Grandma Barb, annoyingly tapping Jack's hand and brazenly pointing behind his shoulder.

'Gran, we're not at the zoo, you can't point and stare!' said Jack, embarrassed by his gran's very vocal observations.

'Not a zoo! I just heard a woman belch. Honestly, Jack, when you said we were going out, this wasn't what I had in mind!' responded Grandma Barb, picking up her glass of cheap red wine and taking a large gulp.

It had been years since Grandma Barb had visited a bingo hall. She never did understand what social pleasure came from sitting in silence while staring at a sheet of paper, and as a result had been ostracized from a local bingo hall some forty years ago for talking during games.

Although he'd already bought his gran her bingo cards for the evening, Jack was starting to wonder if his plan had been a little too ambitious. The hall housed well over two hundred people and that didn't include the bar area outside, or the area at the front with the glowing fruit and slot machines by the entrance.

'Honestly, darling, I'm far too trolleyed for this. Can't we just sit at the bar?' asked Grandma Barb, resting her elbows on the table and rubbing her forehead, the day's busy socialising finally catching up with her.

'No, not yet, we've got food coming. That'll sober you up, I promise.'

Jack could sense Grandma Barb's energy was fading, and he was beginning to feel a little bad for dragging her out after an already long day, but he needed a wing man, and what better wing man to take to a bingo hall than a drunk elderly lady!

As Grandma Barb lowered her head to the table a pepperoni pizza and ten sticky chicken wings were placed down.

'So I've got a pizza and chicken wings. Is that everything?' said a friendly, if rather common, female voice.

Jack looked up at the waitress and recognised her instantly.

Dressed in the company's trademark pink polo-neck T-shirt, her long blonde hair tied into a high ponytail, was Carly's friend Lauren. She certainly looked a lot fresher and more steady on her feet than the last time they had met, the very sight of her filling Jack with a new-found hope that his master plan was indeed about to pay off.

'Hey, I know you. Yes, we met at that wedding

a few weeks ago,' said Jack a little too excitedly, causing Lauren to stare down at him and take a step back from the table.

'I er, shared my *cigarette* with you,' Jack said, before Lauren had a chance to step further away.

'Oh yeah ... you were that bloke that went to school with Carly—'

'University,' cut in Jack a little patronisingly.

'Whateves. You all right?' asked Lauren, without sounding interested.

'Yes, great .... is Carly working tonight?'

'Er yeah, she's somewhere,' said Lauren, looking up and down the length of the bingo hall. 'Oh there she is,' added Lauren, pointing ahead of her.

Jack turned his head sharply in that direction.

'Carly, your mate's here!' called Lauren, gesturing towards Jack.

When Carly came into view she was standing holding a plate of pizza in each hand. Jack sprang up from his seat and hurried towards her, at which she dumped the pizzas on the nearest table and began to walk away.

'Carly! Carly!' Jack yelled, quickening his pace.

'Ladies and Gents, eyes down,' announced the bingo caller, the hum of chit-chat and laughter soon quietening.

Carly burst through the doorway of the main hall and found herself in the relative peace of the bar area, customers sitting with their eyes down studying their bingo cards with purpose as the caller announced each number. The sound of Jack's voice was like a bellow as he followed her in, he not caring about interrupting the proceedings.

'Carly! Carly!' he called as the bingo players tutted and tried to shush him.

Although Jack didn't seem to mind about the scene he was making, Carly was embarrassed and eventually stopped to face him by the flashing slot machines at the front entrance.

'What are you doing here?' she hissed, making her annoyance known.

'I … I was worried about you … when you didn't attend class this week,' said Jack, struggling to catch his breath after his short sprint through the hall.

'We both know why I didn't come to the class, Jack, and quite frankly I don't appreciate you seeking me out at work!' said Carly, mortified by her Cambridge-scholar ex's presence at her workplace, which she felt was beneath her at the best of times.

'I wasn't, I swear, my flatmate and I just decided to step out for a game of bingo!' said Jack, his attempt at a plausible explanation so unconvincing it was almost comical.

'Flatmate? That old lady is your flatmate?' said Carly, pointing into the hall at the distant table where Jack's grandmother could just be seen gulping from her wine glass.

'Flatmate, grandmother ... Let's not get bogged down by the specifics.'

Carly let out a small laugh at Jack's pathetic approach.

'Okay, well I hope you both enjoy your evening,' she said, turning, ready to walk away.

Before she could go any further Jack stepped into her path, using his tense body to block her.

'Look, I'm sorry, okay? I'm sorry I was a shit boyfriend when we were nineteen, I am. But right now, I don't care if you forgive me, or if you even like me, but I do care about you, about your talent ... and I'm not going to let you throw it all away for a second time. Why do you think I went into teaching in the first place?'

'For the holidays?' Carly answered nonchalantly.

'Well you're wrong. It's really all about the pension!' replied Jack, making them both laugh, and breaking the tension.

'Jack, it's just a little evening class. It's really not a big deal whether I come or not,' said Carly, her tone decidedly softer but her attitude rather defeatist.

'It might not be a big deal to you, but it is to me. You have to come back to the class. This week Margery wrote a monologue about a polar bear ...'

'A polar bear? Original!'

'No, no, it wasn't. It was dull and ridiculous, and Clive wrote a bloody sonnet!'

'A sonnet, wow, that's really impressive!'

'Yes, and if we were in fact covering sonnets it might have been! The man's an imbecile who completely undermines what I'm trying to teach. I need you back in my class, Carly,' said Jack, making no attempt to disguise the pleading in his voice.

Carly couldn't help but feel touched that Jack cared enough to seek her out and beg for her return, especially as she was in fact desperate to go back to his class. It would certainly be better than driving along the A12 all evening, which was what she'd ended up doing the previous Monday.

'If I come back do you promise not to come here again?' said Carly, looking Jack square in the eye, making her terms clear.

'Cross my heart,' said Jack, his voice so low and sincere it gave Carly the distinct impression that he would agree to run through the bingo hall completely naked if it guaranteed her return.

Carly smiled and gave a small nod, which Jack took as a yes. He felt relieved, if a little smug, that tonight's plan had turned out exactly as he'd hoped.

'Er, Jack, I think you might want to check in on your gran,' said Carly, her face morphing into a look of concern.

Jack turned and looked over to where his gran had been sitting.

'Oh shit!' he exclaimed, and sprinted back towards their table, Carly following behind him.

Grandma Barb's collapse had gone unnoticed, everyone else's attention on their bingo cards and tablets. Jack reached her within seconds and knelt to the floor beside her, resting her head on his lap.

'Gran, are you okay?' he asked, his voice etched with concern.

'Oh hello, darling ... you know, I think I may have had a little too much to drink,' said Grandma Barb, her speech slurred. She gave a drunken giggle.

'Hello, Mrs ... *Lewis?*' said Carly, looking to Jack for confirmation of his grandmother's name. Jack nodded his head.

'What do you say we get you somewhere a little more peaceful?' suggested Carly, her voice soft and caring as she and Jack helped Grandma Barb to her feet.

'How does she know my name?' asked Grandma Barb, as heads turned at the small commotion.

'She's a friend of mine,' replied Jack.

'Oh, he's had lots of those, darling!' said Grandma Barb, her words followed by a drunken cackle as Jack and Carly each took a hold of an arm and led her carefully out of the hall.

The first-aid room at Pinky Bingo was nothing more than a six by six foot square. A cheap black plastic chair rested against one grubby cream wall and a small white handbasin stood in one corner. The first-aid box was well stocked with plasters and anti-bacterial wipes but not a whole lot else.

Grandma Barb sat on the plastic chair with her handbag resting on her lap. Although she was sitting upright, she still looked a little green around the gills.

'Here you go, Mrs Lewis,' said Carly, handing Grandma Barb a glass of water.

'I'm fine, really, honestly. I can't be doing with all this faffing … Really, I'm fine,' said Grandma Barb, too proud to accept the water from Carly.

'Just drink the water, Gran,' instructed Jack, standing in the doorway of the tiny room. He felt embarrassed by her refusal to cooperate.

Grandma Barb huffed loudly and grabbed the glass, spilling some of the water onto her hand-bag as she did so.

'It's okay, we've all been there,' said Carly kindly, unfazed by Grandma Barb's brashness.

'I once got so drunk I used my handbag as a sick bag on the way home and thought nothing of it until I had to dive in there to fetch my door keys!' said Carly humorously, leaning back on the wall behind her.

Jack tilted his head to one side and gave Carly a nostalgic smile, catapulted back to the very start of their teenage romance when they were both first years at Pembroke College.

'Um, now that's not completely true, is it,

Miss Hughes, because if I remember correctly I was actually the one forced to dive into said handbag after you decided to take a lie-down outside your room.'

Carly had been so drunk he could only get her as far as the wrong side of her bedroom door. With no hope of her managing to reach her bed, Jack had brought her bed to her, joining her for a night on the floor with her pillows, duvet and the wastepaper bin, which he'd felt to be a much better vomit vessel than her handbag. He got little sleep himself that night due to Carly's drunken snoring, but he'd felt it wrong to leave her, and was the first up in the morning to fetch them both the ultimate hangover cure of a bacon sandwich and a cup of tea.

Jack had forgotten all about that night until this moment. Their first night spent together. It hadn't been romantic or filled with mind-blowing passion, but Carly still remembered it.

'Well, that's truly disgusting! But thank you for your help … sorry, I didn't catch your name, dear?' laughed Grandma Barb, enjoying the reminiscing between two old friends.

'It's Carly.'

'Cara?'

'No, Carly …'

'Well, it's been lovely meeting you, Cara,' said Grandma Barb, reaching out her hand for Carly to shake.

'Gran, Carly, her name is Carly,' interjected

Jack.

'Then who's Cara?' asked Grandma Barb with a look of utter confusion on her face, her hand still clasping Carly's.

'No one, no one is called Cara!' said Jack, his tone jokey, if a little patronising.

'It's okay, Mrs Lewis, you can call me whatever you want, as long as it's not late for dinner!' quipped Carly, at which Grandma Barb let out a huge raucous laugh, revealing her yellowing crooked teeth, and finally let go of Carly's hand.

'I'm sorry, dear, I have a terrible case of octogenarian! One day you'll understand,' said Grandma Barb, laughter still in her voice as she wiped her eyes, unconcerned about smudging her mascara.

'Now tell me, dear, are you Jewish?' asked Grandma Barb bluntly. She took a large gulp from her glass of water.

'Gran!' snapped Jack, shaking his head, fully aware of where Grandma Barb was about to direct the conversation.

'No, I'm not …'

'Ah, but are you single?'

'Afraid not,' said Carly, holding up her left hand to display her engagement ring.

Grandma Barb shrugged her shoulders. Although Carly hadn't provided her with the answers she had so desired, at least she'd tried at seeking a suitable partner for her grandson in the kind and pretty girl before her.

'Gran, I told you, Carly's just a friend,' said Jack, concealing his embarrassment at his Gran's meddling.

'He was a journalist, you know, for one of the big papers, but then—'

'Okay, well, you're clearly feeling a lot better, so I think it's time we headed home,' cut in Jack. He removed the half-drunk glass of water from her hand and thrust it at Carly before hoisting Grandma Barb off the plastic chair by her arm.

'Was lovely meeting you, Cara,' called Grandma Barb as Jack hustled her out.

Suddenly all alone, Carly stood and stared at the scuff marks on the wall, baffled by Jack's behaviour. She poured the leftover water from Mrs Lewis's glass down the small sink and wondered why he'd been so quick to shut her down. What *was* it about Jack's past he was so desperate to keep secret?

CHAPTER 7:

'There you go, now if you want to turn yourself round,' said Brenda with the kind of practised professional warmth that spoke of years of experience, zipping up the wedding dress Carly was standing in.

Brenda wore her hair in a short, honey-coloured bob and had perfectly manicured hands, her hair and her soft-pink fingernails all the evidence needed that she was a woman who took great pride in her appearance.

Brenda knelt to the floor of Blushing Brides' large changing room and gently positioned the dress so it rested perfectly on the grey carpet beneath them.

'Now would you look at that? That looks absolutely beautiful on you, that does ... What do you think?'

Carly nodded her head in gentle agreement. She did look beautiful; that much was true. Wearing little make-up and with her long, light ginger hair in a messy bun at the side of her head, she still looked stunning.

The dress was simple, a plain white gown with

only a small diamanté trim across the bust, and cut off the shoulder, displaying the flawless pale skin of her shoulders and arms.

The image in front of her was surreal; so much so that Carly struggled to recognise herself.

She had thought about moments such as this. Standing in a wedding dress for the first time, going through the process of finding the perfect one with her mother by her side as she prepared to spend the rest of her life with the man she loved ... but Carly's experience couldn't have been further from the fantasy she had once held in her mind.

Carly felt nothing.

Not nervous, not complacent, not even angry at the absence of her mother or the injustice and impending doom of becoming Craig's wife, Carly simply felt numb. As if she was standing outside her own body and watching someone else, waiting to see how the rest of their story would unfold, choosing to forget that the forthcoming events involved her.

Waiting for the big reveal were Lauren and her five-year-old daughter Sophia, who Carly could hear was starting to get restless as she ran around the shop squealing and causing havoc. She caught sight of Brenda's face in the mirror, her thin lips turned down in disapproval at the sounds coming from outside the changing room.

'Shall we show your friend?' suggested Brenda, eager to calm the situation, and opened the cream curtain behind her to lead Carly out.

'Here she is ...' announced Brenda as Carly stepped onto the shop floor to the sight of Lauren tickling a giggly Sophia with one hand while trying to keep hold of her champagne flute with the other, both of them sitting on the silver crushed-velvet couch.

'Oh Carls ... Look, Sophia, look at Auntie Carly. Doesn't she look beautiful?' gushed Lauren.   Awestruck, Sophia went quiet, her blue eyes following Carly as she glided towards the full-length mirror next to the couch.

'So when's the big day?' asked Brenda, placing her hands into Carly's hair, untying her messy bun and letting her pretty locks fall down over her shoulders, then brushing her fingers through them.

'The 2nd of January ...'

'Oh soon,' said Brenda, raising her thin greying eyebrows in surprise.

'Yeah, it's all happening a bit quicker than originally planned—'

'Oh, I see ... Well if you need us to take this out a little at the front that won't be a problem,' said Brenda, directing her attention to Carly's stomach and patting it down as if to gauge how 'far along' she was.

Lauren let out a filthy cackle. She was the only person in the world privy to the knowledge that Carly had been religiously taking the pill in secret for quite some time.

'No, no, no. That's not what I meant,' said Carly, her cheeks flushing in embarrassment.

'Oh, apologies,' said Brenda, quickly removing her hands. 'So have you booked your venue?' she asked, anxious to change the subject.

'Er, yeah. St Peter's Church and then The Royal Oak in Romford.'

'Oh …' said Brenda, surprised that a bride as pretty and elegant as Carly should be holding her wedding reception in such a run-down establishment as The Royal Oak in Romford, a working man's pub, famous locally for once having its kitchen closed down by the Food Hygiene Standards Agency after a rat infestation.

In the silence Carly felt no need to mention that the pub was on a busy main road and its function room, unsurprisingly, had no another bookings for the whole of January; another wedding day arrangement made courtesy of Craig without her prior knowledge.

'So what do we think, ladies?' Brenda said. 'Is this the one? Or would you like to try on another?'

'No, this'll do,' said Carly dismissively, running her hands over the dress as if finishing up a business deal, eager to get the small talk out of the way and return back to work.

A look of concern flashed across Lauren's face. She climbed up from the couch and stood next to Carly by the mirror.

'"This'll do"? Carls, come on, I know it's not

exactly been what dreams are made of, but it's still your wedding dress. Are you really gonna settle for "this'll do"?' asked Lauren, bothered by her friend's complete lack of enthusiasm.

Carly turned to face Lauren.

'Well it was how I picked a husband, so it's how I'll pick a dress,' Carly said curtly, snatching the flute from Lauren's hand and pouring the remainder of the champagne down her throat, before stomping back into the changing room, leaving Brenda, Lauren and Sophia on the shop floor, all of them dumbfounded by her impromptu outburst.

Carly struggled as she reached behind her and started tugging at the zip on the back of her dress, not wanting to wear it a minute longer, desperate to free her body from the garment in the way she was unable to free herself from the suffocating situation she found herself in.

Jack slammed his key fob against the reader outside Grandma Barb's flat and pushed his body weight against the heavy metal door to open it. Feeling hot and sweaty from his run from his car, he moved as fast as he could in an effort to make up as many precious seconds as possible.

It was Monday evening, and Jack was running late for his creative writing class. Given the slow-moving London traffic, there wasn't really time to go back to the flat after school and collect what he needed for Wanstead House, but today he had no choice.

After oversleeping that morning and having to wait behind Grandma Barb for use of the bathroom, Jack had rushed out of the front door, leaving all of his paperwork and writing prompts behind on the kitchen table.

Jack was greeted in the hallway by Betsy, sniffing his shoes and wagging her tail, excited to see him; but he was in too much of a hurry for the welcome-home parade, and rushed straight past her down the long hallway towards the kitchen.

'Jack! Is that you?' called Grandma Barb from the living room.

'No, it's the Rabbi!' Jack called back sarcastically at what he felt to be a ridiculous question.

In the kitchen Jack headed straight over to the table in the corner and hurriedly picked up a pile of papers and a white plastic shopping bag containing a selection of 'autumnal' objects.

'I thought you had your class tonight?' Grandma Barb called from the living room.

'I do, and I'm running late for it. I forgot to take all this with me this morning.'

'Well I'm pleased you passed by, now I can give you this before I forget,' said Grandma Barb, entering the kitchen with a glass of red wine in one hand and a folded newspaper in the other, which she placed on top of the pile of papers balanced on Jack's forearm.

Jack glanced down and saw it was the property section from the local paper.

'What is this?' asked Jack, pausing for the first time since tearing through the front door. 'I thought you liked having me here ...' He looked up at his grandmother in disbelief.

'I also like penguins, darling, but I don't want one living in my spare room and eating all my food for the next five years!' answered Grandma Barb matter-of-factly, without a hint of discomfort or guilt. She took a large gulp from her wine glass.

Jack shook his head, unwilling to process what Grandma Barb was suggesting.

'Gran, I'm sorry, I haven't got time for this right now. We'll talk later, okay?' he said, dropping the paper to the kitchen table, before placing a kiss on Grandma Barb's cheek, a gesture that was rather out of character, but one he felt necessary.

'I'll be sure to circle the affordable ones!' Grandma Barb called out as Jack hurried away, escaping the conversation.

It was 7.40 p.m. when Jack finally pulled up outside Wanstead House. He drove into the small packed car park and spotted the only remaining space. It was the one that was always vacant because, being next to the giant oak tree, it was the most difficult one to manoeuvre into.

With no time to scour the streets for an alternative, Jack slipped the gear stick into reverse, and without using his mirrors, swung his black

Mini Cooper into the space. There was a loud crunching sound as his back bumper smashed into the large tree trunk behind him.

'Oh shitting hell!' Jack yelled to himself, clumsily shifting the gear stick back into first gear and jolting the car forward, before slipping it back into reverse and swinging it into the space once again, this time cautiously using his mirrors and moving much more slowly. He turned off the ignition, grabbed the pile of papers and plastic bag from the passenger seat and climbed out of the car.

Jack ran around to the back of the car to inspect the damage, and was not in the least bit surprised to see the silver trim of his bumper hanging off.

'Urgh!' he groaned.

'Is everything okay, Jack?' called Beryl from the entrance of the building.

'Yes, thank you, Beryl!' Jack called back, pretending to be ever so grateful for her show of concern.

'You have a class full of students in here waiting for you, Jack!' Beryl called, her need to state the obvious infuriating him still further.

'Yes, Beryl, many thanks for the update!' Jack yelled, failing to contain his frustration, at which Beryl scurried back inside, leaving Jack feeling mildly guilty at his shortness towards her.

With no time to sort the damage to his car,

Jack knew he had no choice but to deal with it later. He pointed his key fob at his car to lock it and stomped his way the short distance into Wanstead House.

Jack dumped his papers and plastic bag down on the classroom table with a loud thud.

'You okay, Jack?' asked Clive before Jack had a chance to apologise to the class for his lateness.

'Yes, yes, not so bad, and yourself, Clive?' replied Jack, trying to show an interest in his least favourite student.

'Um, yes, well, no, well, I was okay. I had a good enough week and good weekend, but then Monday happened, and well, I'm struggling somewhat with some issues relating to my son, but ...' As Clive rambled on in his monotone drawl, Jack looked around the table and felt a deep stab of disappointment.

There were all the usual faces but Carly was nowhere to be seen. Her vacant seat the cherry on the top of what had so far been a disastrous evening.

'That's great, Clive, really, well done with that,' interrupted Jack, making it all too apparent that he hadn't been listening to a word Clive had been saying. 'Sorry I'm late, everyone,' he announced, making an effort to hide his upset at Carly's absence and glad of the distraction of the class before him. 'I er, ran into some car trouble en route.'

Jack swallowed hard and opened the plastic bag he'd brought with him and gradually pulled out its random objects. He placed his grandmother's vase decorated with autumnal leaves in the middle of the table, then added a small plastic pumpkin.

'Do you want this door shut, Jack?' asked Clive, pointing at the door and climbing to his feet before Jack had a chance to respond.

'Er, yes, thank you …' replied Jack, his attention on his writing prompts.

'Whoa, whoa, hot tea coming through!' said an alarmed voice from the other side of the large white door.

Instantly recognising the voice, Jack looked round, but not quite able to believe it,
not wanting to get his hopes up, he numbed his feelings until the door swung open. There stood Carly, dressed in her usual Pinky Bingo work attire, between her hands a red-and-white-patterned mug.

'Sorry, I just went to get a tea while we were waiting,' she said coyly.

Feeling nothing but sheer glee at the sight of her, Jack beamed a wide joyous smile, and fought an odd inner urge to rush over and hug her.

'I'm really pleased you're here,' he said quietly, unsure as to whether he'd spoken loudly enough for her to hear.

Carly smiled a tight smile and made her way to her seat at the far end of the table.

'Right. So autumn is upon us, so I thought these objects might make some useful writing prompts for us tonight,' said Jack, enlivened by Carly's presence and ready now to address his class with his usual rhythm and bounce.

'Right, who would like to read what they've got?' asked Jack.

It always amused him how such a simple question could cause a group of adults to all simultaneously look away from him, as if they believed that by not making eye contact they could make themselves invisible.

'I don't mind going first,' said Andrew, who was sitting on one side of Jack.

With no one else feeling brave enough, Jack was happy to let Andrew hold court.

'Great, by all means, Andrew,' he encouraged.

Andrew cleared his throat loudly as his small eyes stared intently at the notebook he held in front of him.

'"The carrot hung from the blue maple tree, before dropping onto the springy marshmallow ground. Legs sprang from the cactus's spikes and it ran through the desert until it found the sea. The birds overhead swooped down onto the gleaming ocean, before soaring high into the cornfields above, keeping their watchful eyes on the jumping salmon."'

Looking awfully proud of himself, Andrew placed his notebook back down on the desk and pushed his small round glasses onto the bridge of his nose, as the rest of the class sat in a stunned silence.

Jack looked over at Carly and he could see her biting the inside of her cheeks, trying to suppress her laughter, whilst keeping her gaze fixed on her notepad in front of her.

'It's not very autumnal,' announced Margery, breaking the silence, her observation mirroring Jack's thoughts exactly.

'I loved it, it's .... it's mind-blowing!' exclaimed Jenni, defending Andrew and shaking her head in disbelief at his genius.

'I was going for something alternative ...' said Andrew with an air of creative arrogance that annoyed Jack, who didn't feel Andrew's work was worthy of it.

'I respect that you were brave enough to do that, Andrew, and forgive me if it's indeed me that's not understanding, but I'm struggling to feel that autumnal theme running through there,' said Jack, trying to give something in the way of constructive critique.

'Well, like I say, it's an alternative piece. I don't expect *everyone* to understand,' replied Andrew, implying that Jack himself was not of the calibre to understand that level of creativity.

'Quite,' said Jack, suppressing the urge to fire off his own smart comment to a paying student, and turning his attention to the rest of the class, and one student in particular. 'Carly.'

Carly rolled her eyes and looked up at Jack with a knowing smile, as if she had been waiting all evening for him to put her on the spot.

'Would you like to read? What with you not being with us last week?' suggested Jack, trying to sound encouraging.

Not wanting to come across as nervous, Carly sat up straight. She exhaled a loud breath and looked down at the notepad in front of her as her foot began to tap under the table in the same agitated manner as it had last time.

'"He clenched his fists and felt a sharp pain. He looked down and noticed the skin across his aching dry knuckles had cracked open. Shoving his hoe into the ground he looked out at the land before him. The bright vibrant colours of summer were now nothing more than a distant memory. The trees' once lush green leaves now beginning to rust, as each one shredded from the high branches, floating to the ground and invading the damp grass below. His eyes squinted from the bright sun above, as a crisp autumn breeze flew through his thin greying hair" – um, that's all I've got. Sorry, I'm not sure it's my best effort,' apologised Carly, feeling a stab of self-doubt.

Jack smiled, proud of the kind of work Carly was able to produce and pleased that somebody in his class had understood the assignment given to them.

'I disagree. It's a good piece. A man at the end

of summer, awaiting winter. The definition of autumn. I like it,' said Jack, reassuring Carly of her ability, whilst hoping Andrew picked up on the subtle dig.

Carly smiled sweetly back at Jack, pleased her reading was over, and feeling a degree happier with her work than she had been only moments earlier.

It was 9.30 p.m, and Jack's students were gradually making their way out of the classroom as another week's lesson drew to a close.

Jack watched as Carly walked slowly towards the classroom door. Wrapped up warmly in a black coat and pink scarf, she didn't seem to be in any great rush to leave; at the same time, judging by the route she was taking, she was deliberately avoiding passing him.

'See ya, Jack,' said Kevin, bouncing out of the classroom with his notepad tucked securely under his arm.

'Bye, Kevin, take care.'

As Carly edged closer to the door, Jack climbed from his seat at the head of the long table and placed himself in her path.

'Oh Carly, before you go ... I never got the chance to say thank you, for looking after my gran the other night.'

'You're welcome. Is she okay?' asked Carly with genuine concern.

'Oh she's fine, she's a walking bottle of Pinto at

the best of times. She'd just had a long day is all.'

'Well I'm pleased she's okay ... I'll see you next week,' said Carly, turning her back on him.

'Are you in a rush to get home?' Jack blurted out. Carly stopped and turned round to face him, her lips pursed and her head slightly tilted quizzically.

'I thought maybe I could buy you a drink ... just to say thank you properly ...'

Jack wasn't sure why he so desperately wanted to spend more time with Carly. Although he was certainly keen to make up for the other week, or more specifically for what had happened on that punting boat with Amy Shepherd. The yearning within him was an unfamiliar one. Even in the three years he had spent with Jess, there'd never been moments when he'd desperately wanted to be in her company.

He wondered if it was feelings of guilt finally surfacing after all these years. Or maybe it was his recent feelings of emptiness ... Or maybe it was quite simply because he was drawn to Carly. To her beauty and kindness, her intelligence and humbleness, in just the same way he'd been drawn to her when they had first crossed paths.

Carly glanced up at the ceiling. She was certainly in no rush to get home, and her curiosity was piqued as to where a drink with Jack could lead. She still wanted to know why exactly he'd been so quick to leave the Pinky Bingo first-aid room at the mention of his journalism career, and maybe this was her chance to find out.

'Yeah, okay. Why not?' shrugged Carly, causing a huge grin to spread across Jack's face.

Both bundled up in their winter coats, Carly and Jack took a slow walk to The George, the same pub they had visited previously. As they passed Wanstead Tube Station, the sight of it sowed a seed in Carly's mind.

'You know, it's been a while since I last went into town,' she said, slowing down to a complete stop. She pointed behind her at the station's large, brightly lit entrance.

Jack let out a small chuckle, surprised by her spontaneity.

'Are you suggesting an evening of debauchery on a school night, Miss Hughes?' he asked with a smile, never having been one to turn down a night out, no matter what the day or time.

'I'm just suggesting something that isn't that run-down pub on the corner,' answered Carly with a smile, pleased at the realisation that Jack wasn't going to take too much persuasion to get on board with her idea.

Jack nodded, and without any hesitation walked straight into the station, Carly following behind him.

Jack and Carly sat opposite each other at a small table in the upstairs section of Hamilton Hall, a large pub that was part of the complex around

Liverpool Street Station.

The ornate nineteenth-century building, once used as a ballroom and first-class waiting lounge, still possessed all its unique character in the form of mirrored walls, grand chandeliers and intricate gold designs of flower garlands and angels along the high ceiling and corners.

It was almost 11 p.m. and the pub was crowded with suited City types enjoying prolonged after-work drinks. Carly felt giddy. She wasn't drunk, but she felt high on laughter, surprised at how much she was enjoying her time with Jack as they reminisced about old times. The memories they shared had been buried so far back in her mind, Carly was astounded she was able to unearth them.

'Yes, that's right! You were supposed to be Michael Jackson, but everyone thought you were Boy George!' laughed Carly, recalling the student fancy-dress party.

'You'd smoked so much weed that night! Frankly I'm surprised you remember anything about that party!' laughed Jack as he took a sip from his glass of cider.

'I know! God, if my mum had known what I was getting up to she would have killed me!' said Carly, shaking her head at a past, much wilder version of herself.

'Ha, well, Cambridge wasn't best known for its party scene, but you certainly made it fun, Miss Hughes.'

'You know, I think you're literally the only person that knows that stuff about me,' said Carly, laughing softly as she allowed herself to relax back in her chair.

A spark of interest was ignited in Jack. He cast his mind back a few weeks to their surprise meeting the night of the wedding. Perhaps it was true, because Carly's friend hadn't seemed to have any idea of the person she'd once been.

'So tell me, am I also the only one that knows you were at Cambridge? Because I remember that friend of yours seemed to think I was just some crazy high person when I mentioned uni …'

Carly looked down at the table, pretending to concentrate on the large scratch etched across the wood.

'You might be,' she answered shyly, avoiding his gaze as she picked up her glass and took a sip from her drink.

'Why have you never told anyone?' asked Jack, sensing her discomfort, but too intrigued to let the subject go.

'For the same reason I don't tell people what I just did in the toilet. Because it's personal and no one cares!'

A silence fell between the pair as Jack stared at Carly, making her squirm.

'What?' she protested.

'I just … I disagree. You should be proud, not so much of your weed and alcohol consumption, but certainly of the academic achievement.'

'What achievement? I dropped out!' exclaimed Carly, finding Jack's words almost laughable.

'But not out of choice. Just by getting in, you achieved something so many people try and fail at!' said Jack, a desperation in his voice as he tried to make Carly understand that she had so much to be proud of.

Carly clearly remembered the day she was accepted to Cambridge, and she knew Jack was right, for that day; that moment, had marked her life's single biggest achievement.

Too scared to open the letter, Carly remembered her Mother soon growing impatient and taking the letter from her and opening it herself. As she read the joyous news aloud, Carly and her Mother screamed and cried and jumped up and down on the kitchen tiles like they had just won the lottery, because in some respect, they had.

Carly had a winning ticket to a life of better prospects and opportunities. A life few people like her would ever be fortunate enough to experience.

Carly and her Mother celebrated her 'win' that night with a takeaway pizza and a viewing of their *Dirty Dancing* DVD, a simple celebration, but an incredibly special memory she held dear.

'Yeah, well, it was a long time ago now,' Carly said quietly, unable to look Jack in the eye and unwilling at that precise moment to let her mind play its constant refrain: 'What Life Could Have Been.'

Carly looked down at the silver watch on her wrist: it was gone eleven. For the first time since she had entered the pub, the niggling thought of May and Craig entered her head. Carly knew she should start making her way back home and felt downcast that the fun she was having with Jack was about to draw to a close.

'I should really get going …' she said, and lifting her glass finished the last of her drink.

The evening had flown by, and she felt a bit short-changed that she hadn't got to find out more about Jack.

'I wasn't trying to upset you,' said Jack, worried he might have offended her.

'It's fine. I'm not upset, really. I just should get going,' said Carly, taking her coat from the back of her chair.

Jack finished up the last of his drink and quickly followed Carly's lead, taking his coat from the back of his own chair and preparing himself to leave.

As Carly stood waiting for Jack, she caught sight of a young man standing along the balcony, only a few feet away from their table. He had a bottle of beer in his hand and was dressed smartly in a crisp white shirt and dark navy-blue trousers, his attire evidence that he had come straight from the office. He was with a small group of friends, all roughly the same age, in their late twenties and early thirties, and he was squinting at Jack as if he was trying to place him.

Jack picked up his brown work satchel from under the table and placed the strap over his shoulder.

'Ready?' he asked, at which Carly nodded.

As they walked towards the stairs leading to the exit, the man in the white shirt swiftly detached himself from the group and approached Jack, placing his hand roughly on his shoulder.

'Jack? It's Jack, isn't it?'

'Er … yes.'

'You were a newspaper journalist?'

'Yes …' replied Jack, embarrassed at failing to remember the person that clearly remembered him.

'Ah, you don't remember me, do you?'

Jack looked into the man's face, and began to feel a little uneasy.

'Tom. We've met a couple of times. Michelle's fiancé; her *ex*-fiancé.'

Jack's eyes widened and he felt his heart begin to race at the uncomfortable knowledge of who was standing before him.

Michelle worked for the paper as a junior reporter and Jack remembered her; if a little too well.

The paper being the sociable enterprise that it was, there were many nights after work spent in City bars and pubs, and it was common practice for Jack's evening to be rounded off nicely with a blowjob, usually in the toilets, by the ever so obliging Michelle. Even after Michelle became engaged, the fun didn't stop, only coming to a sudden halt once Jack finally left the paper, and he and Michelle's paths hadn't crossed again.

'Yeah, she told me all about you—' said Tom, with a note of passive-aggressiveness.

'All positive, I'm sure—' interjected Jack with a cocky smile. He stepped forward, desperate to end their interaction, but was forcibly stopped by the placement of Tom's heavy hand on his shoulder.

'After I found a picture of your knob on her phone.'

Carly stood silently next to Jack, her eyes darting frantically between the two men. She was curious, if not a little excited, to know what was going to happen next.

Tom took a step back and turned away.

Relieved, Jack turned to Carly and gave a gentle shake of his head, when almost in slow motion, Tom turn back round. Lifting his clenched fist into the air and without an ounce of hesitation, Tom punched an unsuspecting Jack square on the nose.

The power of Tom's punch sent Jack on a direct descent to the floor, empty glasses clanking loudly as he knocked into the nearby laden table, and slumped to a pathetic heap on the pub's worn patterned carpet.

'Whoa, whoa, whoa!' exclaimed a shocked

Carly, instantly dropping to her knees to where Jack lay on the floor, just as a pal of Tom's came rushing over to pull him away.

The group of friends rushed down the stairs and out of the pub, not waiting to be forcibly removed by the bouncer.

'Oh shit, your nose is bleeding,' said Carly, intently inspecting it.

'Of course it's bleeding, I just got punched in the bloody face!' snapped Jack, taking his humiliation and frustration out on Carly.

'Well if you will sleep with other people's fiancées …' Carly replied jovially, unfazed by Jack's temper as she took his face delicately between her hands.

Jack's eyes met Carly's pretty grey-blue eyes as they searched his face.

'I never slept with her. It never went beyond blowjobs!'

'Right … because anything else would've been indecent,' said Carly, finding Jack's feeble remorse rather pathetic.

The pair maintained eye contact for a moment longer, and as Carly held Jack's battered face in her hands she was able to see past the dirt bag that did stupid things with people he shouldn't. She could feel his vulnerability; she remembered someone kind and loving and she ached to know more about the man that to her seemed so lost.

Scared of the feelings suddenly simmering inside her, Carly looked away.

'You need to sit up and try and keep your head forward. Stay there and I'll grab you some ice and maybe a brandy,' instructed Carly, letting go of Jack's face and disappearing out of sight towards the bar.

CHAPTER 8:

'You didn't need to bring me home. Really, I'm a big boy,' said Jack, his speech slightly slurred, the result of two double brandies and a swollen nasal passage.

Carly looked up at Jack's bruised face and couldn't help but scoff a laugh at the sight of him. With one of her tampons hanging out of his left nostril, Jack looked rather dishevelled, his ego just as bruised as his throbbing nose. His brown satchel hung lazily halfway down his bent arm as he held on to an old discoloured pub tea towel, a makeshift ice pack, now nothing more than an icy, cold, sodden rag. Jack placed it over his nose, hoping its coldness would ease the pain a little.

'Indeed you are, but I'll feel better knowing you got back in one piece,' said Carly as they walked the last few steps down the concrete path that led to Jack's grandmother's flat. After they'd taken the tube back to Wanstead, she'd driven Jack home in his battered black Mini. She'd enjoyed the unexpected extra time they'd spent together, even if it was courtesy of Jack being punched in the face. It was now past midnight, and they were the only people out in the silent grounds.

'But you've had to come miles out of your way,' said Jack, feeling guilty for the burden he had put on Carly.

'Don't feel bad. Really, the more time I spend away from home the better!' she quipped, making light of a situation she did in fact take very seriously.

Jack was intrigued that Carly should display so little enthusiasm when it came to returning home to her soon-to-be husband.

'Care to elaborate?' he asked, removing the tea towel from his face, the movement causing his satchel to fall to the ground, at which he let out a defeated huff.

'No,' Carly replied bluntly, bending to the ground to rescue the satchel and placing the strap over her shoulder as she stood waiting for Jack to find his door key buried in his coat pocket.

'Okay, I guess this is where I leave you ...' she said, lowering Jack's satchel from her shoulder and handing it back to him along with his car keys.

'What? Don't be silly, come in,' said Jack, pushing open the metal street door then leading Carly to his grandmother's red front door.

'No, it's late ... I don't want to wake anyone.'

'You're coming in to wait for a cab, not your

chopper,' said Jack, accepting his satchel back from Carly and pushing the front door open.

Jack went inside, dumped his satchel down on the green carpet by the front door and was greeted by an excitable Betsy.

'Hello, old girl,' he said in a hushed voice, bending to give Betsy a quick ruffle on her head before walking down the long darkened hallway towards the bathroom.

Betsy turned her attentions to Carly, who was hovering by the front door, reluctant to go any further into unfamiliar surroundings in the dark. She knelt to the floor to say hello to Betsy and was met with a waft of Betsy's halitosis.

'Oh Jesus!' Carly blurted out, shocked into standing up just as the hallway burst into light.

'Jack! Is that you?' Grandma Barb called out, exiting her bedroom at the very end of the hallway, dressed in a light pink dressing gown, a chunky novel in her hand and her spectacles pushed up onto her head.

'Oh hello, dear!' she said when she saw Carly, then turned to the open bathroom door, through which she could see Jack standing at the sink, inspecting his face in the bathroom mirror.

'Jack! What on earth happened to you?' said Grandma Barb, rushing to Jack's aid as Carly stayed where she was.

With Grandma Barb fussing over her wounded grandson and the light now on, Carly was able to take in her surroundings, and looked in awe at the display of framed postcard reproductions that took up both walls of the long green hallway.

'It was just a simple misunderstanding!' Jack explained from the bathroom as Carly took a slow stroll to admire Grandma Barb's collection, when one small picture, about halfway down, between two doors, caught her attention. It was one she was familiar with: *Bathers at Asnières* by Georges Pierre Seurat, an Impressionist piece, a print of which used to hang in large poster size on the stairway of the house Carly grew up in with her mother. Her mother loved the painting depicting workers enjoying a day off by a clear blue lake. Some were basking in the bright sunshine, while others were taking a refreshing dip, the scene peaceful, but not without a sense of fun and enjoyment.

Mesmerised by a picture she hadn't laid eyes on in years, Carly recalled sitting alongside her mother in the National Gallery, where the real thing, the original, monstrous-sized painting, hung proudly. It had been their last trip to the National Gallery before Carly left for Cambridge; a happy memory, but one she had deeply buried.

'Forgive me, have we met before?'

Carly's attention was diverted from the picture as Grandma Barb appeared by her side.

'Carly! You met her at bingo!' Jack interjected loudly from the bathroom.

'Ah yes, Cara. Lovely to see you again, dear.'

'Carly!' Jack called, correcting his grand-mother.

'Yes, Cara, that's what I said!'

'Oh forget it!' huffed Jack, too tired and drunk to correct his grandmother for a second time.

'I'm so sorry, Mrs Lewis, did we wake you?'

'No, no, I was still awake reading. Are you an art scholar, dear?' asked Grandma Barb, nodding towards the prints on the wall, assuming as usual that every person she made contact with was an esteemed academic.

'No, no, just a humble admirer. When I was growing up we didn't have a lot of money, so my mum, she used to take me and a packed lunch to museums and galleries a lot. They were free and the heating was always on.' Carly chuckled lightly, trying to ignore the tightness in her throat.

'She sounds like my type o' gal, your mum!'

'Yeah, she was a very smart lady,' Carly said quietly, her eyes drawn back to *Bathers at Asnières.* Grandma Barb noted the past tense in which Carly had spoken, and the sadness in her voice.

'Let me get you a drink,' she suggested, breaking the sombre mood and walking with purpose towards the kitchen at the end of the hallway opposite the bathroom.

'Oh no, I'm not staying—'

'Nonsense. What kind of host would I be if I

didn't make you a drink!'

Grandma Barb walked towards the door on her right, and a little reluctantly Carly followed, Betsy at her heels.

Standing inside what Carly presumed to be a darkened spare room, Grandma Barb flicked on the light.

The room was relatively small, and in many ways really quite ordinary. A tired looking arm chair that didn't look all that comfortable sat beside a large yucca plant that was in desperate need of repotting; however what was unique about the room, really was quite wonderous.

All four walls were lined with heavy, over-loaded, wooden bookcases, with a short one under the large window at the back.

Utterly astounded by Grandma Barbs vast personal collection, Carly looked round the small room in absolute awe, taking a few short steps forward to take a closer look.

Every shelf was crammed with books, from thick encyclopaedia's, battered looking cook books as well as serval versions of Oxford English Dictionary's.

Carly noticed a copy of Life of Pi alongside The Kite Runner, as well as copy of Paul O'Grady's autobiography.

'You have...your own.....library?' said Carly, undeniably impressed. 'I'm very jealous!'

'Ha! You think this is something, that's not all!' said Grandma Barb, making her way over to the furthest corner of the room towards the wardrobe door in the wall.

Grandma Barb opened the door and as she did so soft pink lighting burst from inside to reveal an inbuilt glass bar.

A mini fridge was tucked away in the corner on the floor underneath a glass topped bar, where a crystal short glass sat with a lipstick stain on the rim. Two shelves hung above, packed with bottles in every manner of colour and size.

'Don't you love it?' Exclaimed Grandma Barb, delighted to show off the unique addition to her personal library.

'Ha, that's amazing!' Carly laughed gently, shaking her head in mild disbelief as she neared closer.

'This was Jack's Father's bedroom, then it was a spare bedroom, but you know Cara, I have two perfectly good bedrooms either end of the hall, so I thought, I'll make this one a home for my babies...' explained Grandma Barb, looking on lovingly at her many books. '...honestly, I swear they multiply during the night! So, I sit, I read, I drink, it really is all my dreams come true!'

'I can tell. It's wonderful.' Said Carly, feeling envious of Jack - being able to live amongst those that appreciated the glory of art and books so greatly.

'Thank you Cara, now I have gin, I have wine, I also have some whisky somewhere if you'd prefer?' said Grandma Barb, standing on tiptoes, as she buried her head into the bar and clanked the bottles as she riffled through them.

'Do you have tea bags?' asked Carly sheepishly, knowing she couldn't possibly have another drink if she was still going to drive her car home from Wanstead House.

'Hmm, suit yourself,' shrugged Grandma Barb, closing the door on her bar and leading Carly along with Betsy down the hallway and into the kitchen.

Grandma Barb walked through the kitchen and reached for the white plastic kettle on the counter.

Carly pulled out the chair that faced the large kitchen window and sat herself down. She unzipped her coat and, sliding it off over her shoulders, let it fall on the back of her chair.

Betsy followed her and stood on her hind legs, resting her front paws on Carly's knees, bidding for the stranger's attention.

'Oh shove that smelly thing away if she's bothering you!' said Grandma Barb, taking a step in Betsy's direction.

'Don't worry, we won't be here bothering you for much longer,' said Jack from the doorway, the tampon gone from his nostril, in his hand a ball of scrunched pink toilet paper.

'Gran, have you got anything for the bruise?'

'Hmm, there's some Germolene in the bathroom cabinet, but I'm not sure it'll do much good,' said Grandma Barb, looking up at Jack, and feeling at a loss at to what else to suggest.

'Are you having a drink?' she added as Jack stomped back out of the kitchen.

'No thank you!' he yelled from the bathroom, making Carly wonder whether she'd been right to agree to stay.

'I think he's annoyed with me,' Grandma Barb whispered as she made her way over to the cupboard behind Carly.

'Oh ... how come?'

Grandma Barb pulled two mugs from the cupboard and on her way to the sink pointed with two tea bags between her fingers at the newspaper property section that was lying on the kitchen table next to a copy of the *Jewish News* and some unopened post.

'Oh, I see ...' nodded Carly, able to connect the dots.

'How do you take your tea, dear?'

'Milk with one, please.'

'To tell the truth ...' said Grandma Barb, pausing to place the mugs down on the work surface. Keeping her back to Carly she stared out of the kitchen window. '... I'd love nothing more than to have him stay here for all eternity. But it's for his own good. He can't spend forever living with Grandma.'

Grandma Barb turned to face Carly and let out a small sigh. She marched back to the cupboard behind her and pulled out a tub of powdered milk and a white paper bag of sugar.

'Whereabouts do you live, Cara dear?' Grandma Barb asked, walking back to tend to the mugs on the counter.

'Not far away, just in Dagenham.'

'And when's the date?'

Carly stared blankly at Grandma Barb and watched as a heaped teaspoon of powdered milk was scooped into one of the mugs. It was the first time she'd seen powdered milk used for making tea …

'Sorry?' asked Carly, realising she hadn't really been paying attention.

Grandma Barb held up her left hand and pointed to her own ring finger, then pointed to Carly's.

'Oh, er … January.'

Grandma Barb nodded and turned back to the kettle that had just finished boiling and poured hot water into each of the mugs.

'I was married once,' Grandma Barb said thoughtfully, the teaspoon tapping the side of the mug with a tinkling sound as she stirred the drinks.

'Oh, I'm sorry. Has it been long? Since …' asked Carly, assuming Grandma Barb was a widow, and feeling uncomfortable at stumbling across such personal ground with a person she barely knew.

'Oh, about fifty-something years now,' replied Grandma Barb, lifting the mugs from the kitchen counter and carrying them slowly over to the table.

Carly looked down at the tea placed in front of her and her eyes widened at the sight of the small yellowish lumps of powdered milk floating to the surface of the muddy brown liquid.

'Thank you,' she said, as Grandma Barb pulled out the chair closest to her and sat down.

'He must have been very young when he died ...' said Carly with great sympathy, wrapping her cold hands around her hot mug, warmth being the only thing the tea was fit for.

'Died? I wish! No, darling. I kicked him out!' Grandma Barb announced, letting out a loud raucous laugh. She leant back in her chair and clapped her hands, her reaction so unexpected and outrageous, Carly couldn't help giggling.

'No, he's still very much alive. Living somewhere near Wembley. Drink your tea, Cara, before it goes cold,' instructed Grandma Barb, flapping her hand at Carly, it not going unnoticed that she was yet to touch a drop.

Carly lifted the mug to her lips and took a small sip, the taste so strong it was almost bitter, the powdered milk not sweet enough to make up for the fact Grandma Barb had forgotten to add the sugar.

'No, really, I shouldn't be so harsh. He wasn't a bad man. He was never abusive or anything like that, but good God, was he boring! He had nothing about him. No interests, no hobbies, never wanted to travel, never wanted to go anywhere, never wanted to open his mind to anything!' Grandma Barb ranted.

'Then why did you marry him?' asked Carly, her question a little blunt, but Grandma Barb's manner made Carly feel as if she was chatting with any other gal pal, rather than an elderly woman; as if no subject or question was out of bounds.

'Because I was knocked up, darling!' declared Grandma Barb. Carly scoffed a laugh at her unapologetic honesty.

'A seventeen-year-old, unmarried mother? No. I had no choice,' continued Grandma Barb, not in the least bit fazed by Carly's direct question. She paused to take a sip from her black tea. 'But one day, I just thought enough already! I knew I couldn't do it. I couldn't spend the rest of my life with him, I just couldn't,' said Grandma Barb forcefully.

'I think that's very brave,' Carly said quietly, looking back down at the milky lumps in her tea, finding it eerie how hauntingly similar Grandma Barb's attitude towards her ex-husband was to her own towards Craig; and Carly envied her courage.

'Have you ever .... walked out of an exam? And you know, you just know you've nailed it? That you've got it in the bag and all will be fine?' Grandma Barb asked Carly, prompting her to look up from her tea.

'Ha, not for a while, but yeah, I have.'

'Well, that's how I walked away from my marriage! I just knew I was going to be fine,' said Grandma Barb, looking Carly squarely in the eye, before a smile spread across her face, exposing her crooked, yellowing teeth.

Grandma Barb's story resonated deeply with Carly.

She knew she could walk away from Craig if she wanted to. She knew that she could find herself a decent job, provide for herself and be self-sufficient, that much was true, but what about May? Carly felt an overwhelming sense of responsibility towards May, and that would never be a situation she could so easily turn her back on.

'So no regrets?' asked Carly, as if she needed confirmation that in walking away from a man she didn't love Grandma Barb had made the right choice.

'Not one,' replied Grandma Barb, just as Jack walked into the kitchen with a tube of Germolene in his hand. He placed the Germolene on the chrome draining board and picked up an empty glass, filling it with water from the sink.

'Oh darling, some post came for you today.'

Grandma Barb sifted through the unopened post on the kitchen table and handed Jack two envelopes. One was white and narrow and already opened, the other larger, with a red edge. Carly noticed the scrappy writing scrawled across it, the typed address in the middle having been crossed out.

Jack looked down at the larger envelope and recognised Jess's handwriting. The envelope had been addressed to them both. He took a large gulp of his water and put down the glass on the draining board.

Jack tore open the envelope, and pulled from it an ornately decorated, black and red invitation: he and Jess were invited to the Bar Mitzvah of his cousin Beth's eldest son James. A Las Vegas-themed Bar Mitzvah at London's Savoy Hotel in November. There was an exact replica of the invite, which she'd obviously received some days earlier, stuck to Grandma Barb's fridge.

Ordinarily the idea of catching up with family in such opulent surroundings would be something Jack would look forward to. However, at this late hour, and after the night he had had, Jack felt nothing but overwhelming tiredness, and tossed the invite behind him onto the kitchen counter, making a mental note to notify his cousin that Jess would not be attending the event.

Jack opened the smaller envelope and pulled out two tickets. He raised a small smile.

'The tickets for the Globe,' he said, handing them over to Grandma Barb then retrieving his glass of water from the draining board.

'Ha ha ha, what a shame!' laughed Grandma Barb, accepting them from Jack and inspecting them. 'You might as well keep hold of them, darling.'

'What are you going to see at the Globe?' asked Carly with genuine interest, and forced herself to take another sip from her tea.

'*Macbeth*. Gran's idea of a gag gift,' said Jack.

'Gag gift?' asked Carly, confused by the notion.

Carly had inherited a love of Shakespeare from her mother. Carly's mother had been a full-time teaching assistant in a school for disabled children and occasional moonlighter in a friend's clothing shop, but her real passion was for the arts. She adored the written word, absorbing everything from Shakespeare to Billy Joel, and was as amazed by the canvases of Monet's water lilies as she was by Warhol's soup cans. Carly's mother opened her mind to everything and encouraged the same attitude in her daughter.

Although not having been granted the privilege of an expensive education, Carly's mother had never felt the gift of knowledge to be out of her reach, or her daughter's, and would often read Carly children's versions of Shakespeare's work. Before Carly was ten years old, she knew the plots and characters of most of the classics such as *Romeo and Juliet*, *Twelfth Night* and *A Midsummer Night's Dream*, without even realising the social and academic significance of Shakespeare.

Carly's own fascination only grew with age.

By the time Carly began to study Shakespeare at school, she was miles ahead of her peers, her knowledge and intelligence making her something of a misfit.

However, at Cambridge Carly finally found her people and her place. She no longer harboured any embarrassment or had to play down her abilities and passions.

To Carly the language of Shakespeare held the same level of beauty as a sunset or a blossoming flower; not that anyone knew, of course. She was fully confident that nobody in her current circle of friends would ever want to join her on something as culturally rich as a trip to the Globe.

'That's how he lost all his hair, darling! Spending the last two years teaching it to fifteen-year-olds!' laughed Grandma Barb, handing the tickets back to Jack.

'So Gran thought booking us tickets to see it was just about the funniest thing in the world, until she realised it clashed with her dirty getaway with Geoffrey!' chuckled Jack, accepting the tickets back from his Gran, his mood lifting as he and Grandma Barb teased each other.

'I'm getting the ferry to Guernsey to meet him. I haven't seen him since the cruise to the Canaries last summer,' Grandma Barb informed Carly, speaking comically from the side of her mouth, as if to make out she was engaging in a secret service mission.

'When do you go?' asked Carly, showing a polite amount of interest.

'Wednesday, so I won't be around for the show this Saturday ... So if you're not busy, Cara dear, feel free to take my ticket,' suggested Grandma Barb. She took a sip from her tea.

Jack's face lit up with joy. He made no attempt to hide his enthusiasm.

'What a superb idea!' he said, knowing enough about Carly to know that a performance of *Macbeth* would be right up her street.

'Oh no, I can't, I have work Saturday,' insisted Carly, not wanting to seem over-keen.

'But they give you holiday, don't they?' said Grandma Barb, refusing to take no for an answer.

'Er ... yeah, they do,' Carly answered hesitantly, one half of her feeling uncomfortable with Grandma Barb's pushiness, the other half loving the idea of an evening of Shakespeare with Jack.

'Then that's settled. I do like it when a plan comes together!' said Grandma Barb, rubbing Carly's hand resting on the table as if sealing the deal.

Carly looked over at Jack. He could sense her bemusement at how easily Grandma Barb had been able to rail-road her into making a date with him, but there were times when he was grateful for his gran's relentless interference.

CHAPTER 9:

Carly was woken by the sound of Craig's 6.30 a.m. alarm. Craig groaned and rolled his body towards his bedside cabinet to swipe the snooze button, as was routine.

When the dark room fell silent again, Craig rolled himself back into the bed and flopping an arm over Carly brashly searched for her breast through her T-shirt.

Carly was tired from the late night, but the unwanted feel of Craig's touch made her instantly alert.

'Right, I'd better get up,' she said, desperate to escape his wandering hands. She lifted herself out of the bed and onto her feet in a movement so swift she almost felt dizzy, needing a second to find her balance. She turned to reach for her dressing gown from the back of the bedroom door and heard Craig let out a disgruntled sigh.

Carly opened the door and sped out of the bedroom into the bathroom before Craig had a chance to open any form of negotiations with her.

When Carly went down to the living room May was still asleep. She crept past her and made her way into the kitchen. Just as she was filling the kettle at the sink she heard Craig's heavy footsteps.

Carly turned to face him.

Craig had only been awake for a few minutes, but he was already fully dressed for work in black combat trousers and a faded black sweatshirt bearing a Barking and Dagenham Borough logo.

'You having one?' she asked, placing the kettle down on its base.

Craig ignored her, refusing even to make eye contact, and stormed over to the bread bin on the opposite worktop. He forcibly lifted the lid of the bread bin, pulled out the plastic bag of bread with a heavy hand and threw two slices into the toaster.

'What's wrong with you?' asked Carly, pleading ignorance as to why Craig was in such a foul mood.

'What do you think!' snapped Craig, opening the fridge door and pulling out the small tub of butter.

'Oh grow up!' Carly hissed, shutting Craig down whilst not wanting May to overhear anything.

'Clearly I'm the only one it bothers—'

Carly left the kitchen before Craig had a chance to finish his sentence. She wasn't willing to spend any more of her energy arguing about their sex life, or lack thereof.

Back in the living room, Carly made her way towards the window by May's bed, and gently opened the curtains.

'Morning, lovey,' said May, her voice a little gruff at being woken so early.

'Morning, May. You sleep well?'

'Not so bad. You were back late last night.'

Carly felt a flutter of panic. It was almost 2 a.m. by the time she eventually returned home. She could remember tripping over Craig's work boots and stumping her toe on the door frame, but although she must have made quite a racket coming in, she was confident she hadn't disturbed May as she crept her way up the stairs to bed.

'Oh, sorry, did I wake you?' apologised Carly, unsure how to approach the subject of her late return home.

'No … well, only for a second. So what happened? It wasn't car trouble, was it?' May asked with concern.

'No, I er, bumped into an old friend. Remember, the one I told you about from the wedding the other week?'

'Oh, your old schoolfriend. What did you say her name was again?' asked May, assuming she'd forgotten, when in actual fact Carly hadn't mentioned a name.

It was then that Craig walked into the living room holding a slice of toast in each hand; clearly it was too much trouble for him to use a plate.

Much as Carly held Craig in contempt, she didn't feel it right after the conversation that had just ensued between them to announce that she had spent the previous evening with another man, however innocent the encounter may have been.

'Jane. Yeah, she'd come for a game of bingo. She asked me to go back to hers for a drink afterwards, so ...' answered Carly, picking up the dirty mugs from the coffee table in front of the TV.

'Ah, that's lovely, catching up with old friends. It's so easy to lose touch.'

'Yeah, I think so. We've arranged to meet again actually, Saturday evening,' said Carly, offering more information than was strictly necessary, but anxious to keep the amount of lies she told to a minimum.

'Where are you going?' asked Craig with his mouth full, plonking himself down on his recliner.

'To watch a show, she had a spare ticket and asked if I wanted to go ...'

'A show, oh how lovely. What one?' asked May, her voice full of interest and wonder.

'*Macbeth.*'

Craig let out a loud laugh, spitting out some of his mouthful of toast onto his work trousers. He picked up the white soggy lump with his short stubby fingers and placed it back in his mouth.

'Why's that funny?' asked Carly, offended by Craig's reaction to a plan she was looking forward to.

'I could not think of anything worse! Sitting with a numb arse listening to some prat spouting a load of shite all night,' declared Craig, before taking another large bite from his toast.

'Well it's just as well you've provided me with plenty of practice then!' Carly hit back, her dig followed by May's signature filthy cackle.

Carly stomped back into the kitchen, wanting to get as far away from Craig as possible.

The staff room at Langston High possessed an overwhelming stench of cooked fish, the smell of Tracy's lunch doing little to aid Jack's throbbing head. He wasn't hungover as such, but his face still felt sore and his head heavy from a late night and little sleep, the bruise at the top of his nose nicely matching the dark rings under his eyes. Unwilling to engage in anything productive during his lunch break, Jack, his phone in his hand, sat slumped in the corner on one of the many worn, brown-cushioned chairs.

Having just finished off a helping of Grandma Barb's chicken soup, Jack was trying to decide whether it was appropriate to message Carly, now that he'd finally obtained her number ahead of their trip to the Globe on Saturday. He wanted to thank her for looking after him last night ... No, really he just wanted to message her for the sheer hell of it! To say hello, ask how she was, how her day was going ... ultimately to plant the thought of himself into her mind ... but he refrained. Jack was enjoying the friendship that was beginning to blossom between them, and certainly didn't want it to end by coming across pushy or needy. Instead of messaging Carly he casually caught up on the day's news headlines whilst listening in on the conversation between Tracy and Vicky from the art department.

'Yeah, so they bought this house out in Cambridge for next to nothing. Five bedrooms, three bathrooms, garage, and even a swimming pool in the back garden. Turns out the previous owner was a convicted paedo and the place was this house of horrors. They couldn't give it away! But my friend didn't care, she was just happy to have scored such a bargain.'

Jack scoffed a small laugh at Tracy's story, which made both the ladies turn their heads to look at him.

'Sorry, I didn't mean to eavesdrop. I just heard you say Cambridge and it caught my interest.'

'Oh that's right, I forgot, aren't you from Cambridge?' said Vicky, pushing her thin dark hair out of her face as she tucked back into her salad.

'No, I'm from London. I went to uni in Cambridge,' Jack replied.

'Oh apologies, I thought you were from there. So did you study at Cambridge University, or a university in Cambridge?' asked Vicky with a mouth full of salad and an air of sarcasm.

'Cambridge University, Pembroke College, to be exact.'

Vicky nodded her head approvingly, if with a sprinkling of surprise.

'And now you work here?' confirmed Tracy, finding it almost laughable that a Cambridge scholar hadn't got any further ahead in life than they had, their own degrees having been achieved at much more modest establishments.

Choosing to ignore Tracy's mocking judgement towards his career choices, Jack swiftly moved the conversation back to its original topic.

'Forgive me for asking, but how much did your friend pay for that house?'

'Really next to nothing, about two hundred grand.'

'Wow, that is a steal!' said Jack, sitting up from his slumped position on the chair.

It had been less than twenty-four hours since Grandma Barb had made it clear that it was time for Jack to flee the comfy nest that was her spare room and find a home of his own.

Jack knew finding his own place at such a low price was unlikely and he also knew that property in Cambridge wasn't usually a great deal cheaper than that in London, but he figured that as he had no current emotional ties a fresh start somewhere new might be something worth considering.

As Tracy and Vicky continued to chat amongst themselves Jack drew his attention back to his phone and typed in the search bar *Teaching jobs in Cambridge.* Within seconds a long list of teaching vacancies in the Cambridge area listed down the screen. With his thumb, Jack scrolled down the list: *Primary School Teacher, Swimming Teacher, PE Teacher ...*

And then, amongst all the irrelevant dross, *Head of English Department – Private School.* Jack tapped into the job's link and read through the job description with interest, the first productive thing he had done all day.

Carly and May had just finished eating their lunch, and now it was time for Carly to help May with a bed bath. The only bathroom in the house was upstairs and it had been over a year since May had managed to summon the strength to climb stairs of any kind, and so it had become part of Carly's daily routine to help May have a wash from her bed.

The procedure wasn't as undignified as it might have been, had May been unable to wash most of her body herself, but she did require assistance in undressing and dressing, as well as an able-bodied person to fetch the necessary water and soap.

As May sat up and leant forward, Carly perched herself on the edge of the bed, and with a pink sponge in her hand, washed May's back, the purpose of which was more relaxation than practical cleanliness. As Carly glided the sponge along May's back, the two women chatted, the closing music to *Loose Women* sounding in the background.

'… apparently she went into labour while in Asda, but she still managed to finish her shop and pay … then she went off to the hospital with a frozen chicken in the boot and the baby's head crowning!' laughed Carly, filling May in on the news of Bonnie from Pinky Bingo's unique birthing experience.

'Blimey, well, it's just as well she kept her tights on!'

'Ha, yeah. She's at Queen's, so I said I'd stop by and see her and the baby tonight on my book round.'

'Ah well, if soppy bollocks gets his way, it won't be long until your friends are visiting you on that ward!'

The thought of carrying Craig's baby filled Carly with nothing more than sheer horror. As an awkward silence fell, Carly dropped the sponge into the soapy bowl of water that was balancing on the small table next to May's bed.

Although it wasn't like May to pry, Carly wondered if she had overheard her earlier conversation with Craig, and if this was May's way of trying to check if all was okay.

With only the sound of the television filling the silence between them, Carly wrapped May's body in a large green towel to dry off. May reached her hand up to Carly's by her shoulder and took gentle hold of it.

'He thinks the world of you, you know that, don't you?'

'Yeah, I know,' Carly said quietly, nodding her head gently.

'I know things haven't been easy of late. I

feel terrible for the amount of strain I must be putting on you both,' said May, blaming herself and her poor health for Carly's obvious unhappiness.

May's ill health was indeed a legitimate excuse for Carly's constant bad mood, and although she felt terrible that May should blame herself, Carly knew she could never tell May the truth. That her unhappiness wasn't a side effect of caring for her; she and Craig had grown apart years ago, and May's ailing health, rather than being a strain, was in fact the only glue keeping them together.

'Don't be silly, May,' said Carly, pulling her hand out from under May's and lifting the bowl of water from the side table.

'You looking forward to your show on Saturday?' asked May, eager to change the subject to something lighter.

A smile flashed across Carly's face.

'Yeah, yeah I am. I just hope it doesn't rain, otherwise it's going to be a long night standing in the wet and cold.'

'Eh? How do you mean?'

'The Globe. It's an open-air theatre.'

May tilted her puzzled head to one side, unfamiliar with the concept.

'It doesn't have a roof. You know, for authenticity.'

'Oh, really? Well, that's different. I'm pleased you're making new friends, lovey.

Sounds like this Jane might be able to teach you all kinds of new things!' said May.

Carly smiled, finding May's ignorance endearing.

Having spent so many years denying how culturally rich her mind was, Carly knew that who she really was under the Pinky Bingo T-shirt was a person no one was likely to understand.

'Tea?' Carly asked May as she made her way into the kitchen with the bowl of water. Jack's image came into her mind and she smiled, the thought of seeing him again being the only thing getting her through the day.

'Oh Jesus, what is that smell?' said Jack, heaving as he walked through the front door and pulling the neck of his jumper up around his nose to mask the dreadful smell that was invading the hallway.

'That smell is your dog!' Grandma Barb barked from her bedroom.

Jack went down the hallway and into Grandma Barb's pink bedroom where he found his elderly grandmother down on all fours scrubbing the worn burgundy carpet with a washing-up sponge, the blue washing-up bowl next to her.

'Where's Betsy?' asked Jack.

'I've shut her in the kitchen. She diarrhoea-ed all over my carpet!'

'Oh no, has she been out today?' asked Jack, walking out of the bedroom towards the kitchen.

'Yes, and she diarrhoea-ed all the way down Stoke Newington High Street as well. Honestly, Jack, you have no idea what a day I've had! Never mind poo bags, I needed a jet hose to keep up with her bowel movements! You need to get that thing to a vet!' ranted Grandma Barb.

Jack opened the kitchen door and was greeted by Betsy, bounding towards him, her tail wagging, then leaping up on her hind legs, vying for his attention.

Jack bent down and scooped Betsy into his arms.

'She seems fine!' he called to his grandmother as Betsy licked his face.

'Tell that to my carpet!' Grandma Barb yelled back.

'Okay, I'll call the vet, but Simon should be back in a couple of weeks.'

'Good! Oh before I forget, darling, will you take a look at the door handle in the living room, it's hanging loose and the door keeps jamming shut,' said Grandma Barb as she came into the kitchen holding the washing-up bowl. She carried it over to the sink and tipped the water away.

Grandma Barb often asked for Jack's help

with small practical jobs around the flat, much to Jack's amusement. She seemed to assume that because Jack was male he was genetically wired with the skills to carry out such tasks, when in truth Betsy was likely to be of more use.

'Yes, but can I take a look at it later, Gran? I've got something I need to do.'

'Let me guess. Marking?' said Grandma Barb, 'marking' always being Jack's go-to excuse when he wanted to wriggle out of a task.

'Er, no, not on this occasion,' said Jack, placing Betsy back down on the kitchen floor.

Grandma Barb turned her head from the sink and pursed her lips, waiting for Jack to tell her more.

'I stumbled across a job I want to apply for.'

Grandma Barb's eyes widened with interest and she nodded her head approvingly.

'Oh, really? That's good news! And does said job come with lodgings?' she asked.

'Ha, no, but it's in Cambridge, so if all goes well, you'll be getting your spare room back soon enough!'

'Brilliant!' exclaimed Grandma Barb, clapping her hands loudly then jokingly punching the air. 'Well, don't let me stop you, darling, you'd better get cracking!' she added as she made her way out of the kitchen, but not before playfully tapping the side of Jack's face with her wet hand.

Jack heard her dutifully close the kitchen door and sat himself down at the messy kitchen table. He opened up his laptop and went about applying for the position of *Head of English Department.*

CHAPTER 10:

It was early Saturday evening and Carly was on her way to meet Jack for the evening performance of *Macbeth*. All she could see before her as she walked through the underground station were black and red spots and she was starting to wonder if maybe she had overdone it with the amount of layers she had dressed in. She was wearing a pink sequined woolly hat, with a matching scarf and mittens, and under her black coat a simple combo of dark jeans and jumper, but with added hidden layers of a T-shirt, leggings and ski socks.

She'd thought it only sensible to be prepared for a chilly evening outside by the Thames, but after the time she'd spent standing on a busy packed train deep underground, Carly could feel herself starting to burn up. Her forehead was wet with sweat under her woolly hat, and her back felt clammy, but she wasn't about to let her discomfort get her down.

Carly held on tightly to the stairs handrail to steady herself and felt a flutter of excitement in her stomach. All week she'd been looking forward to this evening, but she was unsure what she was looking forward to most: the Shakespeare, or being with Jack.

Jack stood outside just by the stations exit and admired the spectacular view of the London Eye, lit up bright red under the dark London sky. He had only arrived at the station some two minutes ago and made sure to stand out of the way of the hordes of moving people around him while he waited for Carly to arrive.

For the first time in a long time, Jack felt positive. This week had a been a good one. Not only had he completed the process of applying for a new job, but also the bruise on his nose was starting to fade nicely, he had caught up on all his marking, surprised himself by mending the door handle on Grandma Barb's living-room door and to-night he was about to enjoy the company of his newest friend Carly.

It had only been a few days since they had last seen each other, but to Jack it had felt like weeks, this evening not coming round soon enough. He struggled to remember the last time he had genuinely looked forward to anything, and wondered if his life was at a point where he was finally able to move on from the all-consuming sadness of the past few years.

The thought was interrupted by the sound of a familiar voice.

'Hiya!'

Jack lifted his gaze from the London Eye and turned to greet a smiley Carly.

'Hi,' he said, leaning in to give Carly a kiss on the cheek.

Carly returned the gesture and pulled away, just as Jack went in to plant a kiss on her other cheek. He took a step back, his second kiss hanging embarrassingly in the air between them as he gazed at her. Carly looked pretty, as was usual, but her pale face was bright red and moist with beads of sweat.

'You look hot,' said Jack.

'Oh thanks,' Carly replied coyly, flattered, if a little taken aback, by Jack's very forward compliment.

'No, I mean, you look *hot*. As if you might be overheating!' said Jack, concerned for Carly's welfare and wondering why the thermal attire on what was a reasonably mild evening.

Carly's feelings quickly morphed into embarrassment that her sweaty and flustered state hadn't gone unnoticed.

'Well, I didn't want to get cold,' she said,

a little concerned that, as handsome as Jack looked, he was dressed unsuitably for an evening of standing outside in the cold, wearing his usual grey coat but no other accessories such as a hat or scarf.

'Right … well certainly no fear of that, Miss Hughes. Let's get you into the open!' said Jack, proceeding to lead the into the cool evening air.

After a leisurely stroll over the Millennium Bridge to the Southbank side of the Thames, the stroll working wonders in bringing down Carly's body temperature, Carly and Jack had found themselves a seat on a wooden bench and were sitting eating the noodles they had purchased from one of the world-food stalls behind them.

The pedestrian walkway was relatively quiet, the crowds of earlier in the day now filtered down to only a handful of passers-by, and lined with small trees barren of their leaves but glowing with blue and white fairy lights, adding a glimmer of magic to the night. Beyond the foggy river, St Paul's Cathedral could be seen in the distance, a picturesque view.

'So did your gran get off okay?' asked Carly, referring to her trip to Guernsey, and took a mouthful of noodles.

'I assume so. I'm not even sure when she's due back. If she's not back this time next month I'll give the authorities a call!'

'She seems great. I hope if I ever get to that age I still have that much get up and go!' said Carly, holding pure admiration for Grandma Barb's fun-loving attitude towards life.

'Yeah, she's great. She's very well travelled and educated. She's had an interesting life,' said Jack, speaking with great pride about Grandma Barb, before shoving a large portion of noodles into his mouth.

'So how come you live with your gran?' asked Carly, having wanted for so long to find out more about Jack, and now seizing the opportunity to dig a little deeper.

'It's just temporary ... Let's just say I've not been the best version of myself these past few years ... Eventually it caught up with me.'

'Is that code for, you cheated on your girl-friend?' Carly asked bluntly, but still able to withhold a judgemental tone.

'Fiancée actually,' said Jack, correcting Carly on the finer details, even if that fact seemed to make the betrayal even worse.

Jack let out a small sigh, pausing on his next intake of noodles and taking a minute to look out at the river as he reminded himself of what a terrible human being he really was.

'She threw me out, but who could blame her?' shrugged Jack, knowing he had no right to be angry or bitter about Jess's decision to end their relationship.

Although Jack's story didn't exactly make him

the world's nicest guy, Carly still found herself sympathising with him. She could see a person that was able to admit they had wronged another, and she felt that to be a rather rare and noble quality.

'I'm sorry,' she said sincerely.

'Don't be. It's taken me some time to realise it, but it was for the best. You know, it's only now that I look back on it, I can see it was really more of a mutual arrangement than a romantic relationship,' said Jack, bringing his attention back to his noodles and twisting his fork into the middle of them.

'How do you mean?' asked Carly, even more intrigued.

'We met just before I left the paper. I remember I had my cousin Will's wedding coming up, and I didn't want to go alone. She was pretty and smart, but that giddy romance, that not-being-able-to-keep-your-hands-off-each-other feeling when you first get together ... it was never there, not really ...'

Carly listened intently and wondered if Jack was making a comparison based on their own past romance, one in which the sex was amazing and they couldn't bear to spend a moment apart.

'... being together, it was more about having someone to attend weddings with and someone to split the bills with. I had someone that would pick me up a birthday card for my mum when I'd so predictably forget, and she had someone that could mend, or at least attempt to mend, the leaky tap in the kitchen, and it worked ... for a while ... until it didn't,' shrugged Jack, not showing a great deal of emotion, but lack of emotion aside, Carly found his honesty refreshing.

'So, did you ever love her?' she asked.

'I'm sure I did, but maybe not in the way I was supposed to,' answered Jack. He forked up more noodles. 'What about you? How did you met your fiancé?' he asked with his mouth full.

Carly hadn't paid a second thought to Craig since she'd left the house, and resented having to think of him now, but as Jack had just revealed so much about himself, it was only right he should have his turn to pry.

Carly leaned back on the bench and looked out at the river as she cast her mind back over the past decade.

'I worked with his mum, May, at the bingo hall. It was right after my mum died and I was struggling, emotionally, financially. Anyway, she was lovely, like so lovely. I moved in with her and her son – Craig.'

Carly paused, not particularly wanting to talk any more about a person she'd wanted to forget about. She turned to face Jack, but rather than taking the hint to move the conversation on to the next topic, he sat silently, looking at Carly with a wide, interested stare, willing her to go on.

'Me and him were, are, the same age, and it

just kind of developed. He was kind, and well, he was there. It was nice, as if I was part of a family again, and it worked well at the start. After my mum died I spent about three years just staring into space. Not wanting to do anything, not wanting to go anywhere or see anyone, so with Craig already being mentally hardwired that way himself, it was fine, but now—'

'You realise you need more?' interjected Jack, taking Carly by surprise at how quickly and easily he knew exactly what it was she was trying to say.

'Maybe?' she replied, looking back down at the box of noodles in her hands, picking up the plastic fork and twisting it in the middle of the portion.

Jack watched Carly as she played with her food.

He felt a deep wave of sadness for her situation. She, above all people, deserved to be happy. He felt completely helpless, knowing from their prior conversations that Carly helped care for May, and no matter how miserable Carly felt, May wasn't someone she could easily walk away from.

'Why did you leave the paper?' Carly asked, wanting to take the conversation away from herself.

The sudden change in topic took Jack by surprise. Determined not to show his discomfort, he looked away from Carly and back at his food.

He knew not answering would create even more questions, and so he buried his feelings, as he was so used to doing, and gave his most well-rehearsed and blasé response.

'I just … fancied a change.'

'And that's it?' questioned Carly, frowning at Jack, finding it difficult to comprehend that he would so readily walk away from a glittering journalism career.

'I know, I don't expect everyone to get it. My dad certainly doesn't. I know I'm a massive disappointment to him,' said Jack, instantly regretting having said it.

'Hey, if you're happy with your decision, then that's all that matters, right?'

Jack smiled at Carly, the first person ever to give a positive response to his drastic career change.

'And for what it's worth, I don't think your dad sees you as a disappointment. From what I could tell he was very proud of you.'

Jack gave Carly a look of utter confusion.

'Your dad. Max, bald guy, prostate the size of Wales?'

'Yes …' Jack answered cautiously, spooked at Carly's intimate knowledge of his father.

'I told you, I volunteer at the hospital. I met him, a couple of times, sold him a couple of books. He was the one that gave me the flyer for the creative writing class. He told me that his son was teaching it, and he seemed *very* proud of you.'

Jack's mouth dropped open. He leaned himself back on the bench, remembering the evening when his father tried to lecture him on his career choices and his wasted Cambridge degree, when another, slightly more disturbing, memory of that evening sprang to mind.

'Miss Hughes, did you sell my father a copy of *Fifty Shades of Grey*?' asked Jack in mock outrage.

'Guilty!' giggled Carly, lifting her hand in admission.

Jack shook his head in disbelief and laughed, feeling a sense of comfort that all this time Carly's presence had been a lot closer than he had realised.

Ten minutes before curtain-up, the foyer of the Globe Theatre was bustling with people. In contrast to the Elizabethan exterior it was modern, with high white ceilings and plush charcoal flooring, not resembling at all the kind of interior Carly had been expecting.
There was the obligatory gift shop, selling overpriced fridge magnets and pencils, and in front of Carly a bar area, crowded with friends chatting and drinking in their groups, the atmosphere busy and alive with the loud hum of conversation and laughter.

Jack led the way, familiar with his surroundings.

'Have you been here before?' asked Carly.

'Yes, too many times, with my students mainly. I think this is my first visit without them!' answered Jack, pulling his wallet from his front trouser pocket and taking out the tickets.

'You're so lucky,' said Carly enviously, looking around her and drinking in where she was, it feeling like an eternity since she had engaged in something so culturally enriching.

'Shall we go through?' suggested Jack.

Carly nodded her head excitedly, at which Jack smiled, finding her excitement endearing.

Following behind other theatregoers, they walked up a short flight of steps and around a red brick wall, then Jack led Carly into a small darkened theatre. There was no electric lighting, the only light coming from the several chandeliers hanging from the ceiling above the stage, each one containing about a dozen or so skinny wax candles.

Carly looked around in equal states of confusion and wonder.

'We're inside,' she said, utterly bewildered.

'Well spotted,' said Jack in his usual deadpan manner, leading the way to their seats past other audience members, tightly packed in on low wooden benches.

'I thought we'd be outside, standing?'

'Oh, right …' said Jack, it finally dawning on him why Carly was wearing so many layers of warm clothing.

'Oh, I'm so sorry, Carly, I should have told you.

So this is the Sam Wanamaker Playhouse. It's new, well in comparison to the rest of the building. It only opened a few years ago, in 2014, I think, or thereabouts.'

Carly looked around the small intimate theatre in wonder; it was only capable of holding an audience of a hundred or so. Even in the dim light she could make out the intricate design on the celling: an angel in the centre of the sky, surrounded by cherubs floating on clouds. There was another tier of seating above theirs overlooking the small stage, already full of people.

'How did I not know that?' said Carly, disappointed that something so wondrous and important had completely passed her by.

'Hey, you don't know until you know,' said Jack, using a catchphrase he often used with his students when they felt down about their lack of knowledge, trying to make Carly feel better as he slid off his coat.

'It's amazing. Thank you so much for this,' gushed Carly, genuinely grateful she had been given the opportunity to accompany Jack to such a magnificent place.

'You're most welcome, Miss Hughes. Now do you need any assistance de-robing?' said Jack, poking fun at Carly's many layers of clothing, and using the light banter to disguise the tightness in his throat Carly's comment had brought on, he being unable to remember the last time somebody had been so happy to be in his company.

'Hey, mitts off, you, I know your type!'

As Carly took off her hat and unwrapped her scarf from around her neck, Jack suddenly felt a queer sick feeling churn its way through the pit of his stomach, and he winced.

'You okay?' Carly asked.

'Yes, yes, all good,' he said convincingly, hiding his worry.

It was not at all uncommon for Jack to suffer from the occasional sensitive stomach. There had been many a dodgy takeaway or greasy burger over the years that had been too much for his stomach to handle. Where most people's stomachs could easily digest trans fats and light bacteria without a worry, Jack's was less likely to play ball, and it seemed tonight was no different.

Jack made a grab for his stomach through his jumper and could feel the bubbling of his gut underneath.

'How are you feeling? Since those noodles?' he asked Carly, lowering himself down onto the bench.

'Fine,' Carly answered sweetly, taking a seat next to Jack with her outdoor clothes bundled on her lap.

Jack smiled tightly at Carly, but she could sense his anguish.

'Are you feeling okay?' she asked kindly.

'Mmm,' sounded Jack through tightly pursed lips. As he nodded his head the churning in his gut turned up a gear, causing a tight knot of pain. The mirrored doors on the centre stage opened and ten or so of the cast appeared, a similar number taking to the upper balcony.

The audience fell silent as the haunting sound of an a cappella Latin chant filled the auditorium. While Carly focused all her attention on the scene in front of her, Jack could only focus on his troublesome gut.

The chant came to an end and the singers all went backstage. The theatre went quiet, and Carly couldn't help hearing the sound of Jack's rumbling stomach, or more accurately the sound of someone passing wind.

She gave Jack a sideways glance, and scoffed a small laugh.

'Are you sure you're okay?' she whispered, keeping her eyes on the stage.

Jack nodded frantically and took a tighter grip on his vibrating stomach when he felt the southernmost part of his bowel make an urgent involuntary contraction. He got up from his seat in one fluid motion, knowing he had no choice but to remove himself from the theatre before something truly terrible happened.

As the three witches took to the stage, Jack began to sidle his way out at quite a speed, forcing the snuggly packed audience to stand in order to let him pass.

'Sorry, sorry, so sorry …' he whispered gratefully as he squeezed urgently by each person, his worried voice met by a series of tuts and groans.

Having watched the comical scene unfold Carly wondered if she should go after Jack and check he was okay. Then figuring that standing outside the toilet door wouldn't offer much in the way of practical help, she decided to stay where she was and embrace the performance she had been so looking forward to, even if it did mean watching it alone.

Carly stood, awkwardly trying to keep hold of her scarf, hat and mittens that were wrapped inside her coat whilst clapping and cheering as the cast of *Macbeth* took their final bow on the small stage.

She felt emotional, having so enjoyed the performance. The high drama, the tears, the blackmail, the gore. She looked around at the adoring audience, and failed to understand why the people currently in her life had chosen to close their minds to a world so full of wonder and intrigue, even going so far as to label it boring. Carly had been so blown away by the performance she'd barely been aware of Jack's reappearance after his dash to the men's room, then his disappearance during the second act so he missed the end.

As the audience began to make their way out she followed suit, hoping to spot Jack in the foyer. When she saw him he was leaning against a glass screen balcony by the stairs, his dark grey coat draped over his arm and a bottle of water in his hand, along with a small white paper bag. He looked so handsome and sophisticated that Carly felt an overwhelming need to be near him, almost as if to claim him as hers.

Jack spotted Carly and gave her a nod and held up his hand to give her a small wave. He was relieved to see her approach with a gleeful expression, having been worried that his early exit might have angered her, or worse, embarrassed her.

'Hey, how you feeling?' Carly asked, struggling to keep hold of her coat and all her other garments.

'Delicate at best, but better. I'm annoyed I missed the end,' said Jack, taking Carly's coat from her and holding it open for her to slip over her shoulders, the act of such simple chivalry making Carly's heart flutter with appreciation for it was a type of attention she never received from Craig.

'Macbeth dies,' she quipped, slipping her coat on and turning round to face Jack.

'No, surely not again!' he laughed. 'I'm sorry I left you!'

'Don't be, you had to do what you had to do ... anyway I had a great time!' said Carly, pulling her pretty hair out from under her coat and placing her wholly hat over her head.

'I'm pleased. Well, whilst I was avoiding causing a disturbance by going back in, I thought to check out the gift shop. Here, I got you this.'

Jack opened the small white paper bag in his hand and from it pulled out two small magnets, placing one in Carly's hand.

Carly looked down at a tiny Globe Theatre, a white building with brown beams, underneath it a red ribbon and the words *The Globe*.

'I got us one each, so whenever we look at our fridges we can remember the night of Noodle Gate!' said Jack with a small chuckle.

Carly was touched that Jack would want her to have a memento of their evening together; and she wondered if it was strange that she was more touched by a simple gift-shop magnet from Jack than she had been by an engagement ring from Craig.

'That's so sweet. Thank you, Jack,' gushed Carly, placing the magnet in her coat pocket before leaning towards Jack and planting a soft kiss on his cheek.

The unexpected contact and the rush of feeling it aroused left Jack momentarily speechless, and he let out a small cough, clearing his throat of any emotion as his cheeks flushed a light shade of pink.

'After you, Miss Hughes,' he said, motioning towards the doors, insisting it was now time for them to leave, while internally pleading with himself to banish the blossoming adoration he felt for a woman he knew deserved better than him.

CHAPTER 11:

'You know, I always thought Macbeth was a woman,' said May the next morning, clinging on to the plastic cup that was threatening to slide from her weakening grip as she sat in her wheelchair.

While Craig was slumped in his recliner in front of the TV, one hand down his stained navy joggers and the other holding a cup of tea, Carly stood folding the dry washing from the clothes horse as she relayed her evening to May.

'Well you're not completely wrong, you're thinking of Lady Macbeth, who is Macbeth's wife, and you see, she's the one that makes him kill the king. But then after he kills the king he kills other people to cover his tracks.'

'Oh blimey! Sounds worse than *EastEnders*!' exclaimed May.

'Yeah, well, you know, people don't realise it, but those same lines of plot have been used over and over again in so many films and soaps. The feuding families, jealous siblings, star- crossed lovers ...' continued Carly, speaking with building enthusiasm.

She was utterly thrilled to have somebody to speak to about such things, it being the first time she had done so since leaving Cambridge, or at least since her mother died. She wondered if she had been wrong to assume for all these years that someone like May would have no interest in such a topic, when her train of thought was rudely interrupted by the blaring sound of the television.

Craig had obviously removed his hand from his joggers and used it to turn up the volume on the TV to drown out her and May's conversation.

'Craig! Do you mind, we're talking!' Carly yelled over the drone of a racing car engine on a replay of *Top Gear*.

'Fucking hell, Carly, no one cares about sodding Shakespeare!' barked Craig dropped the TV remote back down on his lap and glued his eyes to the screen.

'I care, you miserable sod!' yelled May.

'Well I don't, and neither does anyone else! Fuck me, Carly, most people would spend a Saturday night off work getting shit-faced, but not you! Coming home and giving us all a fucking English lesson!' fumed Craig.

'Well maybe if you'd spent less time getting shit-faced you wouldn't be digging holes in the ground for a living!' yelled May, embarrassed by Craig's rudeness.

Although May might have been insulted by Craig's behaviour, Carly wasn't. She was used to it, and hadn't expected anything better from Craig, knowing that his closed-mindedness came not just from a place of ignorance, but also from a place of fear. He was afraid of not understanding, and for that she pitied him.

Carly refused to be annoyed and remained calm. She took the last pair of Craig's black socks from the clothes horse and rolled them into a ball.

'You know, you don't have to understand it, Craig, you don't even have to like it, but you are allowed to open your mind to it,' said Carly, placing the ball of socks on top of the pile of washing and lifting it from the floor.

'Well maybe you should run off with this Jane! You and 'er seem to have so much in common!' Craig snapped back with a menacing laugh, unaware of how appealing the offer was.

'Don't tempt me!' replied Carly as she walked with the washing held in her arms up the stairs and as far away as possible from Craig.

Jack, dressed in nothing other than a pair of black boxer shorts and his Homer Simpson slippers, sat alone at Grandma Barb's kitchen table in front of his open laptop. One hand wrapped around a lukewarm cup of coffee, he stared into the glowing screen in front of him at an unsent email to his cousin Beth.

All week he'd been putting off RSVP-ing to James's Bar Mitzvah, dreading the idea of having to inform his cousin that Jess would not be attending and thus making her aware that he was in the midst of yet another failed relationship.

Jack let out a deep sigh and leaned himself back on the kitchen chair. He pulled his cup of coffee to his bare chest and let his gaze drift up to the fridge in front of him, where a small magnet in the shape of the Globe Theatre was helping to hold in place the dreaded Bar Mitzvah invite on the fridge door.

Jack smiled at the sight of the magnet, happy to let his mind play back the memory of his evening with Carly, and he wondered, would it be such a bad idea to ask Carly along to the Bar Mitzvah as his plus-one? After all, he enjoyed her company more than anyone else's, but would it be appropriate? She was after all engaged to another man, a man whom she held little affection for, but another man nevertheless.

However, a Bar Mitzvah wasn't as formal an event as say, a wedding. It was merely a glorified thirteen-year-old's birthday party, Jack told himself, trying to justify asking another man's fiancé to a glamorous event at London's Savoy.

As Jack pondered, he looked over at Betsy curled up on the kitchen floor by the open door. 'What do you think, old girl? Should I ask her?'

Betsy lifted her tired head and let out a loud groan, unusually high and laced with the sound of discomfort or pain, and taking Jack by complete surprise. He watched with concern as Betsy struggled to climb to her feet. Once Betsy was upright he saw the pool of blood she'd left behind her on Grandma Barb's kitchen floor.

'Oh no, no, no!' said Jack as he urgently pushed back on his chair and rushed over to Betsy, who scurried out of the room.

Jack stood in a panic in the kitchen doorway, alternately turning his head to the pool of blood on the floor and the hallway down which Betsy had gone, not knowing what aspect of the emergency to attend to first.

Carly was in her bedroom, putting away her clean washing, when she heard her mobile phone ring. She hung her pink work T-shirt in her wardrobe and meandered over towards the bed where her phone was resting on top of the unmade duvet. She picked it up, and smiled to herself when she saw Jack's name displayed across the screen. As happy as she was to be hearing from him, Carly was a little hesitant to answer the call with Craig in the house.

The phone in her hand, she neared the bedroom door, and hearing that Craig was still downstairs, no doubt staring aimlessly at the television with a hand tucked into his pants, she felt it safe to answer, swiping the screen and placing the phone to her ear.

'Can you come over?' Jack barked down the phone, his tone resting uneasily with Carly.

'Hi, I'm good, thanks, how are you?' Carly replied sarcastically.

'Sorry to be so blunt, but I need help! I need to get Betsy to the vet, and I can't get her out from under the bed, and I need somebody to hold her while I drive, or somebody to drive while I hold her. I have no idea when my gran's coming back, and she's going to go spare when she sees the bloodstain on the kitchen floor and—'

'Okay, okay, calm down … What's happened?' said Carly, interrupting Jack's panicked rant.

'She's bleeding, from behind. I called the vet and he said to bring her by now, but I can't get her out from under the bed. I'm so sorry but I didn't know who else to call …'

Carly watched Craig walk in and disconnect his own phone charging on his bedside table. She flashed him a tight smile, acknowledging his presence, then turned her back on him.

'It's okay, try not to panic. I'm on my way …' she said quietly, and ended the call.

'Who was that?' asked Craig, his finger buried deep in the back of his mouth as he picked his teeth.

'Er, my friend Jane, she's got some kind of emergency with her dog. I'm not really sure what's happened, but I think I should go and make sure she's okay…'

Craig grimaced, failing to source any sympathy

or understanding.

'It's a bit short notice, ain't it? Are you even gonna be back in time to cook the dinner?' he asked, removing his finger from his mouth and wiping the spit-soaked finger on his joggers.

Carly looked at Craig with pure revulsion and placed her phone in her jeans pocket.

'Well, that's the nature of emergencies, Craig, they're often brought on with little notice. And if you're worried about your dinner, there's an oven in the kitchen you can use. Big metal glass thing with hobs on the top, you can't miss it!' said Carly as she brushed past Craig and left the bedroom, rushing down the stairs before he had a chance to respond.

Jack and Carly were waiting anxiously in the veterinary surgery. It was over an hour since Betsy had been taken away to be examined. Carly sat on one of the hard plastic chairs and watched Jack as he paced the small empty waiting room whilst nervously biting his thumbnail. The surgery was only open on Sundays for emergencies, the silence and solitude doing little to ease the tension.

'Should I try and call him again?' Jack asked, startling Carly. He was referring to Betsy's owner, Simon. Jack had already tried to call Simon multiple times, but received no answer, his location in the Middle East not always providing the best phone signal.

After finally dragging Betsy out from under Jack's bed, Jack had held her in his lap on the journey to the vet's as Carly drove. Betsy had bled and whimpered throughout the entire journey and displayed little energy. Judging by her condition, Carly felt it unlikely they were about to receive anything but bad news, but she didn't want to scare Jack, and tried to remain a positive influence.

'No, try him again when they give us an update. It'll do no good worrying him until you have some actual news,' she said, trying to sound reassuring.

'Yes, yes, you're right, you're right,' said Jack, continuing to pace the waiting room.
'Thank you for being here,' he added, pausing for a moment, his voice strained with anguish.

'You're welcome,' said Carly, just as the door in front of her creaked open to reveal the vet on the other side.

He was a tall Asian man, of middle age, with a prominent amount of grey in his short black hair.

'Would you like to come through?' he said in a tone of voice that gave nothing away.

Jack and Carly followed him into the consulting room and stood behind a black, rubber-lined table. The vet went over to the other side of the table and stood next to his nurse, a young, pasty-faced boy with dark spiky hair, dressed in a dark green overall.

'So we've run some tests, and we've found that Betsy has a large, what could be a cancerous growth in her stomach,' said the vet, his sombre expression indicating that the situation was indeed as awful as it sounded.

Jack closed his eyes, placed a hand over his open mouth and let out a deep sigh as the vet confirmed all his most dreaded fears.

'Okay, so where do we go from here?' said Jack, trying to rationalise the next step.

The vet glanced away momentarily, taking a second to think before he spoke.

'Betsy is … very old, and in a great amount of pain. The growth is very large, and I'm afraid to admit there isn't a huge amount else we would be able to do for her now.'

'But you can make her comfortable, surely, with painkillers or something?' said Jack, reluctant to digest what he was being told.

'Indeed, we can ease her pain as best we can, but she is very poorly. The truth is it's unlikely she'll make it through the night. The kindest thing to do at this stage might be—'

'No, no, you can't,' interrupted Jack, not wanting to hear the vet's suggestion.

'Jack …' said Carly, placing her hand on his arm, trying to calm him as best she could.

'No, you don't understand, she's not even mine! I'm just looking after her for a friend … he can't return home to a dead dog. I can't tell him that

I fucked this up. How am I going to explain to him that I couldn't even look after a poodle!' exclaimed Jack, his voice high, as if he was on the verge of tears.

'I understand this is difficult, I do, but honestly, this isn't anything that you've done wrong. Betsy is very old and has been very sick for a long time. Now I can administer some pain relief and you can take her home but the chances are you'll wake in the morning to find her gone,' the vet informed them with great seriousness, his eyes darting between Jack and Carly. He was addressing them both, possibly mistaking them for a couple.

Jack looked desperately at Carly as tears began to surface in his eyes. He seemed to be willing her to say or do something that could change the inevitable.

'Could we have a minute?' Carly asked, subtly taking some control over the situation.

'Of course. Let me fetch Betsy for you,' said the vet, beckoning to his young nurse to follow him out to give Carly and Jack a moment of privacy.

The nurse and the vet left the room and shut the door behind them. The moment the door was shut Jack rubbed his hands over his reddening face and let out a deep frustrated breath.

'Oh God, what on earth am I going to tell Simon?' he said, his hands covering his mouth, as his sad brown eyes looked up towards the ceiling.

'He'll understand,' Carly said softly, gently rubbing Jack's arm. 'He'd want you to do what's best for Betsy.'

Jack nodded his head, absorbing Carly's words, knowing that, as harsh as the reality was, she spoke perfect sense.

The creak of a door broke the sombre silence, and the vet walked in cradling Betsy in his arms. She looked incredibly weak, hanging like a lifeless soft toy in the vet's hold. Her dark eyes met Jack's, minus their usual excitement and joy, indicating that all was not as it should be.

Jack met the vet halfway into the room, and lovingly took Betsy from him, cradling her in his own arms.

'Hello, old girl,' said Jack softly, looking down at Betsy as he held her close.

'I'll give you both a minute with her,' said the vet as he walked back out of the room, pulling the door to behind him.

Carly moved in closer to Jack, her nose catching a waft of Betsy's distinctive odour. Suppressing the urge to gag, she lifted her hand and stroked Betsy's soft curly fur.

'So the doctor tells me you've not been very well, old girl, which is a little inconvenient, because I've become quite accustomed to having you around ...'

Carly felt a tightness develop in her throat as Jack spoke so lovingly and with such kindness, indicating that he had indeed made his decision.

'I'm sorry you're stuck here with me, but I promise to tell your daddy what a brave girl you were,' said Jack quietly, before planting a soft kiss on Betsy's head.

'Would you fetch the vet?' asked Jack, his voice strained as he looked up at Carly and a single tear ran from his right eye.

Carly nodded, forcibly pushing back her own developing tears before leaving the room in search of the vet.

Jack and Carly sat in silence. Carly had parked her car in a tight space just behind Jack's black Mini along the busy main road in front of Grandma Barb's block of flats.

Jack had Betsy's pink dog lead clutched in his hand as they both stared out of the windscreen, neither of them knowing what to say to each other.

Jack had remained quiet the entire journey home, not wanting to interact with Carly through fear of breaking down in front of her, but his silence seemed to highlight his sadness even more.

He looked down at his lap where Betsy had sat only a couple of hours before. As well as feeling heartbroken, he couldn't shake the feeling of complete and utter failure, which rested as uneasily with him today as it always had.

'Are you gonna be okay?' Carly asked sympathetically, taking a hand from the steering wheel and stroking Jack's forearm gently.

'Hmm, yes, I'll be fine …' said Jack unconvincingly. Tears sprang from his eyes and streamed down his face. He lifted his hands and urgently wiped the tears away with the heel of his hand, wanting to wipe away his devastation.

'It's okay to be sad, you know,' said Carly reassuringly.

'God, I don't even know why I'm so upset! She wasn't even my pet!' said Jack through a small chuckle, trying to make light of his heartbreak.

'She might not have been your pet, but she was your friend.'

The very poignancy of Carly's words caused Jack's bottom lip to tremble, and he was a little ashamed of how easily she was able to break him.

'Oh God!' he laughed, embarrassed, and held his sobbing head in his hands as he cried genuine tears of love for his dear departed friend.

Carly manoeuvred in her seat and leant over to give Jack a well-needed hug.

Jack willingly rested his tired weeping head on Carly's shoulder and inhaled her scent of sweet perfume and hairspray, the smell a familiar and welcome one.

As Carly wrapped her arms around Jack's body, she found his slender frame folded perfectly into hers, just like it always had done, and she held on to him tightly, enjoying the feel of his body on hers, not wanting to let him go.

'I should let you get back,' said Jack, reluctantly pulling himself away, embarrassed by his outpouring of emotion.

Carly unwrapped her arms from Jack as he straightened himself up in his seat, preparing to leave.

'Thank you for today, I'm sorry it was ...' said Jack, trailing off, too emotionally exhausted to find an end to his sentence.

'It's okay, I'm always here ...'

'So, I'll see you tomorrow?' asked Jack, referring to Monday's writing class.

''Course,' nodded Carly.

Jack reached for the door handle and just as he was about to open the car door, he paused.

'Oh shit.'

'Everything okay?' asked Carly, hoping whatever was bothering Jack might cause him to stay with her a moment longer.

'I don't think I asked anybody to do a reading tomorrow night.'

Jack liked to open his class with a reading. Every week he'd ask somebody to volunteer themselves to read something that meant something to them, whether it be an extract from a novel, a poem, or even something they had written themselves, all in an effort to get people's creative juices flowing, which was no mean feat.

'Would you mind doing it?' asked Jack.

'Er, yeah, okay, I'll see if I can dig something out,' Carly agreed hesitantly.

'Thanks,' Jack mouthed, genuinely grateful, knowing just how much Carly hated being put on the spot to read aloud.

'See you tomorrow,' said Carly, feeling an overwhelming desire to be near to him, even if it was only for a few more seconds. She reached for Jack's hand that was closest to hers and gave it a gentle reassuring squeeze.

Jack looked down at their connected hands and smiled up at Carly, enjoying the softness of her touch.

'See you tomorrow,' he echoed as he slipped his hand out from under hers, finally opening the car door and stepping out onto the pavement.

It was still early evening when Carly returned home, but it was already dark and there was a sharp wintery chill in the air. She placed her key in the front door and pushed it open.

May looked over the second she heard Carly step inside. She and Craig were watching TV, just as Carly expected. May was sitting up in her wheelchair while Craig was slumped in his recliner, his eyes glued to the television screen with his hand as usual tucked into the front of his jogging bottoms.

'Everything okay, lovey? How was it?'

Carly paused by the front door. As she stood and absorbed May's simple question, all the day's emotion seemed to catch up with her, and she felt an overwhelming rush of sadness. Sadness for the death of Betsy, sadness for Jack's tragic loss, and sadness for her own miserable situation, of having to return home to a place she simply didn't want to be.

Carly felt her insides finally crumble as all her raw emotions freed themselves.

'It was really, really sad,' she said, her voice high and strained as she broke down by the front door.

'Oh lovey, come here. What happened?' said May, reaching out her arms to beckon Carly over for a hug.

Carly moved slowly towards May as she wiped her eyes with the back of her hand and sobbed.

'What on earth happened?' May said as Carly accepted her comforting embrace, letting her head rest on her shoulder as she stood leaning over her chair.

'The vet had to put the dog down,' Carly sobbed between short sharp breaths. She lifted her head to wipe her damp face again with her hand.

'She was very old and really sick, but it was just so sad!'

While Carly explained the devastating details to May, Craig refused to lift his gaze from the television.

'Oh lovey, I'm so sorry. Craig, Carly's really upset,' said May, her son's lack of attentiveness not going unnoticed.

'What?' Craig barked, lifting the remote to

pause the TV, annoyed that Carly's emotional breakdown was interrupting his show.

'Carly, she's upset …' May said softly.

'Yeah, why? It was a dog, it wasn't even your dog,' said Craig, bemused by what he felt to be a complete overreaction.

'That's a bit rich coming from a grown man who cried at the end of *Toy Story*!' Carly snapped back, her mood quickly switching from sadness to frustration in a matter of seconds.

Craig chose not to respond to Carly's smart comment and pressed the play button on the remote, resuming his programme and choosing to end any further conflict with her.

Carly's upper lip curled in disdain. Not wanting all her contempt to rise up and ruin an already difficult day, she marched out of the living room and stomped up the stairs.

'Carly lovey, where you going?' May called after her.

'I'm having a bath and then I'm going to bed!' she called back, and stormed into the bathroom, slamming the door behind her.

CHAPTER 12:

The heating in Jack's classroom only had two settings: 'on' or 'off', with the 'on' option being only a couple of degrees lower than Hell itself, the stifling heat doing little to hold the attention of thirty very bored teenagers in what was the final lesson of the day.

'What tactics does Lady Macbeth use to manipulate her husband?' Jack asked a sea of blank, uninterested faces.

With no one willing to offer an answer, Jack decided to pick on Ollie Hill, a bright boy who could go far if he just applied himself every now and then.

'Ollie, fancy taking a stab in the dark?'

At the mention of his name, Ollie pulled his attention away from the window overlooking the empty tarmacked playground, the barren sight clearly much more interesting than Jack's teaching.

'How does Lady Macbeth manipulate her husband in the passage we've just read?' asked Jack, leaning his behind on the front of his desk, a copy of *Macbeth* in his hand.

'Er… seduction?' answered Ollie with great uncertainty in his voice, flipping his floppy blond hair out of his eyes.

'Not quite the answer we're looking for, Ollie, but good to see where your head's at!' replied Jack, as a small rumble of laughter sounded from his students.

'No, she goes on the attack. She uses blackmail, she brands him a coward, she's emasculating him,' continued Jack, lifting his weight from the desk and beginning to pace the small floor of his cramped classroom, when he was interrupted by the sound of a mobile phone buzzing.

'Okay – whose is it? Hand it over,' ordered Jack, frustrated by what was the third mobile phone interruption of the day.

Jack stood silently looking out at his students, waiting for somebody to own up.

'I think it's coming from your desk, sir,' said Maria Christodoulou, a smug sporting type who always seemed to have an answer for everything.

Jack tuned in his hearing to the sound, which did indeed seem to be coming from his desk.
He marched over to it and opened his top drawer, where his mobile phone was alight and vibrating. Across the screen an unrecognisable row of numbers was displayed, but Jack was quick to notice that *Cambridge* was given as the number's area.

Jack hesitated, knowing it would be hypocritical of him to answer the call, but curiosity about his job application quickly got the better of him.

'I'm so sorry, I need to take this,' he announced.

Outraged gasps sounded from disgruntled students, well aware of the injustice of Jack's behaviour.

'I'm sorry, I know. Maria, can you read on? I'll be five seconds.'

Jack swiped the phone to answer and held it to his ear before he'd even left the classroom.

'Hello.'

'Oh hi, Jack Lewis?' It was a very well-spoken female voice.

'Yes, speaking,' answered Jack, stepping into the corridor and pulling the classroom door shut behind him.

'Right, yes. Sorry, Jack, I assumed you'd be teaching, I was just going to leave a message,' said the woman, sounding a little disorientated at having to engage in conversation.

'Oh er, free period,' spluttered Jack.

'Oh okay, great. This is Pamela Harrison, deputy head at St Augustin's. You applied for our Head of English position?'

'Yes, that's right,' answered Jack, lifting his gaze from the floor to take a peek through the window at his unsupervised class. The sight was disappointing, but by no means surprising. No reading or work of any kind was taking place. Students were aimlessly walking around, a few were sitting on tables scrolling through their phones, while others talked and laughed amongst themselves, the scene not exactly one of anarchy, but certainly one he was keen to restore some order to.

'We were really impressed by your application and we'd love to invite you for an interview … Jack, are you still there?'

'Yes yes, still here, sorry, bad reception. That'll be great!' Jack added quickly, pulling his attention away from the window to focus on the matter in hand.

'Okay. What I'll do, Jack, is send you over all the information you'll need. The interview will be in two parts: a presentation and then a formal interview as well as a tour of the school … so what I'll do, Jack, is email you all the details, and if you have any questions, don't hesitate to give me a call.'

'Okay, great, that sounds perfect,' replied Jack, struggling to take it all in.

'Brilliant, I look forward to meeting you, Jack, goodbye.'

'Bye,' said Jack, and swiped the phone to end the call.

Jack leaned his head back on the wall behind him, wanting to take a moment to absorb the opportunity that now lay before him.

'Huh,' Jack mused to himself, feeling chuffed if a little surprised to have had a response to his application so soon.

A wide smile spread across his face as he allowed himself to feel excited about what could just be the long-awaited fresh start. At the sound of a teenage girl shrieking from the other side of the thin wall he promptly slipped his phone into the pocket of his trousers and turned towards his classroom door, ready to channel an authoritative persona and establish some much-needed calm.

'Right, Dylan, Mikayla, off the desks! Can we resume some order and get back to work!' announced Jack as he stepped into the room with a new-found sense of purpose.

Beside May in her wheelchair, Carly and Lauren were huddled around the living-room coffee table stuffing envelopes with wedding invitations and sticking on stamps. Thanks to Craig's interference, Carly hadn't been able to put off the task any longer and bury her head in the sand, and though she resented him recruiting Lauren to help her with a task for which she had little enthusiasm, she was enjoying the chance to spend time with her friend. Now that they'd both had their work hours reduced, they didn't see each other so often.

'So then, he walks with me to the cash point, makes me draw out half the money for the cost of the dinner to give to him! I'm telling you, May, never again! All this internet dating is just a con ... I think I need to meet a man in the flesh, you know?' said Lauren, filling May and Carly in on her most recent dating disaster.

'I agree, lovey. God knows who you're meeting on these websites. You go out for a drink and before you know it, you could be chopped into pieces and thrown in the Thames!'

'Jesus Christ, May!' exclaimed Carly, her shock only making May and Lauren laugh.

Lauren pressed down the home button on her phone that was resting on the coffee table amongst the cream envelopes and invitations and checked the time.

'Oh, is it that late? I gotta go and collect Sophia,' she said, quickly getting to her feet. 'Lovely seeing you as always, May.' Lauren gave May a soft kiss on the cheek, then crossed the room to pick up her handbag and coat from the stairs.

Carly stood up too, happy to abandon her task.

'So I'll catch you at work when? Thursday?' Lauren asked Carly as she pulled on her coat.

Carly hadn't informed Lauren that her Monday nights were currently being spent at Jack's creative writing class. She froze, caught off guard.

'Why, you not working tonight, love?' asked an inquisitive May.

'Yeah, I am,' said Lauren, failing to sense Carly's panic as she slipped her handbag over her shoulder.

'Yeah, right, so I'll see you in a couple of hours

then,' said Carly, giving Lauren a meaningful look and willing her to go along with what she was saying.

'Right,' nodded Lauren, a good enough friend to pick up on Carly's signal, as a wicked smile spread across her face.

'You know what, Carls, I'm already running a bit late – would you mind giving me a lift to the school? You'll be all right for a few minutes, won't you, May?' Lauren said.

May nodded her head, not wanting to stand in the way of Lauren arriving late to pick up her daughter.

'Er yeah, 'course. I'll just grab my keys,' said Carly, frantically trying to think of some sort of plausible story to tell her friend.

Carly and Lauren walked the few short steps to Carly's car in silence. Carly pointed her key fob at her car, unlocking it and causing the lights to flash. Lauren opened the passenger door and climbed into the seat while Carly went round to the driver's side. She opened the car door, and before she had even sat down, Lauren said, 'What are you doing tonight?'

'I'm not doing anything, I'm just keeping out of the house,' answered Carly, placing the key in the ignition and pulling at her seat belt, not willing to match Lauren's wicked excitement.

'So, what? You doing extra shifts at the hospital or something?' asked Lauren, quick to assume Carly was going somewhere mundane.

To Lauren's surprise, Carly remained curiously silent as she pulled her car out of its parking space.

Not wanting to offload a barrage of lies onto her most trustworthy friend, Carly simply smiled coyly, causing Lauren's eyes to widen in excitement.

'Oh my God! It's that bloke, isn't it, the one from the wedding, the one that came to work?'

Carly's mouth dropped open in shock that Lauren had managed to put the puzzle together so quickly and accurately.

'What, how have you even come to that—' spluttered Carly.

'Because I'm not stupid, Carls! So, what? Are you and him—'

'No, no, he's just a friend. He's teaching a writing class that I've been going to on a Monday night, and that's all,' Carly confirmed, keen to make sure Lauren didn't get the wrong idea.

'A writing class? What the fuck? Like, teaching you how to write?' asked Lauren, her level of ignorance never ceasing to amaze Carly.

'No, a creative writing class, for stories and poems and stuff.'

Lauren sat back in her seat. She was utterly dumbfounded as to why Carly was being so secretive about something that to her seemed so incredibly dull, and for that reason she couldn't help but feel there was more to Carly's story than she was letting on.

'So that guy, he kept saying you and him met at uni?' asked Lauren, trying to put together all the smaller pieces of information she had.

Carly remained silent. She felt uncomfortable, and frustrated, that a secret she had kept so well for so many years was about to be rumbled.

'Carly?' barked Lauren, desperate for Carly to tell her more.

'Yeah, He ... he was my boyfriend at uni,' Carly confirmed, letting out a deep huff and taking a hand from the steering wheel to anxiously rub her forehead.

'What! So you did go to uni? What uni? That bloke, he was so, I dunno ... posh. Was it a fancy one? Did you go to some posh uni?' asked Lauren, firing off question after question, not stopping for breath, ready to burst with indignation at having been denied such defining information about her best friend.

'Cambridge, I went to Cambridge,' Carly answered bluntly, trying to remain calm, but resenting having to reveal her most closely kept secret.

'CAMBRIDGE!' screamed Lauren. 'Fucking hell, Carly! Why did you never say?'

'What? What do you want me to say? Once ... years ago, I used to be smart, like really fucking smart! But I dropped out when my mum got sick, and now, I'm working at a bingo hall, caring for an invalid and about to marry a gravedigger!

How's your luck!' shouted Carly, banging her hand down on the steering wheel, finally releasing all that she once was out into the atmosphere.

'I can't believe you never told me any of this,' said Lauren, shaking her head with her mouth dropped open.

'We're here,' Carly said curtly, pulling the car up across the road from the school, and ready for Lauren to leave.

Lauren looked out the window at the other parents loitering in the playground behind the black iron railings and then looked back at her friend. She could sense Carly's upset, knowing more than anyone how frustrated Carly had always felt about her situation, but it was only now, after all these years of friendship, that she truly understood where it all stemmed from, with everything Carly felt finally making perfect sense.

'You're still really fucking smart, Carls. You're always boring me with shit I don't give a fuck about,' Lauren teased, breaking the tense atmosphere between them. They both started laughing. 'It's true! Who else would make me watch a programme about that Pompey volcano thing?'

'Pompeii,' said Carly, correcting her friend.

'See! I know you don't need to hear it, but, mate … I mean … me, I'm stuck with this life, but you …' Lauren paused, knowing exactly what she wanted to say, but struggling to find the words. 'Just, have a long hard think before you post those invites, yeah?'

Carly nodded and turned her head away from Lauren to look out through the car's windscreen as she felt tears of pure frustration filling her eyes. Her friend might not have always known the finer details, but she knew her well enough, and they both knew Carly was capable of more than she was settling for.

'Bye, babes, thanks for the lift,' said Lauren, sensing it was time to leave. She opened the car door and climbed out, just as the school bell rang out over the playground.

Carly sat nervously tapping her foot under the table as Margery spoke to her with great enthusiasm about her pending trip to Jamaica.

'I go out there every winter, Carly. I can't bear the cold, it does nothing for my bones, the chill … once I'm there I stay for at least a month.'

'Wow, that sounds amazing. That's what I need, a home in a tropical climate,' Carly replied, using the conversation with Margery to distract her from the sheer dread of having to read her chosen piece aloud tonight.

Carly glanced round and up at the small clock on the wall. The class was about to start. She felt a wave of nauseating nerves wash through her stomach and began to fidget with the corners of the scrappy piece of paper in front of her on the table. Her gaze drifted over to Jack, sitting as usual at the head of the table. He was staring blankly at Mandy as she spoke, nodding his head where appropriate, umming and ahing at all the correct points. Carly watched and felt a small smile tug at the corners of her mouth at just how patient Jack could be, a quality she never realised he possessed in such abundance, never once making Mandy aware of just how dull her laborious story was.

'Well, I'll be sure to watch out for those stray French fries in future, Mandy. Terribly hazardous!' quipped Jack, glancing over at the time above Carly's head, ready to wrap up the conversation and get his show on the road.

'Right, well, it's 7.30, and I think we are all here,' he announced, darting his gaze towards Carly. 'So before we get started, Carly has very kindly offered to open tonight's class with a reading of her choosing.'

The rest of the class turned their attention to Carly. With so many sets of eyes on her, she felt even more nervous, her tapping foot now on overdrive.

'Er, so this is just something I wrote, quite a few years back, and um, well, it's no masterpiece, but it's a piece that meant something at the time, and er, yeah, just recently seemed to make sense to me again somehow, I dunno ...' said Carly, unable to disguise her squirming anxiety. She let out a deep huffy breath and blinked hard before placing her hands flat on the table and focusing solely on the sheet of paper before her.

'"Grief ... is a motherfucker ..."'

A light purr of laughter met a few shocked gasps, the class split fairly equally in their reaction.

Carly glanced up from her sheet of paper and over at Jack. He was sitting with his chin resting on his hand, and she was relieved to see his eyes dance as a small laugh fell from his mouth, his reaction giving her the confidence to continue.

'"I wish I could be more eloquent than that and maybe write me a song about it, but unfortunately I possess nothing in the way of musical talent. In my recent experience, grief has been like watching a storm from the window of your house. You see it coming and gradually it gets nearer, but never in a million years do you think that a bolt of lightning will hit *your* roof, causing *your* house and everything in it to burst into flames, destroying everything to ash. But unfortunately, that's exactly what happens. And one day, it's not just some old aunt that you've not seen in six years, but someone whom you love and cherish, whose passing leaves an unimaginable dark void in your heart ... "'

Aware of whom Carly's piece was referring to, Jack was alert to the strain in her voice. As he sat silently listening, he felt a wave of guilt wash over him. For Carly was the kind of person who would drop her plans on a Sunday afternoon to assist him with a friend's sick dog, yet, during what was the most devastatingly painful time of her life, he selfishly obsessed over his own feelings of abandonment, desperately seeking affection in the form of a blowjob from Amy bloody Shepherd.

Not wanting to distract himself from Carly's reading, Jack quickly shook off his feelings and forced himself to refocus.

'"… I feel like we pay a price for love. Not in a bitter way, but maybe the more your heart aches with a person's passing, the luckier you are? Lucky to have had a person in your life that meant so much to you, because I don't believe that's a gift that everyone is privileged enough to receive in their lifetime. Grief is not a unique experience. It's not something that only a few people will ever go through. It will happen to everyone at some point or another. So maybe crying until your eyes burn feels like utter shit, but I think it means you were lucky to have loved someone so very much. None of us will go on forever, and let's be honest, who'd want to? So we should make the most of every day, and not wait until we get that terminal diagnosis to start ticking things off that bucket list. And so I dedicate this to you, the kindest, bravest, smartest person I'll ever know. Sleep well, and I'll see you on the other side."'

Carly let out another deep breath, this time one of relief. She could feel her cheeks burning from the emotionally charged material as well as from her general fear of reading aloud, but she felt proud of her piece, and proud to have made it through the reading without crying.

The class sat in shared reflective silence for a moment, and then turned their attention to Jack, as if awaiting his next instruction.

Jack let out a small cough, clearing his own tightening throat.

'Thank you, Carly. So do we have any thoughts on the piece we've just heard?'

Melody, sitting opposite Carly and next to her friend Jenni, raised her hand.

'I'm not sure how I feel about the use of language. It was a nice enough piece, but I personally think you ruin it with the swearing,' she said.

Carly was taken off guard by such negative and speedy feedback, and she was left wondering if Melody was aware of just how patronising she sounded.

'Bit harsh,' Margery said in Carly's defence. 'Carly's just bared her soul and—'

'What's the issue you have with swearing?' Carly interrupted, grateful for Margery's efforts, but willing to take on Melody herself.

'I wouldn't say I have an issue—'

'Clearly you have an issue,' Carly countered, her unexpected bluntness causing Melody's cheeks to flush in embarrassment. She felt shocked at being challenged by someone who in her opinion was a lesser individual in a cheap Pinky Bingo T-shirt.

'You open a reading about grief with the word "motherfucker". It's grotesque,' Melody responded, her tone again so patronising it was almost preacherly, urging Carly to see the error of her ways in all that she was portraying.

'Yes, yes, it is, and in fact the term is so grotesque that I felt its meaning and vulgarity perfectly emphasised the awful, terrible, physical agony of grief,' responded Carly, desperately trying not to raise her voice.

As the other students sat in awe of the heated scene being played out in front of them, Jack sensed it was time for him to intervene, and so he pushed back on his chair and climbed to his feet.

'I think—'

'You're wrong, there are other words you could have used,' said Melody, so riled she was unconcerned about interrupting Jack.

'I'm not wrong!' snapped Carly, completely outraged by such ignorance.

'The word is grotesque and ruined what could have been a beautiful piece. It was wrong to have used that word,' Melody hit back, her calmness aggravating Carly further because it gave the impression that she was winning at whatever game was being played between them.

Not wanting to seem hysterical, Carly inhaled a deep breath before replying.

'I'm not wrong. I'm not wrong and nor are you. Writing creatively is a form of art, and art is subjective. It's not wrong, nor is it right, it's open for interpretation, it's a matter of opinion. You don't like it: that's fine, but don't sit there and tell me I'm wrong.'

Somewhat proud of her rather dignified response, Carly made confident eye contact with Melody, refusing to be intimidated or belittled by her snobbery.

'I think you have a coarse mouth,' Melody replied, her brash insult taking everyone by surprise. A nervous giggle released itself from Andrew as he looked sheepishly at Jack.

'*Well,* I think—'

'I think it's time we moved on to characterisation,' announced Jack, interrupting Carly. He clapped his hands together, doing what he could to draw his class's attention to other matters and to end the increasingly tense interaction between the two women.

As Jack spoke to the class regarding that week's topic Carly shot Melody her best filthy look, making her disdain clear. Jenni caught sight of Carly's silent attack on her friend and responded with her own look of repulsion, making Carly smile. She was thriving on the controversy, almost going as far as to be enjoying it.

Jenni placed her hand on Melody's forearm and gave it a squeeze.

'Are you okay?' Jenni mouthed to her friend.

Melody nodded her head, and it was with that reassurance that Carly allowed her attention to be drawn back to Jack's teaching.

It was 9.35 p.m. when Jack's class finally wrapped for the night.

Melody and Jenni hastily packed away their notebooks and put on their coats, making a joint effort to avoid any eye contact with Carly, their obvious awkwardness amusing Carly immensely.

Carly couldn't resist poking at them further.

'See you next week, ladies!' she said with a sickening grin and a small wave towards the pair.

'Bye,' Melody responded, reluctant to engage with the pleasantry as she scurried out of the room behind Jenni.

Clive and Andrew were still present as Carly took her usual time packing away her notebook and putting on her coat. Not only was she in no rush to head home, but also she wanted to speak with Jack and ask him how he was doing after yesterday's trauma with Betsy.

With Clive and Andrew talking happily between themselves Carly made her way over to Jack who was stacking a pile of class papers on the table, packing away for the evening.

'Nice to see she's still in there,' said Jack. Not quite understanding what he meant, Carly gave him a puzzled look.

Jack smiled an amused smile, and for the first

time since they had become reacquainted, Carly felt bashful in his presence, taking note of just how charmingly handsome he looked. Dressed in a simple blue shirt and trousers, he'd rolled his sleeves up to his elbows so his strong forearms, with their light covering of fine dark hair, were on display. He looked relaxed, but polished and smart, Carly's observation delaying her response even longer.

'Your little spat with Melody,' said Jack, keeping his voice low in the presence of Andrew and Clive.

'I prefer the term debate.'

'Call it what you will, it's good to see the old Carly is still in there. Reminded me of the old days,' smiled Jack, referring to the Carly that he first fell in love with. The fiercely intelligent and confident Carly who was never scared to challenge anyone, even Cambridge professors.

Jack's gentle reminder of who she once was made Carly feel sad that the earlier version of herself had lain dormant for so long, but equally she felt relieved to know it was still hidden away somewhere deep inside her.

'Night, Jack, see you next week,' said Andrew as he and Clive made their way out.

'Yes, goodnight ... Anyway, for what it's worth, I really liked your piece,' said Jack with great sincerity, his tone masking the awful discomfort he felt about having been the world's worst boyfriend at the time the piece was written.

'Melody didn't,' grimaced Carly, still harbouring some bitterness.

'Fuck her. Fucking snob!' said Jack, his outrageous opinion of one of his students causing Carly to laugh out loud in shock, making Jack laugh also. He was happy to have succeeded in making her feel better.

'Thank you. How are you feeling?' asked Carly as the last of her laughter left her mouth.

'I'm okay, thank you for asking. Although my gran came back from Guernsey late last night. She was upset, more so than I thought she'd be, so much so in fact that she wants to sit shiva for Betsy tomorrow night,' said Jack with a small laugh and a shake of his head as he put the last of his papers into his satchel and placed it over his shoulder.

'She wants to sit and shiver?' asked Carly, assuming she'd misheard something.

'No, not sit and shiver, she has the heating on! You sit shiva, it's a Jewish thing. Essentially it's drinking and eating and chatting with your family the night of a funeral.'

'Like a wake?' asked Carly, trying to make sense of a custom she was unfamiliar with.

'Yes, kind of. The religious folk do it every night for a week after a funeral. You light candles and say prayers, but on this occasion we won't be taking it that seriously, this is merely an excuse for my gran to get rat-arsed!' explained Jack, walking towards the door with Carly and switching off the light in the classroom.

As the pair walked slowly out into the brightly lit foyer and headed for the exit, Jack felt unsettled. There was no reason for them to see each other now until next week's class, and the thought sat uncomfortably with him because he didn't want to wait that long to see Carly again. He opened the narrow wooden door that led outside and gestured for Carly to walk ahead of him out into the dimly lit car park.

A desperate idea slipped straight from Jack's subconscious and out of his mouth.

'You should come along,' he suggested.

'Oh, I wouldn't want to impose on a family thing,' said Carly, unsure as to why her instant reaction was to reject the idea.

'Trust me, you wouldn't be. It's just me and my gran, and instead of mourning a family member, it's a friend's dog!' said Jack, aware of the ridiculousness of his gran's plan and embarrassing himself by not being able to think of a better suggestion for a social meeting.

'Er … yeah, okay. Sounds fun,' said Carly, still a little unsure as to what it was she was agreeing to exactly, but willing to engage in anything that meant she didn't have to spend another evening stuck at home with Craig.

'Okay, great. I'll see you tomorrow then. About eight o'clock?'

'Okay, yeah, I'll see you tomorrow. Should I

bring anything?' asked Carly.

'No, just you; is more than enough,' said Jack as he flashed Carly a handsome smile one last time.

CHAPTER 13:

It was 8 p.m. on a chilly and damp Tuesday evening. In her hands Carly held a dark bottle of red wine she had purchased en route from a Sainsbury's Local. Although Jack had assured her it wasn't necessary to bring anything tonight, she felt it the right thing to do.

Carly walked the last few steps towards the metal street door of Grandma Barb's block of flats and pressed the number 75 button on the cold steel keypad. A dull buzz sounded through the keypad's small speaker and seconds later she heard the heavy metal door release its locks.

Carly pushed her body weight onto the door to open it and felt a small wash of apprehension as she stepped inside the concrete hallway. She felt unsure as to what to expect from the evening and the fact that she felt underdressed wasn't helping. She was wearing her usual Pinky Bingo clothes, having falsely informed Craig and May yet again that she was working. It was a pattern that was beginning to worry her, making her wonder just how much longer it would go unnoticed that the amount of hours she worked no longer matched up with the figure in her bank account.

Not wanting her worried mind to distract her from her evening, Carly pushed aside any negative thoughts, just as the bright red door in front of her slowly opened, revealing a smiling Jack on the other side. He was dressed smartly, presumably still in his work clothes, wearing the trousers, grey jumper and white shirt combo Carly had seen him in before. His feet were resting comfortably inside yellow Homer Simpson slippers, an endearing sight that made Carly laugh inwardly to herself.

'Loving the footwear,' she quipped, opting for subtle wit over a standard hello.

'I dress to impress!' replied Jack, secretly squirming at not thinking to remove his slippers before opening the door.

As Carly stepped inside the flat's long hallway, she noted the aroma of fish and cooking oil hanging in the air, its potency a little overpowering.

'I see you've learnt your lesson,' said Jack, pointing at the bottle held in Carly's hand.

Carly looked down at the bottle and then back at Jack with a frown, having failed to understand the joke.

'Bringing your own drink, best to avoid the tea at all costs,' said Jack, keeping his voice low so that Grandma Barb wouldn't hear him.

'No comment!' replied Carly, remembering all too clearly Grandma Barb's acquired tea-making methods.

Carly followed Jack down the long hallway and into the kitchen, where they found Grandma Barb. She was wearing a white pinny decorated with green teapots over a cream cashmere jumper and a long, smart, grey skirt. She placed a small ceramic black bowl down on the kitchen table amongst a host of highly piled plates of food. The table was longer than Carly remembered, having been opened to make extra room for all the many plates of food that populated the crisp white tablecloth.

The food on offer was a very beige affair. Small round fish balls, flat potato latkes, cheese, crackers and humous, and a large plated challah bread as the central focal point. There were small bursts of colour in the form of cherry tomatoes, olives, gherkins and a plate of bright orange smoked salmon. Each place setting was lovingly pieced together with floral napkins folded into wine glasses and cute floral teacups and small matching plates, making it clear how much effort Grandma Barb had gone to.

'Cara dear! Welcome. I'm so pleased you're joining us tonight!' exclaimed Grandma Barb as Carly walked further into the kitchen.

'Carly,' said Jack, a correction Grandma Barb blissfully ignored.

Grandma Barb reached out her arms and rushed towards Carly with a joyous smile on her face, pulling her near for an overfriendly welcoming hug, before planting a sloppy wet kiss on the side of her face.

'This is for you,' said Carly, once finally released from Grandma Barb's tight hold. She presented her with the bottle of wine held in her hands.

'Oh, thank you very much. How lovely,' gushed Grandma Barb, accepting the bottle from Carly and heading straight for the cutlery drawer by the sink in search of the corkscrew.

'Jack, take her coat, for goodness' sake!' Grandma Barb ordered, at which Jack jumped to attention.

Carly slipped off her coat and handed it to Jack, revealing her Pinky Bingo T-shirt.

'Oh, have you come straight from work, Cara dear?' asked Grandma Barb over the sound of the cork being yanked from the bottle's top.

'Er yeah, I guess that would make more sense,' answered Carly, her enigmatic response not lost on Grandma Barb or Jack, but each with the good grace not to question her answer.

'Sit, sit!' Grandma Barb fluffed, pulling out the chair closest to Carly and beckoning for her to sit down.

While Carly made herself comfortable at the kitchen table, Jack took her coat into Grandma Barb's darkened bedroom. Before placing it down on the bed, Jack couldn't help himself and held the coat up to his nose. He closed his eyes and deeply inhaled, absorbing the comforting aroma of perfume and washing powder, the familiarity of Carly's sweet fragrance making his body ache, making him long to be close to her in a way he knew wasn't possible.

Instantly realising the oddness of his action, Jack quickly pulled the coat away from his face, dutifully placed it down on Grandma Barb's neatly made bed and made his way back into the kitchen.

A couple of hours later Carly, Jack and Grandma Barb were still sitting at the kitchen table eating, drinking and chatting. The more Grandma Barb drank the more she spoke, barely pausing for breath, or the input of anyone else.

Jack, nursing a glass of red wine, and having heard Grandma Barb's stories one too many times, was glad of the fact someone else was there to listen, not that Carly seemed to mind.

Grandma Barb was a well-educated, well-travelled woman, and it seemed she enjoyed nothing more than talking to any willing individual about the interesting life she had led.

'You know where I did love, oh it was an island south of Italy.'

'Oh um, Sicily,' answered Carly, placing down the cup of bitter dark tea that Grandma Barb had insisted on making for her.

'No, no, where all the mobsters come from,' replied Grandma Barb, dismissing Carly's answer with a short wave of her hand.

'Sicily,' said Jack, with a small nod towards Carly.

'It begins with S …'

'Still Sicily,' repeated Jack, Grandma Barb completely ignoring him as she placed her forehead between her hands and rubbed her tired drunken head.

Carly and Jack smiled at each other, neither of them willing to offer anything further until Grandma Barb was able to process her own thoughts.

'Oh, I have a magnet!' Grandma Barb yelped, springing up from her chair and walking with a comical drunken wobble over to the fridge.

Standing by the fridge door, Grandma Barb scanned over the many colourful magnets that cluttered it. The magnets were her most prized possessions, one purchased from every destination she had visited over the past thirty-something years.

'Ah Sicily!' announced Grandma Barb, pulling a small square magnet from the door and causing the invite to James's Bar Mitzvah it was securing to fall onto the lino floor.

Grandma Barb knelt to the floor to pick up the invite, and with the magnet in her other hand, waddled back to the table.

'Wonderful place, have you been, Cara?' asked Grandma Barb, placing the magnet down next to Carly's small china teacup.

'No, I can't say I have,' answered Carly, looking

at the small but stunning picture of a lush green hill dwarfing the clean white hotels and villas that rested upon on it, above the hill a clear sunny blue sky and below it a deep blue sea, the word *Sicily* written across the top of the picture.

Grandma Barb slumped herself back down in her chair between Jack and Carly and gently tossed the invite that had fallen from the fridge door onto the table next to a small used plate and an almost empty glass of red wine.

Carly looked up from the magnet, her gaze drawn to the large red shiny dice that stood out on the invitation's black background.

'Wow, that looks fancy,' she said, struck by the contrast between its shimmer and opulence and her dull, store-bought wedding invitations.

'Yes, my great-grandson's Bar Mitzvah … can you believe I'm old enough to have a thirteen-year-old great-grandson!' laughed Grandma Barb, jokingly running her hands through her blonde curly hair. 'Talking of which, I spoke with Beth the other day, she told me you're still yet to RSVP,' she said to Jack, wagging her finger at him while making a grab for her wine glass with her other hand.

'No, I know, I will. I just haven't got round to it yet,' said Jack with a tired yawn as he stretched his arms over his head, the evening having finally zapped all the energy from him.

Grandma Barb knew her grandson well. She knew that the last thing he would want to have to do at a family event was explain the absence of his fiancée. However, that was no excuse for his tardiness in replying to his cousin.

'So it's nothing to do with you being downcast about not having a plus-one?' teased Grandma Barb before gulping down the last of her wine.

Jack remained silent, giving a slightly embarrassed sideways glance to Carly.

'Well, personally, I can't wait. It's at the Savoy, Cara! Three-course dinner, open bar, and they're putting Granny Barb up in a room at the Savoy for the night, can you believe it?' Grandma Barb bragged, hardly believing her own luck at being treated to such luxury.

'Wow, that sounds amazing. Well if you need a date, Jack, you have my number!' quipped Carly, pushing back on her chair and taking her cold, barely touched tea over to the sink, readying herself to call it a night.

A wide grin spread over Jack's face. He knew Carly was merely making a jovial comment, but he had enough moxie to push her suggestion further.

'Would you like to go?' Jack asked Carly outright, his tone casual and cool, well disguising how desperate he was for her to say yes.

'Oh no, I was just joking!' said Carly, turning round from the sink to face Jack.

'I wasn't,' responded Jack, still effortlessly cool.

'But I wouldn't have anything to wear … and

I'm not even Jewish,' said Carly, genuinely feeling unworthy of such a glamorous event and looking for any plausible reason to excuse herself.

'It's not a cult gathering! You don't have to be a member to be granted access,' chuckled Jack, finding Carly's excuse laughable.

'Yes, Jack's right, it's a celebration, all are welcome!' interjected Grandma Barb.

Carly stood for a moment in silence by the kitchen sink and smiled a sweet shy smile at Jack, making him wonder what she was thinking.

He knew maybe asking Carly was crossing some kind of line, for he wouldn't greatly appreciate another man requesting the company of his fiancé to such an event, but Jack convinced himself this was different. He and Carly went way back. He'd known her longer, probably even better, than her fiancé, and the ball was firmly in her court. If she didn't want to come, she could simply say no.

'It does sound amazing,' said Carly, knowing she would only regret letting such an opportunity pass her by.

'So is that a yes?' asked Jack, his eyes wide in anticipation of Carly's answer.

'Okay, why not?' shrugged Carly with a jovial eye roll, pretending she was being persuaded into something so as to hide how desperate she was to be a part of it.

'Tremendous! Oh Cara, we're going to have

a wonderful time. I think this deserves a toast!' announced Grandma Barb, her excitement about Carly's attendance at the Bar Mitzvah making her rather animated.

'Gran, I think Carly wants to head off,' said Jack, doing his best to save Carly from any more of Grandma Barb's anecdotes.

'Oh hush, I'll be quick!' barked Grandma Barb, lifting her now empty wine glass.

'To our dearly departed friend Betsy, may she rest in peace. To her owner Simon, we wish him long life. To my new friend Cara, and to my favourite grandson Jack, for finally moving back to Cambridge and out of my spare room! L'Chaim!'

Carly stood still, frozen in shock at the kitchen sink, as Grandma Barb lifted her empty wine glass to her lips and cackled loudly on realising it was empty. Carly's mouth dropped open as she watched Jack take a small sip from his glass of wine and then glance at her, uncomfortably shifting in his chair.

'You're moving to Cambridge?' Carly uttered over Grandma Barb's laughter.

'No, well, maybe, but not yet. I have an interview in a couple of weeks, but it's Cambridge, not New Zealand!' said Jack, trying to reassure a stunned Carly.

Indeed Jack was right, geographically Cambridge wasn't all that far away, but to Carly, it may as well have been the other side of the world. She had no business there, not any more, and with her responsibilities at home never allowing her to venture too far, she knew that, if Jack moved to Cambridge, the likelihood of ever seeing him again would be slim.

'He's a Cambridge scholar, you know, Cara. Did he tell you that?'

'Yes ... it's been mentioned,' nodded Carly, her voice low.

'I was so proud of him, and then he got his job at the paper, he was a senior reporter, but then a few years back—'

'Gran, Gran, I think Carly wants to get going,' interrupted Jack, keen to shut Grandma Barb down before she exposed him even more.

'Yes, yes, I need to go now, but good luck with the interview, Jack, and thank you for a lovely evening,' spluttered Carly, feeling overwhelmed by sadness at the thought of Jack moving away, the rush of emotion taking her by complete surprise and making her desperate to escape.

It was almost midnight when Carly finally pulled her car up outside the small house she called home. She was relieved to see all the lights were out, a sign that both of them inside would be soundly asleep.

Carly turned off the engine and took a minute to herself before climbing out of the car.
She let out a deep breath and folded her arms over the steering wheel, slumping forward awk-

wardly and accidently pushing down on the car's horn.

'Shit!' she whispered, bolting herself back upright and hoping the sudden loud noise hadn't woken anybody.

Carly leaned back in her seat and pondered. The whole way home the same uncomfortable feeling had been stewing inside her. The mere thought of Jack leaving for Cambridge bothered her, and it bothered her that she was bothered. She wondered if it was Cambridge she minded, the city holding such significance for them both. Or was it more that she just couldn't bear the thought of his going away?

Carly was finally forced, in the privacy of her car, to acknowledge the uncomfortable, albeit inconvenient, truth. She was falling for Jack; in the exact same way she had fallen for him all those years ago. That oh so familiar feeling of desperately wanting to be near him, wanting to absorb every ounce of his being, relishing every moment of time she was able to spend with him.

There was no way she could admit her feelings out loud; and anyway, what would he even see in her? she told herself. He was an academic, with fancy credentials, surrounded by people that led full and interesting lives, and she worked at a bingo hall. She was a grown woman with real responsibilities, people that depended on her, and she knew the fantasy of a relationship with Jack could remain only that.

Carly knew no good could come from admitting her feelings, and so she took a deep breath, pulled her key from the ignition, suppressed her emotions and forced herself to climb out of the car.

Carly pushed open the street door as carefully as she could and crept into the darkness of the living room. She walked silently past May who was snoring gently in her bed and went slowly up the stairs.

Carly pushed her bedroom door open and was startled to see Craig sitting in the dark bolt upright on the bed.

'Shit, Craig, you scared me!' said Carly, clutching hold of her chest as her heart raced and closing the door shut.

With Craig awake, Carly felt no need to creep around in the dark and flicked on the bedroom light. On top of the bed's messy covers Craig sat wearing his usual scruffy jogging bottoms and grey bed T-shirt, in his chubby hand a half-used silver-foil pack of contraceptive pills. His face was stern and his eyes cold as he stared blankly at Carly standing open-mouthed in shock by the bedroom door.

'What are you doing? Where did you get those?' barked Carly, lunging forward to make a grab for the pills, but Craig was quick and pulled them away before Carly could get her hands on them.

Craig's silence was disconcerting. Carly knew

by the look on his face there was no point in fob-
bing him off, telling him the pills were some sort
of painkiller or allergy relief, and she wondered
how long he had been sitting alone in the dark
waiting for her, mulling over his discovery.

Carly felt dread overcome her, knowing a row
was imminent, and so she felt no need to hold
back and was the first to go in on the attack.

'Why were you going through my things?' she
barked angrily, making a second lunge for the
packet, but Craig was fully expecting it and
swiping the packet away from Carly got up from
the bed, his movement causing her to fall forward onto the messy duvet.

'I was looking for a pair of tweezers for the hair
on my mole,' said Craig, distracting Carly as the
image of the large hairy mole on his upper leg
came into her mind and made her cringe in disgust. Taking a pause from her anger, she sat herself down in the space Craig had just vacated.

'How long have you been taking these?'
shouted Craig, his sudden loud aggression laced
with a strong air of hurt.

'Shut up, Craig, you'll wake May!'

'How long?!' Craig shouted louder, his seething
fury beginning to frighten Carly.

'It's none of your business,' Carly answered
nonchalantly, refusing to match Craig's state of
agitation.

'None of my business! Are you having a laugh?'
Craig yelled, pacing the bedroom floor as his

cheeks reddened with anger, tears beginning to surface in his eyes.

'Oh calm down, Craig,' Carly said coldly, standing up and walking over to her own side of the bed. She pulled at the hairband holding her ponytail in place and tossed the black elastic down on her bedside table. 'We don't even have enough sex to make a baby anyway,' she said with a small laugh, trying to make light of the increasingly tense situation.

'Yeah and don't I fucking know it!' he shouted back, unable to find anything humorous in their conflict.

Carly stood still and watched Craig as he continued to frantically pace their small bedroom, unsure as to what her next move should be and desperately hoping their arguing hadn't woken May.

'Carly, I'm gonna ask you this once, and I want you to answer me honestly,' Craig said calmly, planting himself in front of Carly with a look of desperation on his face.

Carly felt her stomach tie itself into knots.

Maybe this is it, she thought.

Maybe Craig had finally received the message and realised for himself that their relationship was over. Maybe he was going to ask her if they should break up. Maybe tonight she was going to be granted the long-awaited get-out, and she'd be finally free of her miserable existence.

Carly braced herself. Along with the nervousness, she could feel a soft note of excitement humming inside her. She nodded her head gently at Craig, giving him permission to ask whatever he needed to.

'Carly, do you think ... that maybe ... you're a lesbian?'

Carly stared blankly into Craig's small peering eyes as any hope and excitement quickly evaporated and sheer frustration took its place.

'Craig. What the fuck is wrong with you!' she blasted, angry at herself for getting her hopes up.

Carly swept past Craig and pulled open the bedroom door, storming through it and slamming it shut behind her, too angry to care if the noise woke May. She marched down the landing towards the bathroom but before she reached it she heard the bedroom door fly open again and the sound of Craig's heavy footsteps.

'Well it would explain a few things!' he shouted down the landing. 'Why you never want to have sex!'

'Craig, if you are too pig ignorant to look past your own nose then I really can't help you!' yelled Carly, refusing to turn round and face Craig. She opened the bathroom door and slammed it shut behind her, at which Craig swung it open.

'Why you jump at the chance of seeing this Jane woman all the time! Why you don't want to have a baby,' said Craig, continuing to rattle off all the logical reasons he had been storing up in his mind.

'Right. Because everybody knows the most common sign of lesbianism is not wanting to procreate!' Carly yelled sarcastically, utterly astounded by Craig's ignorance.

Craig turned to close the bathroom door in what seemed like a pointless effort not to wake May. In closing the door he blocked out the light seeping along the landing from the bedroom, but they stood there in darkness, it not occurring to either of them to switch on the bathroom light.

'Well I'm fucked if I can figure you out, Carly!' hissed Craig in a whisper.

'Did it ever occur to you, Craig, that maybe I'm fucking knackered!' Carly hissed back, also anxious to keep her voice down. 'I look after May, I clean this house, I cook your dinners, I wash your clothes, I volunteer at the hospital, I go to work and I come home late, and maybe the idea of having a baby on top of all that might just be too much for me!' she ranted, her irate explanation not at all untrue, but Carly was fully aware she was skirting around the real reason: she didn't want a baby with a man she didn't love.

'Then give up the job, you'd get more on benefits than what they pay you!' said Craig, as if proud of himself for having magically thought up a solution to all their problems, but Carly felt herself seething with anger.

The fact that Craig would rather her troubles

be eased by her quitting work than by him offering anything in the way of help in the home made her blood boil, his refusal to lift a finger in the house being one of the things on her long list of things she despised him for.

Her job was the only piece of freedom she obtained. It was the only opportunity she ever had to leave the house and currently the only excuse she could use to see Jack. Carly knew she would never be able to reason with Craig's ignorance, and so she had nothing further to say, already tired but now mentally exhausted.

Resenting Craig for having ruined a lovely evening, she ran her hand through her long, light ginger hair and pushed it away from her face, and felt no shame in being the one to surrender.

'It's late and I'm tired. I need to sleep, and I'm going to do that in the spare room,' said Carly, brushing past Craig and opening the bathroom door.

'So that's it, you're just going to leave it there?' Craig called, annoyed that all their arguing had failed to resolve anything.

'That's right,' Carly called back, as she walked down the landing. She opened the door to the spare room and shut herself inside.

Carly threw herself down on the bed fully clothed and closed her eyes. She could hear the sulking footsteps of Craig walking from the bathroom and back down the landing and she held her breath, fully expecting him to enter her room.

Carly heard the footsteps stop and the dull thud of Craig closing their bedroom door, the sound filling Carly with a great sense of relief, for she would finally be allowed to enjoy a night alone in bed without him.

CHAPTER 14:

It was almost 6 p.m. on a Friday evening. Carly had only half an hour until she needed to leave the house ahead of her evening volunteering at the hospital. She dished up three plates of shepherd's pie and took two of them into the living room. Craig was lying on the sofa in his scruffy work clothes with one hand protecting the television remote.

Carly walked up to May who was sitting up in her wheelchair and graciously placed her dinner down on the wooden manoeuvrable table in front of her.

'Thanks, lovey,' May said gratefully, awkwardly picking up the cutlery, ready to tuck into her meal.

'You're welcome,' said Carly as she took a seat at the end of the sofa, abruptly dropping herself down on Craig's feet.

Craig slid his feet out from under Carly, their clumsy interaction being the first time they had acknowledged each other since Craig's return home from work.

'Where's mine?' asked Craig, sitting himself up

from the sofa.

'In the kitchen,' Carly answered curtly, leaning forward to pick up her cutlery from the coffee table in front of her.

Craig let out a loud huff and resentfully pulled himself from the sofa and skulked into the kitchen.

It had been almost two weeks since Craig's discovery of Carly's pills and the pair had barely spoken since.

Neither Craig nor Carly had confided in May, but unbeknown to them, May had been woken by their rowing that night and was fully aware that all was not well in paradise.

The atmosphere in the house was always tense when they were both present, so much so May was grateful for the times one of them was out.

She couldn't say for certain, but she reckoned they were sleeping separately, with Carly using the spare room. From what she had heard, their rowing hadn't seemed directly linked to her, but that didn't stop her feeling that she was at fault. May worried that her sheer presence meant Craig and Carly were denied the right to hash over their differences in the way a young couple should.

She loved them both dearly and wanted nothing more than for them both to be happy. After a fortnight of little softening from either party, May felt it was time to step in and right all that was wrong.

Craig returned from the kitchen, sat himself down on his recliner, as far away from Carly as he could get and loudly began to tuck into his food.

'So I've been doing some thinking …' began May, swallowing her mouthful.

Carly turned her head to face May, but Craig paid less attention, flicking his gaze between his plate and the television.

'… what with the wedding not being all that far off, I thought maybe it's time for us to start thinking about living arrangements.'

'How do you mean?' asked Carly, with a mouth full of shepherd's pie.

'You two don't want to start your married life with me here getting in the way—'

'What are trying to say?' asked Craig, willing his mother to get to the point, his involvement coming as a surprise to Carly.

May placed her cutlery down on her table and looked up at the low ceiling.

The pause in conversation prompted Craig to look at his mother, and both he and Carly instantly noticed the tears beginning to form in May's eyes.

'I just want you both to be … to be like other couples. Me living here with you both, it's too much pressure. I think it's time I looked into going into some kind of residential care.'

'And where do you suppose we'll get the money for that!' blurted out Craig, outraged at what to him seemed a ludicrous suggestion, given the family's finances.

Astonished at Craig's tactlessness, Carly knew it would be up to her to intervene.

'Aside from that ... May, this is your home,' said Carly, placing her plate and cutlery down on the coffee table and nearing May to take her weakening hand into her own.

'But things are only going to get worse and it's unfair to expect you both to take on that burden when you wanna start a family of your own,' said May as a tear fell from her eye, all of her pent-up emotions and anxieties of the past two weeks seeping out of her. She brushed the tear away with her hand.

'May, we *are* a family, the three of us.'

'You know what I mean,' said May, her voice breaking as she tried her hardest to hold it together after so much worry about the impact the demise of her health was having on her loved ones.

While May quietly sobbed, Craig and Carly looked at each other and felt a mutual sense of guilt, knowing the friction between them was what had led to this very conversation.

Although Carly still held on to a great amount of anger towards Craig, her love and respect for May overshadowed her resentment. Carly couldn't let May believe that her health and presence were the main reasons for the contempt she felt for Craig, and so Carly gave her best in the way of a defeated smile to Craig, which he returned, a silent agreement to call time on their fractious behaviour.

'Mum, when, if, the day should come when you need more help than we can provide, we'll discuss a home, but until then you'll be staying here,' said Craig, lacking much in the way of tenderness, but saying all that needed to be said.

'He's right, May, much as it pains me to say it,' said Carly, at which May let out a soft laugh through her sadness. 'Until that day comes, we'll all be staying here together,' said Carly with a reassuring smile, hiding her anguish at the thought of such an arrangement.

Carly lifted herself from the sofa and wrapped her arms around May.

May too wrapped her arms around Carly and held her tightly.

'Be happy, lovey. Do what you need to do to be happy,' May whispered into Carly's ear.

Carly pulled her body away and looked quizzically at May. Completely taken off guard, she stared at May, unsure if she had heard her correctly.

Does she know? Carly asked herself.

Was May aware of how deeply her unhappiness was cutting through her? Was she giving Carly her blessing to seek happiness elsewhere? Carly wasn't sure.

'Eat your dinner, lovey. You need to get yourself to that hospital, those books won't sell themselves!' said May, as if brushing their

troubles away, keen to move on from the sadness.

Carly sat herself down on the sofa and, desperately trying to make sense of what she had just
been told, looked back at May. As May picked up
her knife and fork from her table she looked lovingly at Carly and gave her a soft knowing smile
and a wink before continuing to eat her food.

'Wait, wait, wait!' Grandma Barb bellowed with
great urgency down the hallway, just as Jack
opened the flat's front door.

Jack turned his head to see his grandmother
doing the closest she could to a sprint towards
him, waving a small Tupperware box in her
hand, its contents wrapped in scrunched tin foil.

'You've forgotten your sandwich!' she said,
handing the plastic container to Jack.

'Gran, I told you, I'll just get something at the
station,' said Jack, refusing to accept the box
from Grandma Barb.

'Now what kind of grandmother would I be if I
sent you out into the world without something
to put in your belly!' she insisted, thrusting the
box at Jack once again.

Jack reluctantly accepted the plastic container, opened his satchel and dropped it inside,
secretly touched that somebody cared about
him so much.

Jack was nervous, the feeling unfamiliar, and
it rested uncomfortably with him, but he was

aware the feeling was quite natural, for today was an important day, the day of his interview in Cambridge.

It would be a busy day, too, what with the journey to and from Cambridge, and then on to his creative writing class, which was maybe why Grandma Barb wanted to make sure he had enough in the way of food.

'Now do you have your mobile telephone on your person?' asked Grandma Barb, fussing with Jack's smart coat as she spoke.

'Yes, I have my mobile telephone on my person,' chuckled Jack.

'Good, call me later and let me know how it's gone. Oh I'm so excited for you, darling. Very best of luck!' said Grandma Barb, pulling Jack's face towards hers with a hand gripping each side, then planting one of her sloppy kisses on his cheek.

'Now go, I don't want you to be late,' said Grandma Barb, releasing Jack and forcibly shoving him out the door.

As Jack walked with purpose along the busy main road under a grey and cloudy sky, his mind was a whirl of thoughts. He wondered how life would change, should he get the job. He wondered if he should start looking at places to rent on the train journey. He wondered how well his presentation would go, and if maybe the train journey should be spent brushing up on it. Of all the thoughts his mind possessed, the one image that stood front and centre was that of Carly.

Exciting as the possibility of starting again was, Jack was terrified by the idea of having to say goodbye to the one person he adored more than any other. Just the sheer presence of her made each moment so much sweeter, but it was important for Jack to remind himself of the uncomfortable fact that always seemed to slip his mind: her future was not destined to be with him. She was unattainable, ready to marry someone else, someone whom she felt great loyalty to, and that situation was unlikely to change.

While Jack tried his best to push down his ever-building adoration, his mind was conveniently distracted by the vibrating of his mobile phone in his coat pocket. Jack pulled out his phone and was surprised to see the name *Brad* displayed across the screen. Although Jack and Brad often spoke, at 7.45 a.m. it seemed rather early for one of their catch-ups. Curious as to what the call could be regarding, Jack swiped the phone to answer just as he made it into the station's entrance.

'Hello.'

'Hiya, Jack. How's things?'

'All's well. You?'

'Um, yeah, good. You on your way to work?' asked Brad a little hesitantly and Jack could sense an unusual uncertainty in his voice.

'Not quite. I'm on my way to Cambridge for an interview,' answered Jack as he secured the phone to his ear using his shoulder and searched his satchel for his Oyster card.

'Oh yes, of course! I'm so sorry, Jack, I didn't realise that was today. Look, I'd better go. I'll give you a call tomorrow,' said Brad, using Jack's plans for the day as an excuse to rush himself off the phone, a behaviour that was most unusual for a chatterbox such as Brad.

'It's fine, I'm not in the interview, I can talk,' Jack laughed nervously, starting to feel uneasy at Brad's out-of-character behaviour.

The line went silent. Jack pulled the phone from his ear to check if Brad had ended the call as he walked down the grey steps that led to the station's already bustling platform.

'Brad, you still there?' asked Jack as he secured himself a position along the station's metal fencing.

'Yes, yes, I'm still here …' Brad answered, and then sighed deeply, the distinct lack of cheerfulness in his voice starting to worry Jack.

'Is everything okay?' asked Jack, concerned for his friend's welfare.

'Look, Jack, I think it's best we speak tomorrow.'

'Brad, you're starting to worry me, what's going on?' asked Jack, his question causing Brad to fall silent once again.

'Brad?' said Jack, wondering once more if Brad

was still there.

'The injunction. It's being lifted,' Brad blurted out, unable to keep the burning piece of information to himself any longer, just as Jack's train pulled into the station.

Jack stood perfectly still. His mind involuntarily catapulted him back to all that had happened three years before. He felt his mouth go dry as his heart raced furiously inside his chest and he watched, paralysed, as his train closed its doors and rolled out of the station, minus him aboard.

'Jack, you still there?' Brad asked softly, bringing Jack back round to the present.

'When?' asked Jack, his voice pitchy.

'In a couple of days.'

'No, I mean when. When are you running the story? I assume that's what this is about,' said Jack, trying to assert himself, keen to get to all the facts he needed.

'Well, in the next couple of days,' said Brad, confirming the obvious.

'Right ...'

'I'm so sorry, Jack. I just ... wanted to be the one to tell you—'

'It's fine. We all knew this day would come eventually,' said Jack, looking up at the grey sky, leaning his head back in an effort to stem the tears that were beginning to surface in his eyes.

'Are you okay, Jack?'

'Um, yes. Um, right, well, Brad, I think, I mean

I'd better shoot, I've got to …' spluttered Jack, barely able to string a sentence together.

'Yes, yes, of course.'

'Okay, bye then, Brad. Thanks for the call,' said Jack, already pulling the phone away from his ear, ready to hang up.

'Jack … ' he heard Brad say, prompting him to apply the phone back to his ear.

'I'm here for you, bud, you know that, right?'

'Yeah … I know. Thanks, Brad,' said Jack.

'And good luck with the interview. I hope it goes well.'

'Yeah, me too,' said Jack, able to raise a small smile.

'Bye, bud …'

'Bye.'

Jack swiped the phone's screen to end the call and slipped it back into his coat pocket. He rubbed his cold hand over his face, trying to push back his emotions, and let out a deep sigh. Jack knew eventually this day would come. The injunction would be lifted, and the press would want to release their story, but he still couldn't believe that that day was now here.

Still unable to talk about that day with anybody outside of a professional setting, Jack knew he wasn't ready for the entire country to find out about all that he had witnessed.

Jack looked up at the digital departures board and saw that the next train would be arriving in three minutes. Annoyed with himself for missing his train, Jack hoped the rest of his day could only improve and was determined now more than ever for this day to mark the beginning of a much needed fresh start.

As Jack walked up the gravel entrance to St Augustin's he was impressed. There was a definite sense of calm about the place. He could hear the music of birds singing, the tranquil sound far from the din of car engines and sirens coming from the busy main road that backed onto Langston High.

The tall Victorian red-brick building was surrounded by well-kempt evergreen shrubs and a neatly trimmed lawn, a sight that made him feel that maybe he had indeed found the perfect place to start his life again – *if only Carly was able to share in it too*, he thought sadly, her never far from his mind.

Throughout his commute to Cambridge, Jack's mind had been preoccupied by the news Brad had given him. He knew the time he'd spent in denial was almost up. He knew that, soon enough, all that he struggled to say would be said for him in the style of a tabloid headline that he would have no control over, and the thought terrified him.

As Jack walked up towards the school's main reception, his thoughts were interrupted by the school bell ringing out. He picked up his walking pace, keen to check himself into reception before droves of teenagers descended on the corridors.

Inside Jack stood on the well-trodden parquet floor as he waited his turn. In front of him was a lanky young man, scruffily dressed in dark blue jeans and a crinkled plaid shirt, and struggling to keep hold of the large beige duffel bag on his right shoulder whilst signing the visitors' book.

A set of glass double doors did what they could to muffle the sound of the last few stragglers making their way along the corridor to their next class and Jack laughed inwardly at the sight of a middle-aged female teacher hurrying along a small group of teenage girls, all dressed in matching burgundy skirts and blazers, and all much more concerned with sharing gossip than making their way to the classroom.

Jack's attention was quickly brought back round by the dull thud of the man's duffel bag dropping clumsily to the floor.

'Oh, I know I'm already running late, but is it okay to use your loo?' asked the man, looking rather flustered as he bent to the floor to pick up his bag.

The chubby receptionist shook her head in frustration and tutted behind the plastic screen that separated them before letting out a loud huff. She was a late-middle-aged lady and wore her hair in a sharp blonde bob, her blunt hairstyle in accordance with her blunt manner.

'Okay, I'll have to show you. The Gents down

here are out of order, the other staff loos are all the way upstairs,' she said, not hiding her frustration at having to leave her position.

'Yes, you, who are you here to see?' the receptionist curtly asked Jack, pointing her fuchsia nail at him through the screen.

'Pamela Harrison, I have—'

'Yes, okay, sign in and take a seat,' said the receptionist, waving coldly towards the signing-in book and getting up from her seat.

Jack did as he was told and picked up the black biro pen that was attached to a lever arch file by a frayed piece of green string. He heard a beep, and looked up to see the receptionist opening one of the glass doors with her key card and ushering the young man through. Jack watched as he was marched down the corridor.

Having signed his name and written down the time of his arrival, Jack found himself alone, and took a seat on one of the four red plastic chairs that lined the wall of the narrow area.
As he sat waiting in mild anticipation, he heard another beep. The door was swung open by a woman around the same age as himself. Her cheeks were a little flushed and she possessed a slight air of irritation about her person.

'Lewis?' she said from the doorway.

'Er, yes …' answered Jack, surprised to be addressed by his surname. Almost as surprised as he was by her appearance. Pamela had sounded professional, experienced, on the phone, he'd assumed she was an older woman, but the woman glaring at him now was not only younger than he'd expected but rather plain, dressed in unflattering black trousers and a tight red jumper that drew attention to a sagging ample bosom.

'You're late, you were meant to be here twenty minutes ago,' said the woman impatiently, brushing her long frizzy hair away from her face.

'Oh, really? I thought my appointment was for eleven,' answered Jack, believing he was in fact fifteen minutes early. Jack stood up from his seat and walked towards the woman at the glass door.

'Have you brought everything you need for the demonstration?' she asked, looking over Jack's person as she marched him at great speed down the long empty corridor.

'I'm sorry, I don't understand,' answered Jack, feeling confused, for he was fully aware he was expected to deliver a presentation, but a demonstration?

'For the demonstration?' the woman repeated bluntly, her patience wearing thin at Jack's vagueness.

'I have a presentation on a memory stick. Should I hand it over?'

'No, no, keep it on you, there's a laptop in the classroom, just plug it in when you get there.'

Jack nodded his head and wisely chose to remain silent for the remainder of his short tour of long corridors and sharp corners.

'Okay, here we are,' said the woman, halting outside a brown glossy door and pushing it open.

Jack followed her inside and was horrified by the sight of a full class of twenty fourteen- to fifteen-year-olds. Although fully prepared to give a presentation, Jack had assumed he would merely stand before a handful of staff members on a professional panel, and he was not at all prepared.

The air was filled with the murmur of chatter, and Jack was impressed by the students' behaviour, considering they'd been left unsupervised, so unlike the unruly behaviour he was used to at Langston High, but it did little to diminish his anguish.

'Sorry for the delay everyone, but our guest speaker has finally arrived,' announced the teacher, making her way over to stand before the four long tables that faced a white smart board.

Jack held back, utterly bewildered as to what was going on, and then felt even worse when he saw what was written on the smart board: *Sex Talk* in large blue letters.

'Right, I don't want to waste any more time, so let's get right to it, shall we?' said the woman, staring hard at Jack, urging him to join her at the front of the class.

Jack stood at the back of the class open-mouthed as the students gradually turned their heads to take a look at the man who was holding up proceedings. Jack was sure a terrible error had been made, and he knew he should say something before it was all too late, but then again, he wondered, what if it wasn't a mistake? What if this was the newest style of teacher interviewing? A style of psychological testing? To throw an unsuspecting person in at the deep end, to witness whether they would sink or swim?

Jack so badly wanted the opportunity to start his life afresh, and so he knew he had no choice but to jump in headfirst.

'Sex, right, sex …' said Jack, gently nodding his head and blinking hard.

Jack made his way to the front of the class determined to display nothing but confidence, experienced enough to know that no one could sense fear in a man more than a gathering of teenagers.

'Thank you for that introduction, Miss—' said Jack, removing his satchel and coat and placing them on the brown plastic chair behind the teacher's cluttered desk.

'Webster,' answered the woman, abandoning Jack and walking to the back of the class to observe his torture.

'So, well, let's begin. I am Mr Lewis, and I am here today to talk to you about … sex … it seems. Er, so, right, what is the most important thing we need to remember when it comes to sex?'

A number of hands were raised in the air, and Jack was surprised by the level of participation.

He decided to choose one of the boys in the second row whose pale skin was littered with large red pimples. Jack pointed at him, giving permission to answer.

'Protection,' the boy answered without a hint of embarrassment or awkwardness, outwardly displaying a sense of self-assurance Jack was impressed by.

'Indeed, protection is very important, and certainly at your age none of you should be engaging in any sexual activity without fully protecting yourselves. However, one day, when I'm sure many of you look to start making babies of your own, protection won't always be such a priority.'

Jack heard a soft knock at the door. He paused as the students turned their heads to Miss Webster at the back and waited for her to speak.

'Carry on,' she said, opening the door and stepping outside.

'But one factor that will always be the most important, whether you're a randy teenager or an old man like me ...' said Jack, at which the students all laughed gently as he casually paced the floor.

'... is enjoyment, and by enjoyment, I mean that to be the case for both parties. And in order for that to happen, there needs to be a level of mutual consent. Is that clear?'

Jack knew he had the class's full attention and was happy to see them all listening and gently nodding, but he was distracted by the aggravated hushed tones coming from the other side of the door that had been left ajar.

As Jack began to wonder what on earth was going on outside, Miss Webster walked nervously back into the class, joined by a smartly dressed lady in a black skirt suit and the scruffily dressed man he'd come across in reception.

All three stood at the back of the classroom, on Miss Webster's face a look of great discomfort. The smartly dressed woman far more resembled the image of a deputy headmistress. Although her face was free from any obvious make-up, her short, light blonde hair was elegantly styled and the mauve scarf that hung loosely around her neck added some softness to her outfit.

From the look on Miss Webster's face it quickly became apparent to Jack that maybe he had been the unfortunate victim in a case of mistaken identity, but with no one signalling for him to stop, he took the initiative to soldier on.

'You see, the most important thing to remember when it comes to sex is that it's not just an activity designed for procreation but for fun, for pleasure, too. Don't be the reason why someone else associates something wonderful with pain, or fear, and if anyone has ever made you feel like that, remember there are people you can speak to. That includes myself and any member of staff in this building.'

Jack saw the smartly dressed woman nod in agreement and smile softly at him, and although the smile helped put him at ease, he was none the wiser as to what exactly was going on.

'Now, I can start talking you through the mechanics, but I'm not sure that's going to be that useful ... at what, fourteen, fifteen years old, I'm sure you're all pretty aware of the basics? So I think what we'll do is open the floor and this is your chance to simply ask whatever you want to ask, and I'll try my best to pass on my ill-gathered wisdom,' said Jack, casually resting his weight on the edge of Miss Webster's desk, settling himself before he was met by a barrage of uncomfortable questions.

A few students raised their hands and Jack made the conscious decision to pick one of the boys again, in the hope that he might be able to relate. Jack pointed at an olive-skinned boy who displayed a dark shadow of thin black hair above his top lip.

'Is it true a girl's fanny smells like fish?' asked the boy, his question followed by his own uncontrollable laughter, as well as gasps of outrage and hilarity from the other students.

Shocked but impressed by the boy's outrageousness, Jack tried his level best to contain his own laughter and chewed down hard on the inside of his cheeks. He looked over at the trio at the back of the class, hoping now was the time for somebody to intervene, but with no sign of that, he knew he had no choice but to answer the question put before him.

'Okay, straight in there! Er, well, like feet or under arms, it certainly has its own … aroma if you will. But like any body part, if it's kept clean there's no reason it should smell of anything untoward,' answered Jack, trying and failing to suppress an amused nervous laugh.

'Right, next question?' said Jack, swiftly moving on to another student, this time choosing one of the girls, a pretty brunette with long hair and large stylish glasses.

'Can you get pregnant from anal?' she asked with an unnerving giggle.

Jack squirmed and rubbed his forehead, starting to show his discomfort.

'Technically, no. But do remember just because that point of entry isn't the baby maker doesn't make it a safer one,' said Jack, moving position from the end of the desk and beginning to pace the floor while he elaborated further.

'Going back to the importance of protection, in many ways an STD is an even bigger commitment than a baby, by which I mean it won't leave home after eighteen years. You could be stuck with that for life, so whatever entrance you use, just make sure to protect it.'

Feeling he had answered a teenage girl's question about anal sex as best he could, Jack inhaled a deep breath. As he mentally prepared himself for the next question, he was interrupted by the sound of clapping by the smartly dressed woman at the back of the class.

'Okay, class, now I want you all to show your appreciation for Mr Lewis's contribution to today's discussions,' she bellowed in a loud assertive voice, her solo round of applause soon accompanied by that of the students.

A great sense of relief rushed through Jack, grateful that the agony was seemingly coming to an abrupt end.

'Thank you, Mr Lewis, really that was certainly ... refreshing. Now, class, may I introduce *Lewis Turner* who will be continuing your sexual health talk from here. Lewis is a sexual health advisor joining us today from CTASH and will be leading the rest of the session's discussions.'

Lewis Turner stumbled to the front of the class and Jack fought the urge to hug the woman who had finally come to his rescue, but rather than embarrassingly embracing a complete stranger, Jack raced to gather his coat and satchel and quickly followed on the coat tails of the woman who had orchestrated his escape.

Safely outside in the corridor, Jack closed the door behind him.

'Jack Lewis, I presume?'

'Unfortunately so,' nodded Jack.

'Pamela Harrison,' said the woman, holding out her hand and offering Jack a firm handshake.

'I can only apologise, Mr Lewis, a terrible case

of mistaken identity, I'm afraid.'

'That's quite all right, I'm sure it could've been worse.'

'Indeed. Now I think I owe you a cup of something warm before we get started,' winked Pamela, taking sympathy on Jack before leading the way back along the corridor. 'But may I say, you handled that excellently,' she added, impressed by Jack's ability to think on his feet.

'Well, maybe if today doesn't work out I could consider sexual health advisor as my next career move,' quipped Jack.

'I'm quite positive it won't come to that, Mr Lewis,' replied Pamela with a warm smile, already sure Jack was just the kind of candidate she was looking for.

CHAPTER 15:

'I remember my thirteenth birthday. I got a hair-dryer! Or was that for my twelfth? Either way, it certainly weren't this extravagant!' said Lauren as she stood behind Carly and pulled up the zip on the sapphire gown that was to be her brides-maid's dress for Carly and Craig's pending nup-tials.

Fortunately for Carly, she and Lauren were just about the same size. In need of a gown for the black-tie event at the Savoy, Carly hadn't had to look any further than her best friend for help.

'I honestly can't even remember how I spent mine. Anyway I'm not sure it's actually a birth-day party as such. It's more to do with becoming a man and all your family and friends give you a shitload of money, or that's at least how Jack explained it,' said Carly, holding her hair out of Lauren's way.

'So when they say thirteen is unlucky for some, I guess that doesn't apply to Jews?' chuckled Lauren, brushing down the back of the dress, making sure it was sitting perfectly on Carly's body.

'Ha, so it seems!' said Carly, letting go of her long hair so it fell over her shoulders and back. She turned her body round and took a look at herself in the floor-length mirror on Lauren's wardrobe door, the mirror also reflecting Lauren's unmade bed, cluttered with an array of handbags and jewellery amongst other accessories being used as part of the dress- up session between the two friends.

'You look beauts, babe, you really do,' gushed Lauren.

Initially when Lauren had picked her bridesmaid's dress, Carly had taken little interest, but now she was grateful for her friend's taste. As nervous as Carly was about attending such a fancy event, the sight of herself in Lauren's dress made her feel more at ease. She felt confident now that she would at least look the part. The floor-length gown would look right with a pair of heels, and the halter-neck design showed off her chest nicely whilst still keeping things modest.

As Carly admired herself in the mirror, she swayed her hips gently, making the bottom of the dress gently flow around her feet whilst the material around her waist and hips clung to her frame just tightly enough to highlight her curves.

'So where does Craig think you're going? You know, just so I know?' asked Lauren, sitting herself down on the edge of the bed whilst filtering through the handbags that littered it.

'He will think that my best friend has taken me on a pre-wedding … overnight … spa day … thing,' rattled off Carly, at which Lauren grimaced at Carly in the mirror.

'Do you not think that would be more believable if you actually had a best friend that could afford that?'

'Yes, but luckily for me my best friend is very resourceful and managed to get us some kind of cheapskate internet deal,' suggested Carly. She sat down on the bed next to Lauren.

'Right … and how are things at home?' asked Lauren in a knowing tone.

'Better. But by better I mean we've stopped giving each other the silent treatment, or at least in front of May.'

Lauren sat with her lips tightly pursed, her unusual silence rather unnerving.

'What? What's wrong?' asked Carly, searching Lauren's face for some kind of clue.

'Nothing, nothing. I dunno, Carls, do you not just think it would be easier to, I dunno, break it off, walk away and start again … like now, before the I do?' said Lauren, standing up from the bed and continuing to rifle through the handbags on it, feeling too awkward to look at Carly.

Carly sat open-mouthed, shocked at Lauren's suggestion.

'Er, no … what about May? I can't just—'

'Yes, I know, you've said it a thousand times!

You're indebted to her, she took you in when your mum died, blah fucking blah! So what? Does that mean you spend the rest of your life miserable while you meet the love of your life in secret?' interrupted Lauren, becoming animated as she stomped around the bedroom, trying not to lose her temper while making her point.

'He is not the love of my life, thank you very much!' protested Carly, trying to convince Lauren as well as herself that Jack was nothing more than a friend.

'Oh pull the other one, Carly! You won't even make this much effort for your wedding day!' yelled Lauren, not believing a word that had come from Carly's mouth.

'Okay, Miss Fix It, what do you suppose I do?' Carly yelled back, secretly hoping Lauren might just be able to offer a solution to all her woes.

Lauren forcibly opened her wardrobe door, dropped to her knees on the carpeted floor and turned to face Carly.

'I suppose you put yourself first for once, 'cause otherwise, all this is gonna end in tears. And you know what, Carls, it will all have been your fault,' Lauren said calmly, pointing her finger at Carly, trying to home in her point, before burying her head in the bottom of her wardrobe.

Carly remained silent as she digested what Lauren had said, unable to put together any kind of plausible response. She certainly didn't want to be the cause of anyone else's unhappiness, but as always, she failed to see how she could walk away without hurting anyone or feeling massive guilt.

'Now I know you said you had some shoes, but I think these would look really good,' said Lauren, pulling out a dark green shoebox and lifting the lid to reveal a pair of silver high- heeled strappy sandals.

Carly smiled at Lauren, and nodded at her suggestion.

Carly knew that no matter how agitated Lauren became with her, it would never stop her from keeping hold of her secrets and for that she was grateful.

It was half past five when Jack walked through the front door of Grandma Barb's flat, a whole hour earlier than his usual home time.

'Is that you, Jack?' Grandma Barb called.

Jack didn't answer and instead continued to walk through the hallway and into the living room where he found his grandmother. She was sitting back on her comfy, cream-coloured armchair with her feet propped up on the matching pouffe. In her hands she held open the newspaper, her small eyes peering over the top of her large spectacles. When she saw Jack Grandma Barb quickly closed the newspaper and folded it in half.

'You're early,' said Grandma Barb, pulling her

glasses from her face and placing them on top of her head.

'I was struggling to concentrate, so I just called it a day,' said Jack, slumping himself down on the sofa and rubbing his hands over his tired head and face.

'What does it say?' asked Jack, his voice muffled through his hands as he nodded towards the paper Grandma Barb had stuffed down the side of her armchair.

'You've not read it?' asked Grandma Barb, surprised.

'No. I've been avoiding it all day.'

'Your name's not mentioned,' said Grandma Barb as she pulled the paper back out from where she had just stuffed it.

'Really?' said Jack, frowning, not quite believing his grandmother.

'Not once, here,' she said, handing the paper to Jack.

Jack accepted the paper from Grandma Barb and unfolded it. As expected, the story was front-page news with a tell-all headline: *Journalist Killed in Horror Stabbing at News HQ.*

Under the headline there was a picture of Peter looking happy and relaxed as he sat on the grass in front of a vibrant flower bed. The picture had no doubt been taken in a public park on one of Peter's precious days off.

Jack stared hard at the picture of his friend, whose face he hadn't seen for several years.

Peter's blue eyes sparkled behind his large, thick-framed glasses, his blond floppy hair a little windswept. Peter was smiling broadly without a care or any idea of what terror lay before him.

Feeling his mouth going dry, Jack licked his lips. Having the story between his hands somehow made it all the more real. Jack allowed his gaze to drop to the byline displaying Brad's name and then to the story.

Journalist Peter Wheat, 29, was fatally stabbed whilst leaving work on 29th September ... as Jack read on, he felt an undeniable tight knotting in his stomach. The newspaper in his hands began to shake with his nervous trembling. He felt a familiar rush of fear and, his vision blurring, struggled to focus on the words in front of him. Jack tossed the paper down next to him on the sofa cushion and rubbed his woozy head for what was maybe the one hundredth time that day.

'I can't read this,' he moaned.

Sympathising with her grandson's distress, Grandma Barb instantly climbed from her armchair and picked up the newspaper.

'Okay, I know what we'll do, darling,' she said, carrying it out of the living room. 'I'm going to put it here, in the cupboard under the sink with all the cleaning supplies ...' she continued, calling loudly from the kitchen, and Jack could hear the opening and then the closing of the cupboard door.

'It's not somewhere you ever venture …' said Grandma Barb, reappearing in the doorway of the living room, 'but you know where it is if you ever change your mind.'

Jack acknowledged Grandma Barb with a small nod of his head. He was grateful for her kindness, but felt far too emotionally drained to interact any further.

'It's wasn't your fault, darling. What happened to that young man,' Grandma Barb said softly, slowly making her way back into the living room and sitting herself down next to Jack on the sofa.

Jack let out a deep sigh, noting that no matter how many times someone told him that Peter's death wasn't his fault, it still failed to resolve the festering feelings of guilt and self-hatred he harboured so deeply he feared they would stay with him forever.

Sensing her grandson's sadness, Grandma Barb took Jack's hand in hers and placed it lovingly on her lap.

'You know, when I feel down, I always find gin a big help,' she said jokingly, squeezing his hand gently.

'I thought maybe you might have some of your special arthritis medicine going …' Jack suggested sheepishly, hoping that his forlorn state might be enough for Grandma Barb to accommodate some mild debauchery.

'Afraid not, darling. That nice young man from

the newsagent's is holidaying at la Costa del Majesty's Pleasure for a while. Have you heard back from the job yet?' asked Grandma Barb, eager to focus Jack's mind on more positive subject matter.

Jack shook his head. Although his morning at St Augustin's had got off to a somewhat peculiar start, he felt the interview itself had gone well. He'd been charming and eloquent and had even found some common ground with Pamela Harrison, her father also once having worked as a tabloid journalist. It seemed the earlier sexual-health hiccup had proved his ability to address a class, leaving the board so impressed they excused him from having to give his original planned presentation.

However, it had been two full days since the interview, and Jack was now beginning to assume the outcome was indeed a negative one.

'Well, if you will talk about anal sex with children you don't know, darling!' said Grandma Barb, letting go of Jack's hand in frustration, just as Jack's phone began to vibrate inside his trouser pocket.

'Okay, you make that sound an awful lot worse than it really was,' protested Jack over the sound of the ringtone. He shuffled in his seat and pulled out the phone from his pocket.

Raising the phone to his eyes, Jack looked down at the screen and felt his heart miss a beat when he saw a phone number with a Cambridge area code displayed across it.

'Who is it?' asked Grandma Barb.

Ignoring Grandma Barb's question Jack swiftly swiped the screen to answer, sure it was St Augustin's calling to offer their apologies for rejecting him, and he wanted to get the disappointment over as quickly as possible.

'Hello ...'

'Who is it?' asked Grandma Barb once again, her interference prompting Jack to stand up from the sofa and move away from her.

'Hello, Jack, it's Pamela Harrison from St Augustin's. How are you?'

'I'm very well, thank you, Pamela, how are you?' said Jack, doing a superb job at burying his anguish.

'I'm well, thank you for asking. I'm sorry it's taken me so long to get back to you, Jack, it's been a busy couple of days.'

'That's fine; but thank you for taking the time to call,' said Jack dismissively, not wanting to prolong the pain of rejection, an unwelcome addition to his current mood.

'Um, yes, you're most welcome,' said Pamela, a little put off by Jack's tone.

'Okay, have a good evening, Pamela,' said Jack, ready to hang up the phone, not wanting to have his time wasted for a second longer.

'Jack, we thought your interview went incredibly well. We thought you made a great impression, not just with the panel but also with the students,' said Pamela with haste, correctly sensing Jack had assumed the worst.

'Really?' said Jack, surprised by Pamela's positivity.

'Who is it?' Grandma Barb asked again, at which Jack flapped his hand at her to go away and then turned his back on her to stand by the living-room doorway.

'Of all the candidates we interviewed you certainly displayed the best credentials and we'd be absolutely thrilled for you to join our team ... that is, of course, if you're still interested in the position?' queried Pamela.

'Yes, yes, that ... that would be fantastic, thank you, thank you so much,' exclaimed Jack, not quite believing his ears, turning back to face his grandmother, who looked up at him from the sofa with a puzzled expression.

'Great. I'll leave you now to get on with your evening, but I'll be in touch over the next few days and we'll get everything sorted.'

'Okay, sounds like a plan!'

'Fantastic, welcome aboard, Jack. Speak soon.'

'Thank you. Bye,' said Jack and swiped his phone to hang up.

'Well?' said Grandma Barb, demanding an answer.

'Get your gin out, Gran! I got the job!' declared Jack with a wide amazed smile.

'Ah! Oh darling! I'm so happy for you!' squealed Grandma Barb, leaping up from the sofa and rushing towards Jack, wrapping her arms around his body and squeezing him tightly.

'Screw the gin! I've got some bubbles somewhere!' said Grandma Barb, letting go of Jack and promptly marching out of the living room.

Ecstatic as Jack was to finally be granted his fresh start, as he stood alone in his grandmother's living room his mind turned to Carly. To leave for Cambridge would mean to leave her behind, and the very thought of doing so made his heart race with sheer panic. How could he abandon the one person who understood him, the person he held such affection for?

Detesting the very idea of never seeing Carly again, Jack looked back down at his phone still held in his hand and considered calling Pamela back to reject the offer. He swiped to unlock his phone and quickly found her number under his most recent calls. His thumb hovering over the dial button, his thoughts racing, Jack heard the sound of Grandma Barb's voice coming from the kitchen.

'Oh darling, will you help me, I can't reach these glasses at the back!' Grandma Barb called, snapping him out of his deluded idea.

Jack looked away from his phone, closed his eyes and inhaled a deep breath.

She's not yours. Not any more.

Jack knew he had to come to terms with the cold hard reality that his chance with Carly had been lost too long ago for it to ever be reclaimed.

'Jack!' Grandma Barb called again.

'I'm coming!' Jack called back, slipping his phone into his trouser pocket and feeling determined not to let himself drown in sadness.

CHAPTER 16:

It was almost the end of yet another Monday night creative writing class and Jack was regretting suggesting one final reading before home time.

As Margery proudly read aloud a poorly written poem about a pen, Jack struggled to remain interested. The past few days had proved eventful. With an official job offer received, Jack had spent the weekend scouring the internet for homes to rent in Cambridge and today he had even gone so far as to hand in his notice at Langston High. Having informed friends and family of his big move, Jack still had one person he needed to tell.

Jack gazed over at Carly, who was sitting in her usual seat next to Margery, and doing a much better job than he was at pretending to be listening to Margery's creation.

'"… and that is why every pen needs a place they can call home,"' concluded Margery, placing her small notepad back down on the table.

A meek round of applause followed, which Margery seemed to appreciate, smiling widely and looking terribly proud of herself.

'Brilliant, Margie, and a fantastic piece for us to end on, I think,' announced Jack with false enthusiasm, ready more than ever to wrap up proceedings for another week.

Jack stood up from his seat as his class readied themselves to depart and it was then he began to feel anxious. He watched as Carly packed her things away and put on her coat, as usual making sure she took her time so she'd end up being the last to leave, a strategy designed to give her and Jack the chance to chat for a while alone, for both of them their most favourite part of the evening. But tonight, Jack felt nervous. For he knew the exciting news he wanted to share with her was also the beginning of a sad goodbye that he wasn't ready for.

Jack waited until everyone else had gone except Jenni and Melody. He wished them a good week and watched them shuffle out before turning his attention to Carly. She approached with a warm smile, holding her notebook close to her chest as she always did.

'I've got my outfit all sorted for the Savoy,' said Carly, casually perching her behind on the edge of the table.

'Then you're a step ahead of me, Miss Hughes. I still need to dig out my tux, it's been a while since I needed to wear it.'

'I'm really looking forward to it,' said Carly, feeling excited, not only about the once-in-a-lifetime grand event, but also the night away from home. What with Grandma Barb enjoying a night of luxury at the Savoy, it had been arranged for Carly to stay the night at the flat. The arrangement of course was completely innocent, with Jack and Carly each having their own bedrooms, but that aside, the idea of spending an entire night together was still an exciting prospect for them both.

'Me too. So, I wanted—'

'I was thinking, if you don't need to rush off do you fancy going to The George for a quick one?' suggested Carly, keen as ever to extend her time away from home for as long as she could.

'Yes, that would be great. But before we go I wanted—'

'Or if you're peckish they've just opened a new fancy burger place on the corner,' interjected Carly once more. Although her enthusiasm for socialising was welcome, her interruptions were making Jack even more anxious about delivering his news.

'Yes, burgers sound great, but before we go, I need to tell you—'

'I'm starving, all I had for dinner was a banana —'

'Carly, I got the job in Cambridge,' Jack blurted out, unable to hold in his words a second longer.

Carly stood in open-mouthed silence, her pretty eyes dancing from side to side. Her look of utter disbelief and shock so obvious it made for uncomfortable viewing.

'What?' she said, desperately seeking confirmation of what she had just been told, hoping she had misheard something.

'The job, in Cambridge. I got it ...' Jack replied, awkwardly fidgeting with his fingers and unable to bring himself to look directly at her.

'I didn't even know you'd had the interview.'

'Yes, it was last week.'

Carly blinked hard, trying to process her racing thoughts, struggling to comprehend that in a matter of weeks the one person whose sheer presence she yearned for more than any other would soon be leaving her life.

Carly was devastated. Determined to keep it from Jack, she gently shook her head, and in an effort to banish the feeling, forced herself to respond positively.

'Yeah, sorry, wow, that's um, that's ... amazing, really, congratulations!' said Carly, her wide smile so forced she was almost animated. She reached out her arms and hugged Jack.

As they held each other for a few short seconds, Carly, grateful for the brief opportunity to hide her heartbroken expression, allowed her face to press into his shoulder.

'So I take it you'll be relocating?' she asked, trying to keep her tone casual, whilst secretly dreading Jack's answer.

'Yes, that's the plan,' answered Jack.

'When do you leave?'

'The 2nd of January, hopefully. Should this flat I like work out.'

'That's my wedding day,' replied Carly, her voice low as she stared blankly out of the classroom window behind Jack, the winter's-night sky so dark that all she could see was her own reflection: her face grief-stricken for the friend she was about to lose.

'A day of new beginnings for us both then,' said Jack, his poignant sentence hanging sadly between them.

Jack looked just as downcast as Carly felt, his deep brown eyes on the floor beneath them.

Unable to carry on with the conversation, Carly felt the sudden need to distance herself from Jack and be alone to process all the feelings she could never admit to in the presence of others.

'I need to go,' said Carly with great assertion, already stepping towards the classroom's open door.

'But what about the burger?' said Jack, regretting the way he'd delivered his news and wishing he'd softened the blow by telling Carly over a drink at the very least.

'Yeah, sorry, you know, I've just remembered I've got some errands I need to run.'

'It's half past nine. Do them tomorrow,' said Jack, refusing to accept Carly's feeble excuse.

'I can't. We're running low on milk and I ate the last banana before I left, but I'll see you on

Saturday, for the Savoy thing,' said Carly from the other side of the door.

Jack swallowed hard and nodded at Carly. He wasn't going to force her to stay any longer if she really didn't want to.

After watching her scurry away, Jack decided to take a moment for himself. He wandered towards the chair at the head of the table and slumped himself down upon it, tilting his head back and gazing up at the cobwebs on the ceiling with a feeling of utter bewilderment.

Carly's bizarre reaction had completely thrown him. Could it be that her feelings ran as deeply as his? he wondered. Jack sighed at the troublesome thought. Even if their feelings did indeed match, he knew there was no fertile ground for their relationship to grow.

He was now moving to a new county and she had responsibilities she felt duty-bound to fulfil. Maybe the pending celebration at the Savoy this weekend was perfect timing, thought Jack, providing one last evening of fun before they each continued with their own separate lives; and he welcomed the idea of having some distance from the agonising feelings of love he felt for someone so out of his reach.

Carly pushed open the front door with little grace and was greeted by the bright light of the TV screen in the otherwise darkened room. She was relieved that Craig was nowhere to be seen;

he often retired to bed fairly early and it wasn't uncommon for the TV to be playing to itself with May sound asleep in front of it.

Carly crept past May and walked through into the kitchen. She closed the door gently behind her and leaning her elbows on the cluttered work surface buried her heavy head in her cold hands. In the darkness of the unlit kitchen, Carly finally allowed all her emotions to boil over and wept uncontrollably into her hands. They quickly became sopping wet from all the tears pouring from her eyes and she felt her nose begin to stream, creating a wet sticky patch on her face.

She pulled her face from her hands and searched the dark kitchen for some paper towel. On the wooden stand where the paper towel usually lived there was only an empty cardboard tube, and so Carly wiped her running nose with the back of her hand and ventured back into the living room to fetch the tissues from the coffee table in front of the television.

Still whimpering quietly to herself as she pulled down the zip on her coat and walked towards the coffee table, Carly was startled by the sound of her name.

'Carly?' said May, her voice hoarse from having just woken.

'Oh sorry, May, go back to sleep …' whispered Carly, pulling several tissues from the box, urgently wiping her nose and eyes, wanting to rid her face of any evidence of her upset, but it was too little too late. May could clearly see her smudged mascara under her puffy eyes and her reddened cheeks were glistening from her tears.

'What on earth's the matter, lovey?' asked May, her voice full of concern.

'Nothing, nothing, I'm fine,' said Carly, still dabbing her face.

'It don't seem like nothing. Is it soppy bollocks? Has he upset you again?' said May, annoyed with Craig.

'No, no, nothing like that,' Carly assured her.

May gave Carly a look of grave sympathy and tilted her head slightly, as if silently granting Carly permission to offload.

Gripping a ball of wet tissues, Carly inhaled a deep breath, slipped her coat off over her shoulders and placed it down on the back of the sofa. She went over to the foot of May's bed and sat herself down comfortably, as she often did.

'It's just, my friend, Jane,' said Carly, still concealing Jack's real identity. 'I saw her tonight at the bingo. She's got a job in Cambridge. She's moving there in a few weeks.' As Carly told her story to May, she could feel her lip begin to tremble and her eyes quickly refill with tears, making it impossible for her to speak any further. She let out a small laugh, fully aware her emotional reaction was somewhat dramatic, dismissing her tears as something silly to be ignored.

'You like her a lot, don't you, this Jane?' May

said softly, able to read how deeply cut Carly was at the news of Jane's departure, her reaction mirroring that of a heartbroken lover.

Carly inhaled a jagged breath as she tried to straighten out her emotions and nodded her head in agreement, before looking blankly away from May at the television. Carly wondered if, now that she was alone with May, she should be honest and finally reveal all of who she used to be: a person with an intellect of an Oxbridge calibre, a person who once had a vibrant land of opportunity laid out before her, and if her flowing tears were not only for the loss of the friend she loved, but also for a past lover and the life with him she never gained.

'I think … I think she just reminds me of a different time,' answered Carly, easing herself into the subject.

'A happier time?' questioned May, Carly's misery clear as day.

Carly turned and looked back at May. She looked weak; her once full rosy cheeks were now drained of any life, their paleness highlighting the dark circles that had formed under her eyes, giving her a look of permanent illness.

It didn't feel right, to offload all her troubles onto a person whose troubles in comparison made hers seem so insignificant it was almost embarrassing.

'Just different,' Carly answered, displaying the most reassuring smile she could.

'You seen that story in the paper?' said May, taking Carly by surprise with her complete change of subject.

Carly shook her head.

'There, I think it's still there on the table,' pointed May, instructing Carly to pick it up.

Carly lifted herself from May's bed and leaned over the messy coffee table to pick up the folded newspaper that was lying next to two dirty tea mugs and the TV remote.

'May, this paper is almost a week old,' noted Carly, annoyed that it hadn't been thrown out.

'Look at him, that young man, on the front page. Was killed, just minding his business leaving work one night.'

Carly let her eyes skim back over the article, which she remembered reading the week before.

'Yeah, I read this. He was a journalist. Some relative was mad at the press for writing a story about a child abuse case. He killed one of the reporters,' said Carly, peering at the happy smiling face of the young journalist pictured in the centre of the front page.

'Doesn't look much older than you, that young man.'

'No, I suppose not … Sorry, May, what's your point?' asked Carly, shaking her head and tossing the paper back down onto the coffee table.

'You never know when your number's gonna be up, lovey. You gotta enjoy your life. And if this Jane is the one that makes you happy—'

'May, what has Craig been saying?' interrupted Carly, shaking her head in despair, finally piecing together exactly what May was trying to imply.

'Nothing, lovey,' said May, holding her hands up in surrender, instantly backing down.

Carly let out a small sigh. It was evident that tonight would not be the night she would be able to have an honest and frank conversation with May, not now that May had let slip that she, like Craig, believed that her unhappiness was a result of her frustrated sexuality.

'I'm going to bed,' said Carly, picking up the TV remote from the coffee table and pointing it at the television to shut it off, the disappearance of its light plunging the living room into darkness.

Carly placed the TV remote back down on the coffee table and walked towards the stairs, happy to end her conversation with May.

'You'll always be my daughter, you know ...' said May, causing Carly to pause at the foot of the stairs. '... whatever team you bat for!' May concluded, her incorrect assumption making Carly laugh inwardly.

'Goodnight, May,' said Carly, shaking her head once again as she climbed the stairs to bed, her head a scattered mess.

Although Carly appreciated May's open-mindedness, she was unsure if May would be so understanding if she knew the full truth. She wondered if May would still love her if she abandoned her to start a new life with another man?

The mere thought of May rejecting her was so unsettling that Carly refused to dwell on it and for the first time felt a sense of relief that Jack would soon be leaving her life for good and she would no longer have to wrestle with her feelings.

CHAPTER 17:

It had been at least three hours since Grandma Barb had left to get ready in her hotel room at the Savoy ahead of James's Bar Mitzvah celebrations and Jack was happy to see the back of her. Having skipped the schul earlier in the day due to 'marking commitments', Jack had quickly grown tired of Grandma Barb's *two thousand years of persecution and you can't even be bothered* lecture and was extremely grateful to have had a peaceful few hours to himself.

With Carly's arrival at the flat imminent Jack was busy adding the finishing touches to his appearance. Dressed in a sharp black tux and crisp white shirt, he fidgeted with his black bow tie, struggling to tie it properly, and regretted not purchasing a prepared clip-on alternative. As he stood in the full-length mirror of his dimly lit bedroom, his fidgeting was interrupted by the sound of the flat's buzzer. Leaving the tie hanging hopelessly around his neck, he left the bedroom to answer the door.

Jack hadn't seen Carly since she'd hurried away from him after the class, and he'd been worried that she might not turn up. Standing by the front door, Jack felt a wave of relief, then inhaled a deep breath to steady his nerves. He pulled down the latch on the door and opened it, instantly mesmerised by the sight of Carly on the other side. She looked stunningly beautiful. Her sapphire gown clung perfectly to her womanly figure and she stood taller than usual in a pair of silver high-heeled sandals. Her hair was worn up in a loose bun with soft curls framing her pretty face; she radiated elegance and poise.

Jack stood open-mouthed in the doorway silently drinking her in, her beauty doing little to suppress the inconvenient love that continued to grow inside him.

Carly smiled nervously. Jack's silence was making her wonder whether she'd got her look wrong and she fidgeted anxiously with the small silver clutch bag in her hand.

'You look—'

'Cold!' quipped Carly as she involuntarily shivered from the cold draught in the concrete corridor.

'Far more than I deserve,' Jack said softly, meeting her sparkling eyes with his, just as the strap of her overnight bag slipped carelessly from her shoulder.

Carly made a grab for her bag with her right hand, and Jack noticed Carly's engagement ring was on the wrong hand, it now acting merely as a decorative piece of jewellery rather than a loving commitment to another.

Did Carly not want them to be mistaken for a couple?
Jack wondered, or did she simply want to forget who she was for the evening?

Maybe tonight, she didn't want to be someone's fiancée, or a carer or a bingo hall worker. Maybe tonight she just wanted to be an ordinary girl, enjoying an evening out with a friend- no preying questions, no awkward explanations.

Jack wasn't sure; but he didn't think it was his place to ask such questions and he certainly didn't want to make Carly feel uncomfortable.

'Here, let me get that,' insisted Jack, reaching for the bag. 'Come in, out of the cold,' he said, stepping aside and welcoming Carly into the warmth of the indoors as he placed her bag down on the hallway floor.

'I don't suppose you know how to tie one of these things, do you? I always struggle with them,' said Jack, pointing to the loose black tie hanging around his neck.

'I can have a go,' said Carly with little confidence as she shut the front door behind her and placed her small clutch bag down on top of her overnight bag.

Carly took each end of Jack's bow tie between her fingers and began to carefully tie it. Her nose caught the aroma of his fresh aftershave, the smell so sexy it was almost arousing, making Carly feel a little bashful as she stood in such close proximity to him.

Jack looked devilishly handsome and incredibly sophisticated, a million miles away from the kind of male company Carly was used to, and it took all her willpower for her not to be completely disarmed by his raw magnetism.

'There, I think that should do it,' Carly uttered softly, gently releasing her hands from Jack's bow tie then taking a cheeky opportunity to pat down his jacket and get a welcome feel of his firm chest.

'You look really ...' *Sexy, gorgeous, stupidly handsome?* A string of embarrassing adjectives went through Carly's mind before she settled on one that wasn't. 'Grown-up,' she said assertively, removing her hands from Jack's suit jacket.

'Grown-up?' repeated Jack, a tad disappointed.

Carly laughed inwardly with a tight smile, aware she could have given Jack more of a compliment, but not confident of doing so without pouring out all the pent-up feelings she'd done so well to suppress. She heard the sound of Jack's phone ringing and watched him pull out the phone from his pocket and swipe to answer.

'Hello. Okay, we'll be right out,' said Jack before swiping the phone again to hang up.

'Our taxi awaits, my lady,' said Jack, returning his phone to his pocket. 'Now let's get you to the ball,' he said with a wide smile, deliriously proud to have Carly joining him tonight.

Carly felt a little disorientated. Ever since setting foot in The River Room at London's Savoy Hotel she had been subjected to an endless stream of friendly strangers that were Jack's relatives and family friends, but now as she stood between Jack and his cousin Will, a flute of champagne held tightly in her hand, she took a moment to catch her breath and absorb her surroundings.

The glamorous function suite was jam-packed with people. Understandably a large proportion of the guests were children, aged between eleven and fourteen, everyone dressed to impress in black tie and cocktail dresses.

Guests stood in small groups chatting and laughing, or milling around the large open area, as the Elvis impersonator sang 'Blue Suede Shoes' in the background. Others were making good use of the large buffet in the centre of the room, positioned under two large crystal chandeliers and offering every kind of canapé known to man. Her eyes lingered on the table decoration, large white feathers on proud display in tall glass vases.

She looked back at Jack and Will beside her as they carried on with their conversation. Will and Jack were the same age, but unlike Jack, Will hadn't inherited the family's bald gene, showing off a thick mop of dark brown hair, and he wore small square glasses over his narrow brown eyes.

Will had lost his wife Natalie amongst the sea of people some time ago but was more than happy to be left to catch up with Jack.

'Congrats on the new job by the way, Jack,' said Will before downing the remains of his champagne.

The sheer mention of Jack's pending move filled Carly with dread and so she made a silent effort to distract herself from the conversation by studying the people in the room, when she noticed a short bald man she recognised.

He was accompanied by a lady a little taller than himself, dressed in a shimmering maroon cocktail dress and with fuzzy blonde hair hanging freely past her shoulders. She walked with a strong sense of confidence and her face was fully made up, her long pointy fingernails painted bright red. Dragging behind the couple was a disgruntled-looking lady, pretty behind her harsh expression, with long dark curly hair running well past her shoulders, and she was dressed in a flattering black gown that accentuated her generous bosom.

The bald man saw Carly looking at him and stared back at her for a second longer than was usual as he tried to place where he had seen her before. Then he noticed his son standing next to her.

Will was the first to notice his auntie and uncle approaching and placed his empty champagne flute down before greeting them.

'Hi, Auntie Di. Uncle Max, you're looking well,' said Will, planting kisses on each of their cheeks.

While Will made small talk with Jack's parents, the moody-looking woman brusquely placed herself between Jack and Carly and tossed her small black clutch bag down on the table.

'You're so lucky you're moving away. I just had to endure a whole journey with Mum telling me I'm crushing Chloe's artistic spirit by not getting her more involved in creative studies and then she told Emily she was getting fat!' she huffed.

Jack turned his head towards the buffet, where he knew without any doubt he would spot his niece loading up a plate. Eleven-year-old Emily's small chubby body was squished tightly into a light blue party dress as she wandered around the buffet with the kind of excitement most children would express at an adventure playground, ducking and diving in-between the hordes of people, grabbing hold of spring rolls like they were well-earned prizes.

'Emily is getting fat,' said Jack, unable to humour his sister on the matter.

'I know, but what can I do, put a lock on the fridge! I swear to God, it's like living with Augustus Gloop! I can't control it! I'm so sorry, we haven't been introduced. I'm Louisa, Jack's annoying sister,' said Louisa, pausing her rant to give Carly a welcoming kiss on the cheek.

'Hi, I'm Carly.'

'Lovely to meet you. This is our dad Maxwell and this is our horrible mother Diane,' said Louisa, her brutal introduction of her mother causing Carly to scoff a laugh.

'Carly, you look familiar, have we met before?' asked Maxwell, staring curiously at Carly whilst warmly taking her hands in his. He certainly looked healthier and fresher than how Carly remembered him, although she was surprised by how short he was.

'Yes. I volunteer at the hospital. I sold you a couple of books while you were in there.'

'Oh my goodness! Yes, of course. Di, this is Carly, she sold me *Fifty Shades of Grey*,' Max announced, elated to be reacquainted with the smart pretty lady he remembered so fondly.

'That was you?' questioned Diane. 'Carly, honestly, for years I've been trying to persuade this man to consider something a little more stimulating, and would he listen! But then he reads—'

'Mum, please! No one wants to hear about your gross sex life!' interrupted Jack, pleading with his mother to stop, Diane not in the least bit fazed by how inappropriate her over-sharing was.

'Gross sex life! See how awful my children are, Carly!' protested Diane, before turning her attention back to her son.

'I must say, I am pleased to see you're still alive Jack, I was starting to wonder! Would it kill you to call your Mother once in a while?' said Diane, to which Jack rolled his eyes and huffed like a moody teenager while Diane fussed with his suit jacket.

'How are you Mother?' Jack asked, sarcastically.

'I'm very well thank you for asking, and all the better for seeing you.' said Diane, finally letting go of Jack, secretly relieved to see that he was indeed alive and well. Jack blissfully unaware of how much his Mother really did worry about him.

'Oh Max, look there's Harriet. You know, all that woman talks about is how clever her daughter is. She's so clever she's been to uni three times and left with no degree and a shedload of debt. Can't stick to anything, that daughter of hers, even marriage. She was only with her husband for six months before it all fell apart. I better go and say hello,' said Diane, clattering across the room to mingle with the woman she had just spoken of so harshly.

'What do you say we get a proper drink? I can't abide all this champagne, gives me wind,' moaned Maxwell, rubbing his chest through his shirt.

'Okay, come on, Dad, let's find the bar,' suggested Jack. 'What would you like?' Jack asked Carly, placing his hand on her lower back as he smiled adoringly at her.

'I'll have a vodka and orange, please,' replied Carly smiling back at Jack, enjoying the touch of his hand on her body.

Jack nodded and proceeded to walk away with his father and cousin, leaving Carly alone with

Louisa.

'So how long have you and Jack been seeing each other?' asked Louisa, her eyes wide with eagerness for all the gossip on her brother's latest squeeze.

'Oh, we're not. We're just friends,' said Carly, quick to extinguish the wrong idea.

'I'm sorry?'

'We're just friends,' repeated Carly.

'No, I heard you. I just ... well, I've just never seen my brother look at any of his *friends* like that before; or girlfriends, for that matter,' said Louisa, astonished to hear that Carly's presence in her brother's life was purely platonic.

Carly smiled, feeling a little awkward at the realisation that her and Jack's feelings for each other were obvious to everyone else, no matter how much either of them tried to deny it.

The Lancaster Ballroom at the Savoy was as elegant as Carly expected. Grand crystal chandeliers hung from the high sculptured ceilings and there were giant arched mirrored doors, but it was the injection of personal opulence that took Carly's breath away, like nothing she had ever witnessed before. The room was set out much as it might have been for a wedding reception, with countless round tables each sporting the same ornate centrepiece of tall black crystal candleholder with four small cubes of red roses at its base, each cube supporting three playing cards.

At the front of the room on the large stage was the DJ booth, behind which was a large screen, the kind of screen one would usually see at a pop concert, illuminating the iconic 'Welcome to Las Vegas' sign.

The black dance floor was lit up with small twinkling lights, resembling stars in a dark night's sky, and a bald, overweight black guy and a very tall skinny blonde woman sang a cover of Ed Sheeran's 'Sing' as the guests entered the room and searched for their tables.

In awe of her surroundings, and wanting to know more about their hosts, Carly turned to Jack.

'What does your cousin do for a living?'

'Beth is an architect and her husband Howard does something to do with buying and selling companies. I'm a little sketchy on the details, but what I do know is that they both make an obscene amount of money,' answered Jack as he led Carly towards a table that faced a long row of small one-arm-bandit machines and a roulette table.

Just as Jack chivalrously pulled out Carly's chair, she felt a tight grip on her arm and turned round.

'Oh would you look at you! Absolute perfection,' gushed Grandma Barb as she grabbed Carly wrists, admiring just how beautiful she looked.

'Thank you, Mrs Lewis. You look lovely,' said Carly in response, and it was true. Grandma

Barb was dressed in a black, long-sleeved gown covered with shiny gold embroidery, looking every inch the glamorous granny, and standing proud in smart black court shoes that gave her height an extra few centimetres.

'Mrs Lewis! Please, Mrs Lewis was my mother-in-law and I hated the woman! We're friends, Cara, call me Barb, please,' insisted Grandma Barb.

'Are you on our table, Gran?' asked Jack.

'No, I'm over there somewhere with all the other old people. I just wanted to check, was everything okay in your room back at the flat, Cara dear? You are staying the night, aren't you?'

Carly never did get so far as to check out her room, but she nodded politely anyway.

'Yes, thank you.'

'Ladies and Gentlemen, boys and girls, welcome to James's Bar Mitzvah!' announced the male singer and compere over the sound of the music, his announcement met with the kind of hysteria seen on a TV talent show with people clapping and cheering.

'Oh I'd better go, it's about to start,' said Grandma Barb, excitedly scurrying away to her table.

Carly took a seat next to Jack, on her other side sat Jack's father Maxwell who was sat beside Diane.

'Jack tells me this is your first time at one of these, Carly.'

'Yeah. This is amazing … are all Bar Mitzvahs as glamorous as this?' Carly asked, looking around the ballroom in complete wonder.

'Oh goodness no, this is something rather exceptional. We held Jack's in a function room above a Debenhams!' said Maxwell with a shake of his head and a small chuckle.

'Now let's show some love for your hosts this evening, Beth, Howard and Toby!' announced the bald male compere over the sound of Elvis Presley's 'Viva Las Vegas'.

The two huge mirrored doors at the back of the room were flung open to reveal Jack's cousin Beth, along with her husband Howard and their youngest son Toby. Holding hands, Howard and Toby were dressed in smart black tuxedos while Beth was dressed in a flamboyant pastel dress. The top half a corset clinging tightly to her large bosom with the skirt a large puffy display of pink and mauve feathers, a high-end gown that wouldn't have looked out of place on a New York fashion catwalk.

The atmosphere was electric as all three, wearing wide smiles for their adoring crowd, strode into the ballroom like pop stars on a red carpet, greeting everyone they passed.

'And now, please put your hands together for the man of the hour! Ladies and Gents, clap your hands, stamp your feet, give it up for my man JAAAMES!'

In the large doorway stood a short, brown-haired thirteen-year-old boy. He was dressed smartly in a black tuxedo, and he had on each arm a scantily clad blonde bombshell, the two women wearing nothing more than a silk boxing robe over black hot pants and a crop top.

James stood at least a foot below his glamorous escorts and although his face expressed a look of boyish naivety, he smiled widely for the cheering crowd and walked proudly into the room with an air of cockiness usually reserved for men much older than himself.

As James walked onto the stage, the compere was eager to get the party underway.

'Right, I wanna see you all on your feet for my man James! Everybody, on the dance floor!'

The sound of Elvis was quickly drowned out as the speaker system began blasting a party rendition of 'Hava Nagila', the Israeli folk song that was played at any and every Jewish celebration.

Without a great deal of prompting, children and adults alike from every corner of the ballroom swarmed onto the dance floor.

Carly looked over at Jack, feeling a little uncertain as to whether she should be rushing towards the dance floor so early in the evening.

'Are we dancing?' she asked.

'We don't have a choice, I'm afraid!' answered Jack, getting up from his chair, reaching out his hand to Carly and pulling her up from her seat.

Jack led Carly to the dance floor, keeping a reassuring hold on her hand, happy to let anyone who might notice assume they were a couple.

Squeezing into a small space at the back of the dance floor, Carly watched in amazement as guests young and old, without any instruction, began to hold hands and form two circles, one within the other.

'I don't know what to do!' laughed Carly with a comical look of panic, as her free hand was grabbed by Jack's Mother Diane who was now stood next to her.

'Don't worry, it'll come to you!' Diane yelled over the music, as the circle began to rotate and pick up pace with the dancing feet of joyous partygoers. The circle suddenly changed direction, taking Carly by surprise and making her laugh as an elderly woman behind barged into her shoulder.

In the centre of the inner circle James was lifted into the air on a white dining chair. He gripped the sides as the chair bounced up and down with ease, a look of elation spreading across his young face as his friends and family danced and sang around him. Carly struggled to remember the last time she had had so much fun.

It was safe to say all festivities were in full swing.

The dance floor was heaving, the one-arm bandits and roulette table were constantly engaged as music boomed and strobe lighting filled the room. It had been at least half an hour since everybody had enjoyed their main course and, with dessert not scheduled until a little later in the evening, the Lewis family had decided to partake in the infamous drinking game *Never Have I Ever.*

Had she been entirely sober, Carly might have had some reservations about playing such a game, especially with Jack's father Maxwell in tow, but it seemed the more she drank, the less her inhibitions gnawed away at her.

Jack, Carly, Maxwell, Louisa and her and Jack's cousin Will were propping up the bar that overlooked the ballroom in all its glamorous entirety as they took it in turns to reveal intimate truths about one another.

'Never have I ever gone to the loo and not washed my hands,' Louisa stated proudly as she side stepped, struggling to keep her drunken body stable in her high heels.

All three men took a sip of their drinks, much to the disgust of Louisa and Carly.

'Ergh, filth bags, all of you!' yelled Louisa with a shaming point of her finger.

'Never have I ever.....' began Jack before pausing for dramatic effect. '... been kicked out of a Burger King,' he finished, looking directly at his sister.

Louisa grimaced at Jack and reluctantly took a gulp of her drink.

'Really, Louisa, a Burger King?' questioned Maxwell, unable to fathom such behaviour.

'Also, never have I ever urinated on the floor

of a Burger King!' continued Jack, laughing, much to Louisa's annoyance.

'All right, Jack!' she barked, her cheeks flushing bright crimson as she furiously willed her brother to shut up.

'Oh Louisa, honestly,' said Maxwell, appalled by his daughter's behaviour.

'Okay,' said Will, graciously trying to steer the game away from Louisa's past behaviour, 'never have I ever … made love wearing socks.' He took a sheepish gulp of his drink, and was followed by Maxwell and a hesitant Jack, who gave an oblivious Carly a sideways glance.

'Er, I think you need to drink, Miss Hughes!' said Jack.

'What? I really don't think I have! I always get really hot in bed!' protested Carly, defending her right not to drink.

'That's interesting, because I seem to remember, the night before Christmas break, the heating in my room failed to come on and you happily removed everything, expect for your socks!'

Carly stood still in bemused silence as she cast her mind back to a particularly cold winter's evening. She smiled wickedly to herself as she recalled how she and Jack had rolled between the sheets before parting ways for Christmas, when she did indeed keep her feet warmly enclosed in her socks all night.

'Blimey, you have a good memory!' said Carly,

finally taking a sip from her drink.

'Well, it was a good memory,' mused Jack.

'Hang on, I thought you said you were just friends?' said Louisa, her speech slightly slurred.

Before Jack or Carly had a chance to answer, they were interrupted by an announcement from the compere.

'Hold up, hold up, I need to get my man James up here on the stage. Give it up for my man James, everyone!' As a weary-looking James climbed onto the stage those on the packed dance floor cheered, others gradually joining them to gain a closer look.

'Now, James, tonight is a very special night, and on such a very special night, a very special guest has taken the time out of his very busy schedule to pay you a visit. James, Ladies and Gents, boys and girls, please would you put your hands together for none other than Mr George Ezra!'

'Jesus, how much did that cost!' exclaimed Louisa over the sound of deafening screams and cheers as a tall, blond-haired man, dressed in dark jeans and a black shirt, and armed with his obligatory acoustic guitar, walked onto the stage.

'Who?' asked Maxwell, the reason for such hysteria lost on him.

'George Ezra, Uncle Max, he's a singer. Kind of a big deal at the moment,' explained Will.

'Come on, let's go down there!' said Louisa,

downing the last of her drink, slamming the empty glass down on the small bar behind her and grabbing hold of Carly's hand.

Carly and Louisa found themselves a spot at the back of the packed dance floor behind a swarm of thirteen-year-olds and embarrassingly excited adults as George Ezra sang his smash hit 'Shot Gun'.

The whole room's attention was firmly fixed on the stage gracing the presence of an international pop star, and Carly couldn't believe her luck that she had been included in an evening of such wonder and excitement as she danced with Louisa to the song she knew well.

'Mazel tov, James,' said George Ezra to James at the front of the heaving crowd on finishing 'Shot Gun'. 'Who knows the song "Hold My Girl"?' George continued in his distinctive low voice. The crowd replied with a loud cheer.

George Ezra picked at his guitar and the cheers faded out as he struck the first chord of the intro. Louisa and Carly began to sway along to the song's slow tempo when a familiar voice spoke into Carly's left ear.

'May I have this dance?' said Jack, bearing a beaming smile.

Carly smiled widely back and nodded her head in delight.

Jack took Carly's hand in his and as the two of them snuggly squeezed into a tight corner of the dance floor Jack placed a hand on the small of Carly's back and held her close.

As Carly pressed her body gently against Jack's, she struggled to recall if there had ever been a time when Craig had held her so delicately and lovingly. As they swayed gently to the song, Carly couldn't help but tune in to the song's theme: it was about a guy desperately wanting to hold his girl while he sheltered her from all her woes. With the lyrics holding such poignancy for her, Carly relaxed and happily placing her cheek next to Jack's felt the spiky texture of his stubble on her face.

Wanting to be nowhere else in the whole world than where she was right now, in the warm embrace of a man she so hopelessly loved, Carly felt sad as she reminded herself that Jack's presence in her life would soon be coming to an end.

Jack was the only person who really knew her and could see all she could be, and still after all these years apart encouraged her to aim for more. Carly knew she wasn't able to let Jack leave her life, at least not without telling him how she really felt, and so she lifted her head and looked into his glistening deep brown eyes.

'You okay?' mouthed Jack, noting a hint of sadness in Carly's eyes.

Carly nodded and, finally letting all her defences and reason crumble, leant forward. As her lips gravitated towards Jack's a clammy hand landed on her arm.

'Oh Carly, look, I've broken my heel!' shrilled an irate Louisa.

Carly promptly pulled her body away from Jack's and turned to face Louisa, just as the song came to an end.

In one hand Louisa held a broken heel and in the other a broken sandal. She stood unevenly with a drunken smile, the left side of her body standing a good two inches below the right, a sight that would have been comical had she not just interrupted such an intimate moment.

'Bloody hell, Louisa!' snapped Jack, trying to regain some composure, but clearly annoyed by his sister's intrusion.

Louisa cackled, blissfully unaware of what was going on, just as George Ezra began to pick up the tempo with the song 'Paradise'.

CHAPTER 18:

It was the early hours of Sunday morning when Jack and Carly finally arrived back at Grandma Barb's flat together. It was safe to say they were both a little worse for wear, having consumed rather a lot of alcohol, but it seemed the cab ride home had worked wonders in sobering them up.

Jack's bow tie was now undone and hanging loosely around his neck and he was minus his black jacket, draped over Carly's shoulders to keep her warm. Carly walked in behind Jack holding her silver strappy sandals in her hand while her feet nested comfortably in a pair of white flip-flops, given out at the end of the evening to the female guests with aching feet.

'Thank you for your jacket,' said Carly, placing her sandals down on the hallway floor and removing Jack's jacket from her shoulders to hand back to him.

'You're most welcome, Miss Hughes, and thank you for coming tonight. I hope you had fun?' he said, accepting the jacket and folding it over his arm.

'I had the best time. Thank you for inviting

me,' replied Carly, feeling sad that their evening was now about to draw to a close.

'Would you like something to drink?' asked Jack in an effort to drag out their time together.

'Oh no, I'm good,' said Carly, holding up her hand to indicate that she had had more than enough to drink for one night.

'Fair enough. So, this is you, at the end of the hall,' said Jack, picking up Carly's overnight bag and slowly walking her towards his gran's bedroom at the very end of the flat's long hallway.

'Gran told me to tell you she's put on all clean sheets and she's left you out some towels too, should you need them,' relayed Jack as he stood in the doorway of Grandma Barb's bedroom.

'I must make sure to thank her,' said Carly, meandering into Grandma Barb's very neat pink bedroom. The thin dark pink carpet and blush floral wallpaper were a little dated, but the room was warm and homely and would happily provide Carly with a decent night's sleep.

'Okay ... Well, goodnight then ...' said Jack, unsure as to whether it would be appropriate to wish Carly goodnight with a kiss on the cheek, but before he had a chance to ponder too much, Carly sat herself down on the large double bed in the centre of the room and began the process of untying her hair, readying herself for bed.

'Night,' she said with a sweet smile, masking her resentment at Jack's failure to make any further move on her, especially now they were in their own private quarters.

Jack nodded and left the room. He gently closed the door behind him and let out a small sigh. He paused outside the door and wondered if he should march back in and finish what had never really been started and pull Carly close and kiss her, but he felt the moment had passed. Over was an evening of high-end glamour and celebration. Now he was back at the flat, he was just a thirty-something loser living in his grandmother's spare room, in love with somebody who was far too good for him. He had had his chance with Carly, and he'd blown it, well over a decade ago. It was over, and it was time he came to terms with it; and so Jack let his feet guide him into Grandma Barb's library where he fixed himself a nightcap.

Jack sat on the edge of his narrow single bed in his dimly lit bedroom, nursing the very last drops of his brandy. He felt relaxed, his shirt undone almost halfway, exposing a thin layer of dark chest hair, his long sleeves rolled up to his elbows. He stared down at the brown liquid in his glass and rubbed his tired head, finally ready to call it a night.

Jack lifted the short-glass to his lips and, as he tilted his head back, he saw his bedroom door slowly ease open. In the doorway stood Carly. Her long hair was down, framing her face that was now free of make-up. If it was at all possible, she looked even more beautiful. Carly's face was glowing, displaying the few delicate freckles at the top of her cheeks that Jack had always loved so much.

'Hi,' said Jack, a little startled by her appearance.

'Could you help me? I can't get the zip undone,' Carly asked bashfully, pointing behind her at her back and meeting Jack by his bed.

'Yes, of course,' Jack replied, standing up and placing his empty glass down on the nightstand.

Carly turned round and gathered her hair, arranging it over her left shoulder out of Jack's way. Jack placed his hands at the very top of the dress and gently pulled at the long zip, drawing it all the way down to the very base of Carly's spine, his knuckles gently stroking her flawless fair skin as he did so. As the material parted itself, Jack could see Carly wasn't wearing any underwear, and found the sight of her naked body alluring. Not wanting to misread the situation, he was quick to remove his hands and stand to attention back by his bed.

Carly turned round to face Jack. She looked him in the eye and smiled a tight nervous smile as she placed her hands on the top of her dress and brazenly slipped it off so it fell to the ground in a heap at her feet and she was revealing all of herself to Jack.

Internally praying she wasn't making a complete fool of herself Carly searched Jack's shocked face. His dark eyes were wide as he excitedly explored her body and he couldn't help but wonder if Carly had been minus her underwear all evening, or if this was something she had orchestrated on their return home. Her body was certainly more womanly than he remembered, the curves to her hips and waist more defined and her pert breasts slightly bigger. Jack noted the absence of her navel piercing, the only remaining evidence of it the small dotted scar above her belly button.

Jack wanted nothing more than to hold out his arms and pull her close, but he remained still, keen to witness her next move. Carly placed a hand on Jack's face and lowered her open lips to his, getting a subtle taste of the brandy he had just finished. Carly slowly pulled her lips away, carefully stepped out of the bundle of material on the floor that was her dress and took a step closer to Jack. With no room behind him, he was forced to sit back down on the edge of his bed, at which Carly placed a leg either side of him, straddling him with her naked body.

She could feel with the most intimate part of herself that Jack was fully aroused. He placed a hand in her hair and looked into her wanting eyes, his body yearning for hers as he rested his other hand in the curve of her waist.

'Are you sure you want to do this?' whispered Jack, letting his hand drift out from under her hair to tenderly stroke her cheek.

'I'm sure,' Carly whispered back, leaning in to plant another gentle kiss on Jack's lips.

Unable to resist each other for a second longer, they began to kiss more passionately, their tongues entering each other's mouths. As they kissed Carly's hand found its way inside Jack's open shirt, and she caressed the soft chest hair that wasn't there when they were teenagers.

Jack wrapped his arms around Carly and pulled her in closer to him, enjoying the taste of her and the feel of her body on his. Just as Carly began to fumble with the buttons on Jack's shirt, he lifted her, swiftly placing her down on her back.

As they continued to kiss passionately, Jack undid the last few buttons on his shirt, Carly holding his body between her open legs and fumbling clumsily with his trousers, desperate to get him naked. Jack pulled off his shirt and tossed it onto the floor and Carly flashed him a smile, finding it amusing that after so many years apart, during which so much in each of their lives had changed, they had found their way back to where they were happiest: making love with each other on a narrow single bed, just as they had done countless times before.

As they lay lovingly snuggled together in Jack's bed, Carly's finger gently joined up the three tiny freckles at the top of Jack's shoulder that made a perfect triangle. They were lying on their sides facing one another under the thin duvet, both utterly thrilled by the unexpected turn in the night's events.

'You've got really good,' Carly said softly, referring to Jack's bedroom antics.

'What? I've always been good!' protested Jack.

'Yeah, you were, but that … was *really* good. Have you been practising?' Carly asked with a cheeky smile and a small giggle.

'Possibly. Maybe a little too much these past couple of years,' said Jack, regretting his reckless behaviour.

Not wanting to dwell on his past indiscretions, Jack turned his mind to the present. Here he was, lying in bed with the only woman he had ever truly loved, and he wasn't willing to contemplate a future that didn't include her in it.

'Come with me,' said Jack, lifting Carly's hand from his shoulder and tenderly kissing the tips of her fingers.

Carly narrowed her eyes and smiled, willing Jack to continue.

'Cambridge, come with me to Cambridge, and we can both start again, where it all began,' said Jack, his voice low as he tried to disguise his desperation for Carly to say yes.

'Jack—'

'I'll be teaching, and you could study again if you wanted or you could write, whatever you want to do. And we would be together and we'd both be happy.'

Although Carly's duty to May was still upper-most in her mind, she found it impossible to deny that, after tonight, everything had changed. She knew she couldn't carry on pretending any longer. She had sacrificed her future to care for her mother, her happiness to care for May, and now: she was tired. There was a life out there waiting for her, one she could share with a man she loved and respected, and she didn't want to keep her life on pause any longer.

'Do you need an answer right now?' asked Carly, knowing the logistics of starting again would need some sorting out before she could fully commit to anything.

'No, of course not. And right now there are other matters that greatly need my attention,' said Jack, nuzzling his head into the nape of Carly's neck and gently kissing her skin. With their bodies pressed closely together, Carly could feel his arousal against the very top of her thigh.

'Round two already?' laughed Carly, elated to be back in the embrace of the man she loved so much.

'Ding, ding, Miss Hughes,' said Jack, his voice muffled as he continued to trail kisses down her body.

Carly felt herself begin to wake. Too tired to go as far as opening her eyes, she turned her body away from the wall she was facing in the hope of curling herself into Jack's body but was met by nothing but empty space. Carly opened her eyes, the thin curtains drawn across the window doing little to shade the light from outside.

Their clothes from last night were still strewn across the floor and a shelf closest to the door displayed a collection of old-fashioned knick-knacks and souvenirs. Next to the large chest of drawers there was a stack of empty plastic storage boxes, ready, she assumed, for Jack to pack up his possessions ahead of his move to Cambridge.

Carly hadn't slept all that well, the thought of Jack's offer keeping her awake. She sincerely didn't want to hurt anybody, but the longer she had lain beside Jack, the less she had wanted to return home.

As Carly lay in Jack's bed lost in thought, she was distracted by a noise from the kitchen. She pulled herself out of bed and reached for Jack's shirt on the floor, opening it up and placing her arms through the sleeves. Wearing nothing but Jack's white shirt, Carly pattered barefoot into the kitchen where she was met by the delectable sight of Jack standing over the kitchen stove in a pair of black boxer shorts and his beloved Homer Simpson slippers.

'Morning!' said Carly.

'Hey, morning,' said Jack, turning his head to display a beaming smile.

'What are you making?' asked Carly, walking

over to join Jack at the stove as the smell of fried food wafted through the kitchen.

'I'm making us bacon beigels,' answered Jack as Carly nuzzled up against him, wrapping her arms around his waist. She felt complete now that Jack was next to her once more.

Jack wrapped a loving arm around Carly whilst his other hand tended to his frying pan.

'You're such a bad Jew!'

'I know,' chuckled Jack, before placing a delicate kiss on top of Carly's messy bed hair.

'But yes, I will definitely have me one of those!'

'Did you sleep well?'

'I slept okay,' shrugged Carly, choosing not to bore Jack with the details of her restless night.

There was a brief silence.

'Have you thought any more … about … what we spoke about last night?' asked Jack, keeping his eyes on the frying pan, wanting to disguise his discomfort as he waited for Carly to answer.

'Yeah,' said Carly, her blasé response giving nothing away.

'And?'

'And … I don't think …'

Jack felt his stomach begin to knot, sure she was about to confirm that starting again with him was something she simply couldn't consider.

'… I can live without you. Which is terribly inconvenient,' Carly concluded, looking up at Jack with a warm smile.

'Isn't it just!' said Jack, suppressing the urge to jump up and down in his underwear. Instead he put his energy into pulling Carly in even closer and placing a soft kiss on her lips.

'But there's stuff I'll need to sort out first. I can't just walk out today,' explained Carly, wanting to make it clear that she wasn't willing to abandon May without first making all the necessary arrangements, even if she wasn't feeling at all sure where even to begin.

Jack released his hand from the frying pan to wrap both arms around Carly.

'I wouldn't expect you to. You do, sort, whatever you need to first. Take as much time as you need, and I'll wait, however long it takes,' said Jack, keen to reassure Carly, and not wanting the woman he loved so deeply to have to worry about something as daft as time constraints.

Carly felt sick with nerves. As desperately in love as she was with Jack, she knew that having to call off her wedding and leave all she had known for the past decade wasn't going to be easy. She was about to cause carnage to those around her, but she couldn't suffocate in a black hole of misery any longer. The time to reclaim her happiness was upon her; and she was desperate not to let it slip through her fingers.

'Take a seat, I'll bring these over,' said Jack, planting a kiss on Carly's head before releasing her body to refocus on his bacon.

'Okay, I'm just gonna grab my phone from my

bag,' said Carly, pattering back out of the kitchen and into Grandma Barb's bedroom.

While Jack waited for Carly to return, he removed the sizzling bacon rashers from the hot frying pan with the tips of his fingers and dropped the bacon down onto a sheet of kitchen towel he'd placed in readiness on the nearby work surface.

As Jack patted the grease from his bacon, he heard the gentle patter of Carly's footsteps.

'Now I know you always liked to mix ketchup and mayo together, but we only have the former, I'm afraid. But I believe there is a bottle of salad cream in the fridge, if that's of any use to you?' said Jack, giddy at having Carly join him for breakfast.

Jack looked round at Carly on the other side of the kitchen. Her eyes were glued to the screen of her phone as a look of horror crept over her face, her pretty eyes widening and her lips parting.

'Is everything okay?' Jack asked.

Carly didn't respond, her mind frantic as she scrolled through her phone.

Carly had twenty-six missed calls, mostly from Craig, the rest from Lauren.

Craig had left countless messages, too, begging her to pick up the phone and call him back. So had Lauren. Carly scrolled through Lauren's messages, and finally came across an explanation.

May's been rushed to hospital. They think she's had a stroke. Craig called me trying to get hold of you. I'm so sorry, but I had to tell him I didn't know where you were,   but I've not told him anything, I swear. Call me when you get this, babes. X

Carly felt light-headed, as if the room was spinning, as she struggled to comprehend what was happening.

She tapped back into her missed calls, and took note of the time, the first call having been received from Craig at 01:42 a.m. Carly felt a lump form in her throat, then a strong feeling of nausea overcame her at the realisation that Craig had tried to call her at the exact moment she would have been slipping into bed with Jack. Carly felt disgusted with herself, disgusted that she had put her sexual fulfilment first, over and above the people who relied on her.

'I ... I ... I have to go,' Carly announced urgently as tears began to surface in her eyes.

'What's wrong? Carly, what's happened?' asked Jack, abandoning his bacon and rushing over to Carly.

'It's May. She's in the hospital, I have to go!' said Carly, so fearful for May's welfare she felt her legs begin to tremble.

'Okay, I'll get dressed, I'll come with you!' suggested Jack, wanting to be by Carly's side in her hour of need.

'What? Are you mad? You can't come with me!' snapped Carly.

'No, of course, I'm sorry. Look, let me know if you need anything. I'll stay here, we'll talk later,' said Jack, realising his suggestion was maybe not the most sensible.

'No, Jack, you don't get it. We're not gonna talk, there won't be a later! Oh God, what the hell was I thinking? What have I done? I can't do this! I can't, I can't do this!' rambled Carly, all her racing thoughts spilling out of her mouth as she became almost hysterical.

'Carly, Carly, calm down, everything's going to be okay ...' Jack said, trying to reassure her as he attempted to place his arms around her, but Carly pushed him away and moved aside, wanting to escape the terrible mistake she had made.

'No, no, it's not. I should have been at home last night, taking care of things. And instead I was here with you!' shouted Carly, making it clear with whom she laid her blame. 'I can't do this. *This*, it can't happen!' she stated as tears streamed down her face.

Jack couldn't believe what he was hearing. A few moments ago he had had everything he had ever wanted, and now, all of a sudden, Carly was so cruelly snatching it away. In pure desperation Jack took Carly's hand in his and placed his other hand gently on the side of her face, using his thumb to wipe away her tears.

'Carly, Carly, Carly, come on, you're upset and in shock and neither of us have had much sleep, but this, *this* between us, it isn't just some kind of coincidence! We've found each other, after all this time. We can't just pretend last night didn't happen!' he said, desperate for Carly to be rational.

'I've been pretending my whole life, why stop now?' Carly replied curtly, her sense of duty to May overshadowing any other emotion as she pulled her hand out of Jack's grip and stormed out of the kitchen.

'You don't understand! You don't understand what it means to do the right thing, to be there for people!' Carly shouted from Grandma Barb's bedroom as she collected her few toiletries from the bed and forcibly shoved them into her overnight bag.

'What I don't understand is why you're so willing to run back to a life that you can't stand! What the hell happened to you?' Jack shouted back, unable to comprehend why Carly was so willing to be subservient to a life she didn't want.

'Life, Jack! Life happened to me! While you were getting sucked off by Amy bloody Shepherd, life came along and took a massive shit on me!' screamed Carly as she hurriedly slipped on a pair of blue jeans and trainers she'd pulled from her bag.

'Right, and what, you think you're the only one that's been shat on? Well I've got news for you, Carly, you're not! But you are the only one that's let it plague the rest of their life!' Jack shouted from the bedroom doorway.

'Oh because life has been *really* hard on you! It

must have been *really* tough when you decided to cheat on your fiancée and give up your career on a whim!' shouted Carly as she stormed past Jack and marched down the hallway towards his bedroom.

'You think I gave up my career on a whim?!' shouted Jack, seething and hurt that Carly should hold such an opinion of him.

Jack stormed into the kitchen and over towards the cupboard under the sink. He reached for the newspaper Grandma Barb had placed there and slammed the cupboard door shut. He marched up the hallway towards his bedroom, where he found Carly stuffing her blue dress into her overnight bag.

'There, that was why I gave up my career. Not on a whim, not because I was bored, but because I killed someone!' shouted Jack, his words bursting from him, he failing to keep the truth buried for a second longer as he threw the newspaper down on the bed.

'What?'

Carly looked at the newspaper lying on the messy, unmade bed. She recognised the headline and the photo of the young man; it was the photo May had drawn her attention to in the newspaper article she'd already read. A young journalist had been murdered due to a story the paper had published.

'I wrote that story, about the child abuse case! Me, that was my story! Then one day I'm leaving work and outside the building some guy, some shaking weirdo who looked like he was on smack ...' Jack paused and looked up at the ceiling. He lifted his hands to roughly rub his reddening face, preparing himself for the next horrific instalment. 'He ran into the building, at Peter, and stabbed him in the stomach four times,' said Jack quietly, his voice tight as he struggled to relive the horror of the moment his friend was unknowingly sentenced to his death.

'He was some friend of the family's and he knew someone that worked on the security desk, but he got the wrong guy. I saw the whole thing. The stabbing, the screaming, the masses and masses of blood ... And afterwards, when it all became apparent who he'd actually wanted to kill, all I could think was thank God he got the wrong guy,' uttered Jack, admitting out loud the shameful initial reaction that had haunted him for the past three years, the guilt prompting Jack to leave his journalistic career for a life less destructive.

Carly stood open-mouthed and stared hard at Jack. Tears poured down his cheeks as he stood before her like a lost child, desperate for some kind of reassurance that everything was going to be okay, but Carly wasn't able to offer anything in the way of empathy.

Carly had her own problems she needed to tend to, and she felt angry that Jack selfishly thought that right now was the best time for him to pile his own issues onto her.

'Please say something,' begged Jack, starting to feel panicked by Carly's prolonged silence.

Unwilling to be another Jack Lewis casualty, Carly hoisted the strap of her overnight bag up onto her shoulder. She was seething with anger that in her own hour of need Jack was behaving like everybody else, expecting her to somehow pacify him, paying no regard to her own urgent predicament.

With no time for Jack's battling conscience, Carly shook her head in dismay.

'You really are an arsehole!' she said, her words cutting through Jack like a dagger to his heart, the pain so agonising he felt his body begin to shake with fear of what was to come next.

Carly marched quickly past Jack and out of the bedroom and within seconds Jack heard the opening then the slamming of the front door, so loud it made him jump.

Jack made no attempt to move.

He wanted to run after Carly to tell her how much he loved her, to beg her to see that he really was a good person, but Jack wasn't so sure it was true.

Alone, mentally and physically exhausted, Jack stood perfectly still in bereft shock. Tears fell from his eyes and rolled down his cheeks as he grieved for a lost love that could never be re-claimed.

CHAPTER 19:

Carly raced through the long quiet corridors of a hospital she knew well. She hadn't contacted Lauren or Craig prior to her arrival, her mind solely focused on being by May's side.

Feeling flustered and out of breath, Carly finally made it to Bluebell Ward and stood by the locked doors outside it, peering through the long window and tapping franticly on the glass, Carly noticed the absence of her engagement ring on her left hand. She tugged at her ring, pulling it off and hurriedly placed it back on the correct hand.

After what felt like an eternity a short African nurse strolled slowly towards the door. The nurse pressed the large green button on the wall to release the door, at which Carly pushed it open.

'Hi, I'm looking for May Penton. Can you tell me where she is?'

The nurse looked Carly up and down, visibly unimpressed by her dishevelled appearance: Carly was still wearing Jack's white shirt with no bra.

'Side room 3, down the end,' said the nurse with a thick accent, her eyes now focusing on Carly's messy unbrushed hair.

Not stopping to say thank you, Carly rushed away, and just before she reached Bay D she saw Craig standing outside. He was dressed scruffily in his usual jogging bottoms and T-shirt, with his phone fixed to his ear. A look of great anguish was etched across his face, causing a huge wave of guilt to crash into Carly for not being with him.

Carly slowly approached, and on seeing her Craig instantly dropped his phone from his ear.

'I've been calling and calling you. Where have you been?'

'What's happened? Is May okay? Lauren said they think it's a stroke,' said Carly, skilfully ignoring Craig's question.

'We're still waiting for the doctor to come back, but yeah, it looks like a stroke. What the fuck are you wearing?' grimaced Craig, confused by Carly's attire.

'What happened, when did you notice something was wrong?'

'About midnight. The foxes were shagging outside the front door. I went down to shoo them off and she was just lying there. Honest to God, I thought she was dead,' said Craig, his voice full of worry as he anxiously stroked his beard.

'Okay,' replied Carly, nodding her head as she processed what she was being told, and ready now to enter the bay and check on May for herself.

'So?' said Craig.

Carly paused.

'So what?'

'So where have you been?' snapped Craig, demanding an explanation.

'Does it matter?' huffed Carly, fully aware it did matter, but not willing to divulge anything.

After hours of radio silence during the most distressing night of his life, Craig felt his temper finally flare. Unimpressed by Carly's blasé attitude Craig forcibly took hold of her wrist and pulled her to one side.

'Yes, it fucking matters. You've been MIA for hours and then you rock up wearing another bloke's shirt. Where the fuck have you been?' he hissed, finally reaching the end of his tether.

'Craig, get off, you're hurting me,' Carly hissed back, seeing the raging temper in Craig's eyes.

Carly pulled away, trying and failing to free herself from Craig's tightening hold, his pressing grip crushing her wrist.

'Mr Penton?' asked a hesitant voice, whoever it was aware they were interrupting a tense encounter.

Craig finally let go of Carly's wrist, pausing their heated exchange to face the young man behind them.

Wearing a greying white shirt and worn brown trousers a young male doctor waited cautiously, his concerned brown eyes dancing between the pair.

'Mr Penton, I'm Dr Levin. I need to speak with you about your mother's test results,' said the doctor.

Craig nodded, and Carly felt sick with nerves, terrified of what the doctor's news would be.

Carly and Craig sat in a dazed silence as they each tried to process what the doctor had said. Carly delicately held May's weakening hand in her own, stroking her tired skin, as she lay lifelessly on the hospital bed. Dr Levin, not ten minutes before, had been able to confirm that May had indeed suffered a very large stroke. May's vegetative state said it all. Like a discarded vegetable in a field, she was unable to command any control over her own body. Wired up to hospital machines and with her mouth gaping open at an uncomfortable angle it was clear all was not at all well.

In spite of the dense fog hanging between them, Carly and Craig had real decisions to make, but as severe as the situation was, Carly refused to be the first to break and was more than happy to process her thoughts in silence.

'I'm sorry.... if I hurt you,' said Craig quietly, rightfully ashamed of his brutish conduct.

Carly glanced away from May and over at Craig.

As angry as she was with him, she knew Craig

wasn't a vicious man, but simply a son, scared about the health of his mother. Carly knew for herself how terrifying and lonely his situation was and finally felt herself soften at his apology.

'I'm sorry I wasn't there,' said Carly, ashamed of not having been present when her family had needed her most.

'What if this is it? What if she just stays like this?' asked Craig, his voice quivering as if about to break.

'Let's just see how the next few days go first,' Carly replied softly, trying not to let her own fear for the future surface.

As silence fell once again, Craig began to fill the void with a nervous tapping on the arm of his chair, the annoying sound radiating around the room, making the atmosphere tense.

'He's ... he's not called Jane. Is he?' Craig said, the strain in his voice making it clear he'd been waiting quite some time to release the nagging question from his mind.

Carly felt her stomach flip. She figured it was naïve of her to think that Craig was going to let the fact that she was sitting at his mother's bedside in another man's clothes drop so easily.

Too ashamed to look at him, Carly kept her gaze on May as she struggled to conjure up a reply.

'Carly?'

Carly sighed, knowing she wasn't going to be able to dodge an explanation any longer.

'It's done,' she said, finally able to look at Craig, but quickly wishing she hadn't. His shocked face was a tired mess. His puffy eyes were kept company by the dark rings under them as Carly confirmed all his worst fears and she felt her sickening guilt resurface.

'So that's—'

'Craig, it's done. That's all you need to know,' Carly concluded, trying not to sound too harsh as she felt the pieces of her heart fall apart at how she'd left things with Jack.

With her own emotions heightened through worry and lack of sleep, Carly felt her eyes begin to flood with tears and quickly began to wipe her eyes with her hand.

Too angry to offer his fiancée anything in the way of a loving embrace, but too exhausted to fight, Craig pushed back on his chair and climbed to his feet and did the only thing he could think of.

'You wanna tea?' he asked.

'Yeah. Tea would be good,' Carly nodded.

With that, Craig left the room, leaving Carly to sob alone for all she had lost on one sorry Sunday morning.

***

It was Monday night, and Jack's final creative writing class, not just before the term finished for the Christmas break but also before he left for good for Cambridge.

The atmosphere in the class was lighthearted, as it was in any class before it broke up for Christmas. Margery and Andrew had each bought with them colourful boxes of chocolates to share that were now littered across the table along with some tins containing home-made fairy cakes Mandy had brought from home, four of which Jenni had inhaled in less than ten minutes.

Despite the air of festive merriment, there was a noticeable absence in the form of Carly.

For the fifth week in a row her seat remained empty, the sight of it so disturbingly upsetting for Jack that he could hardly bear to look in its direction.

Jack hadn't heard, spoken to or seen Carly since the morning she'd stormed out of Grandma Barb's flat. Although any involvement in each other's lives now seemed a remote possibility, that didn't stop Jack from constantly thinking about her. Jack had held his phone in his hand countless times over the past few weeks, staring down at Carly's number and hovering his fingers over the call button. He was desperate to hear her voice, longing to know how she was. Jack was anxious not to repeat the mistakes of his nineteen-year-old self and allow what they had to disappear so easily into the abyss, but something stopped him each time.

Carly was only a few short weeks away from marrying an honest man, a man who had by all intents and purposes been there for her over the past decade in a way that he hadn't, for her or anybody else, and he knew he had to respect her wishes and let her go.

Jack expertly pushed the thought of Carly into the deepest crevice of his mind, unwrapped a golden toffee penny, tossed it into his mouth and began to address his class.

'So it seems to me that the festive season is a time of year where a spot of writing seems rather common, whether it be Christmas cards, extensive to-do or shopping lists or indeed your own letters to Father Christmas asking him ever so nicely to leave that brand-new Lamborghini parked in one of the designated spaces out front,' said Jack, pointing at Kevin with a cheeky wink.

'I'm not sure I've been good enough for the Lamborghini this year!' chuckled Kevin.

'Then that makes two us! But it did get me to thinking that maybe letter writing in general is becoming something of a forgotten art, and I thought a fun exercise for our final class would be to simply write a letter. It can be to whoever you like, indeed Father Christmas, even yourself, maybe even somebody who is no longer with you this time of year,' instructed Jack, at which his thoughts instantly turned to Carly.

'So shall we give it fifteen minutes, and then maybe we can share what we've all got?' asked Jack, his question met by the obligatory nods of agreement.

With the class falling silent ready to put their

pens to work, Jack pulled out his chair at the head of the table and sat himself down. In front of him on the table lay a black biro and a few scraps of paper. With no pressing commitments to fill the next fifteen minutes, Jack picked up the pen and on the back of a scrap of paper made some notes of his own, surprising himself at how easily he began to pour out his heart to a person that meant everything to him.

CHAPTER 20:

It was New Year's Day, and the night before Carly and Craig's wedding.

Although Carly had never been the type of girl to spend a lifetime fantasising about the night before her wedding, she never imagined it would be spent like this.

In her hand Carly held a champagne flute, the champagne having been poured from a miniature bottle that Lauren had expertly smuggled into May's hospital ward. The two friends sat either side of the foot of May's bed and toasted tomorrow's pending nuptials.

'Here's to you, babe, my best mate and partner in crime, and to you, May, the world's best mother-in-law,' said Lauren, her sad eyes meeting Carly's.

May didn't respond, just like she hadn't responded to anything for weeks.

May lay in her bed completely motionless, staring up towards the ceiling into a picture of nothingness.

Not a great deal had changed since May was first admitted to hospital. The stroke she had suffered had been severe, and although an operation had eased some of the pressure on her brain and she was now breathing unaided, her future remained bleak.

After a blur of a Christmas, the festive period had been filled with what felt like an endless barrage of information from different doctors and consultants, and Carly and Craig had finally made a heart-breaking decision. Once the wedding was over, May's care would be handed over to a specialist facility able to meet her needs.

What with their joint concern over May, Carly's doubts about marrying Craig had been allowed little time to surface. In the coming days, once May was moved to her new home, their new life would begin, and it was only now as Carly and Lauren toasted to the future that the oh so familiar sick feeling of dread returned to Carly. She downed her champagne, hoping for it to somehow numb her.

'Easy, tiger! I've barely got enough for a glass each here!' laughed Lauren, holding up her tiny green bottle.

Carly didn't laugh, nor did she react in any other way.

She looked over at May and was filled with an overwhelming sadness for what was now a stranger locked inside a failing body. Gone was May's cheerful smile, replaced by an awkward gaping mouth that no longer served any practical use. May's once glistening eyes were vacant and dull, showing no sign of life or compre-hension, but the one change that really upset Carly was the state of May's hair. No longer me-ticulously maintained the way Carly had always kept it, it was now greasy and untamed.

Lauren pulled herself off the bed, and walked around to join her friend, wrapping a loving arm around Carly and planting a kiss on the side of her face.

'Everything's gonna be okay, babes. May's gonna get looked after like a queen, you'll see. And you know … you can … go back to work, you know … full-time … and …' Lauren trailed off, struggling to suggest anything positive about the bleak future that lay ahead for her friend.

Carly's mind suddenly catapulted her back to a happier time when she'd been curled in the warm embrace of Jack, and he'd promised her a future where she could study or write, be the person she really was, a picture in such contrast to the one Craig painted, where Carly was bare-foot and pregnant, tending to everyone else's needs and never her own.

Carly looked at Lauren and smiled a tight, sad smile.

'You know, it's not too late, babes. It's not,' whispered Lauren, as if worried May might hear.

But it was too late.

Just like before, Carly had disappeared, hurry-ing out on Jack and letting her problems become paramount as she switched off from the outside world. After all she had said to Jack, Carly couldn't imagine he was waiting around for her to get in touch and she remembered his moving date was tomorrow – *a day of new beginnings for both of us.*

'Yeah, it is. And anyway, he had very questionable morals,' said Carly, referring to Jack's shocking revelation.

'Maybe, but none of us is perfect, babes, even you!' said Lauren as she downed the last drop of her champagne.

Carly looked down at May and took her lifeless hand in her own. Indeed Carly was not perfect, a fact she didn't need to be reminded of. When Craig and May had needed her most, she was planning her escape with another man, a fact she would never fully forgive herself for and one she was determined to make up for.

'See ya, May. I'll be sure to bring you in the photos of tomorrow,' said Carly, keeping her voice light, as if pretending all was okay in her worried mind.

As Carly lifted herself from the bed, May's hand tightly gripped hers. It was the first and only sign of consciousness May had shown for weeks and Carly wondered if she should call for one of the nurses to alert them, but almost as suddenly May's hold loosened, her hand lying dormant once again in Carly's.

Jack felt a little worse for wear. It was almost

midday and as he went through the motions of packing up the last of his things, ready for his big move to Cambridge, he was still feeling the after-effects of the farewell party Grandma Barb had insisted on throwing him the night before.

Although the only guests in attendance at Jack's party were himself and Grandma Barb, that hadn't stopped them finishing three bottles of red wine between them, the wine leaving its legacy in the form of a pounding headache.

'Now are you sure you don't want me to make you something to eat before you go? I picked up some fresh challah from Grodzinki's only this morning!' Grandma Barb called from the hallway as she approached Jack's bedroom. She stood in the doorway with a look of insistence on her face, as if making Jack a snack for the road was the most important thing in the world.

'Er, yes, okay, a sandwich might be nice, actually,' replied Jack, willing to let Grandma Barb carry out one last grandmotherly duty as he rubbed his aching head. 'I don't suppose you could do me a side order of aspirin with my sandwich, could you, Gran, my head's—'

'Pha, amateur! There should be some in the kitchen drawer,' said Grandma Barb, walking away, leaving Jack in complete awe as to how someone of her advanced years should be suffering so much less than himself this morning.

Jack hoisted up the last of his plastic boxes from his unmade bed and carried it to the front door, placing it next to the three others, before joining Grandma Barb in the kitchen.

'Now have you got everything, darling? If you're short of room in that tiny car you can always leave some things here to pick up another time,' suggested Grandma Barb as she buttered bread with all the grace of a five-year-old, all the butter concentrated in the centre.

Standing in the kitchen doorway, Jack couldn't help but raise a small smile at his grandmother's subtle ploy for him to come back and visit.

'Thank you, Gran,' said Jack, hoping Grandma Barb could sense his gratefulness to her for having been his best friend and rock in what had been a turbulent few months.

Unwilling to engage in any kind of New Age sentiment, Grandma Barb kept her back turned as she carried on buttering the bread and smiled a tight smile that she hoped would stifle her tears.

'Aspirin's in that drawer over there,' said Grandma Barb, pointing with her butter knife to the drawer in the furthest corner next to the oven.

Jack made his way over to the drawer, yanking it open and pulling out a battered box of aspirin, not completely convinced it was still in date, but not caring enough to check.

He snapped two pills from the silver-foil pack and tossed the box back into the drawer, then went to the kitchen sink to fill a glass of water, just as Grandma Barb snapped the lid back on the butter tub and took it back to the fridge.

'Oh darling, this is yours, you don't want to forget it. It's a good one!' exclaimed Grandma Barb, pulling Jack's Globe Theatre magnet from the fridge door. As Jack swallowed his pills, Grandma Barb walked over to him. She placed the magnet in the palm of his hand.

Jack looked down at the small souvenir and felt greatly unsettled by the feeling of devastating loss it brought him, a feeling he had done pretty well to ignore for at least the past half an hour.

'It's okay, Gran, you keep it!' said Jack, waving the magnet at Grandma Barb in the belief that she was unaware of its huge sentimental value.

Grandma Barb pulled out a block of cheese and a tomato from the fridge. Jack's forlorn state hadn't passed her by; for she had raised enough children and witnessed enough in the way of broken hearts to know when something was awry. Although Jack hadn't chosen to fill her in on the details, the fact that Carly hadn't been around, or even mentioned, since the night of the Bar Mitzvah told her all she needed to know.

As Grandma Barb made her way back over to the work surface next to Jack, she placed the cheese and tomato down, and gently closed Jack's hand back around the magnet.

'What is for you won't pass by you, darling,' she said softly, looking into her grandson's sad eyes, wishing she could do something to magic all his pain away.

'What if it already has?' said Jack, keeping the sadness out of his voice. Today was Carly's wedding day and the day of no return with regard to any kind of future with her.

'Trust Granny, darling! She's old, and she's seen it all before! Now are you having tea with your sandwich?'

'No, no, a sandwich is more than enough,' said Jack, pulling out a chair from the kitchen table and expertly dodging Grandma Barb's lumpy tea for one last time.

'You look beautiful,' gushed Carly as she took Sophia's delicate face between her hands and kissed her shiny blonde hair. Sitting on the edge of her bed, Carly then proceeded to fuss with Sophia's small white dress, making sure it was sitting just right on her tiny frame.

'Now, where have you put your flower petals?' asked Carly, readying Sophia for their departure.

'They're downstairs.'

'Okay, you go and find them, then we'll get ready to leave?'

'Okay!' beamed Sophia, running out of the bedroom and straight into Lauren as she came up to the doorway.

'Careful, careful!' Lauren called after her daughter as she disappeared down the stairs, conveniently giving Lauren and Carly a few precious minutes alone.

As Carly stood up from the bed and looked down at her gleaming white wedding gown, she felt precisely nothing, as if the misadventures of the past few months, the constant battering of high emotions, had left her empty, drained of feeling.

'You look beauts, babes, you really do,' Lauren said lovingly to her dearest friend, and she was right.

Carly looked the epitome of beauty. Her simple white gown fitted her perfectly with her lace veil adding a touch of classic elegance. Lauren had styled Carly's light ginger hair in a stylish up-do, just as she had for Carly's night at the Savoy, soft loose curls framing her pretty face.

'Thank you. So do you,' said Carly, Lauren's sapphire-blue gown inconveniently stirring a much fonder memory.

Lauren neared her friend, and took hold of her hands, gripping them tightly. 'She'll be looking down at you now, and she'll be really proud, babes,' said Lauren through a tight smile of love and admiration, and for the first time in her life, Carly was grateful that her mother wasn't there to witness the catastrophe that was her life.

'You ready to do this?' said Lauren, trying to ignite some kind of excitement.

'Ready as I'll ever be,' smiled Carly, willing herself to feel something, even if it was resentment.

'I found my flowers, Auntie Carly, and Mr Postman brought you letters!' announced Sophia, waddling into Carly's bedroom and struggling to keep hold of her flower basket as well as the letters held in her small hands.

'Soph, you're dropping them everywhere, you'll have nothing left for the church,' huffed Lauren as she released Carly's hands and dropped to her knees, scooping up the loose pink flower petals that had rained down onto the carpet.

'Here you go,' said Sophia, thrusting a small pile of letters at Carly.

'Thanks, Soph.'

Carly mindlessly sifted through a Chinese takeaway menu, a gas bill, a circular from a credit card company and a small white envelope, *For the attention of Miss C. Hughes*, the address neatly handwritten in black ink. Intrigued as to who the letter was from, Carly tossed the mail down on her bed and proceeded to open the envelope. She pulled out a small piece of good-quality stationery and noticed straight away Grandma Barb's name and address printed along the top in a purple italic font. Carly sat down on the edge of the bed and held the letter up to her eyes.

Dear Carly,
I should probably start by first apologising for the intrusion of sending mail to your home address. I hope you don't mind, but I managed to source your details from an extremely reluctant Beryl at Wanstead

House, but I suppose it's good to know she handles students' information with the upmost responsibility!

I realise I could easily have sent you an email or text message asking how you were, but I feel there's something sentimental, maybe even romantic, about receiving a handwritten letter. I mean, no one ever prints off an email or a screen shot message to keep forever in a box of memories, do they?

The past decade of my life has been full of one too many regrets. I've lied, I've cheated, I've engaged in careless behaviour that has hurt others and even destroyed my own happiness.

However, when I'm with you, I don't want to be that horrible git that cheats and lies. I want to be decent and kind; I want to be better.

Of course, I realise this is a ludicrous responsibility to rest on your shoulders, but that's how you make me feel, Carly. As if merely having you near allows a better part of me to finally shine, a part I'm happy to be seen by those who may have thought less of me.

I never could have imagined in a million years that we would re-enter each other's lives, and although our re-encounter hasn't ended in the kind of blissful romance each of us might have hoped for, I'm grateful you did, for you, Miss Hughes, are and always will be the most wonderful thing to have ever happened to me.

I beg you to never forget how special you are. You are loving and kind and insanely intelligent.

I sincerely wish you every happiness, Carly, and if being back in the bosom of your family is what truly makes you happy, then I respect your choice.

I suppose there's nothing else left to say but to wish you Happy New Year, by which I mean only good things for the coming year.

All my love, forever and always,

Jack x

PS: Please see enclosed my new contact details. Should you ever need anything, from a listening ear to a bacon beigel, you'll know where to find me!

Carly's eyes read over the last words of Jack's letter with the kind of disappointment felt at the end of an enthralling film or song: she was gutted that it had come to an end all too soon. She looked back inside the envelope, where as stated was another small piece of paper containing Jack's newest address, but it wasn't enough.

Carly wanted more.

She wanted to know how he was, she wanted to know how he'd spent his Christmas, she wanted to know if he was excited about starting his new job, she wanted to know if he too was experiencing the same level of heart-wrenching, earth-shattering devastation that she was, at the very notion of their never seeing each other again.

Carly sat motionless on the edge of her bed and felt her throat tighten as she bit down on the fresh lipstick on her bottom lip. She urged it not to tremble and break her composure, but for the first time in weeks, Carly was finally feeling something. The kind of wave- crashing, heart-stopping, all-consuming, star-aligning love she had been willing herself to feel for years; and it was all for Jack.

'You okay, babes?' Lauren asked hesitantly, but before Carly had a chance to answer, her thoughts were interrupted by the sound of a car beeping outside.

'Oh it's here, the car's here!' flapped Lauren, striding over to the window to confirm the specially hired white black taxi had pulled up outside.

With no time to mull over her emotions, Carly stood up from the bed and quickly folded the letter back into its envelope. She pulled at the top of her dress and tucked the envelope inside her bra, out of sight and close to her heart.

St Peter's Church in Dagenham was a pretty church. A thirteenth-century building that wouldn't have looked out of place in any quaint village, but which was almost a kitsch novelty on a busy main road in Dagenham.

With Carly's Father having never been in her life, Carly had bestowed on Lauren the task of walking her down the aisle. As the two friends stood closely side by side in the porch of the church, Lauren took one last chance to check over Carly's appearance.

'Right, I think we're all good to go,' said Lauren, fidgeting with Carly's veil, making sure each soft pleat hung perfectly across her face.

'I love you, babes, I really really do,' gushed Lauren, dabbing at a tear in the corner of her eye with the tip of her newly manicured finger.

'I love you too, and thank you, for doing this,' said Carly, almost embarrassed at the unconventional role she was asking of her best friend.

'Are you joking? This is literally my life's biggest honour.'

Carly took a large deep breath, just as the music from the church organ began to sound.

The church doors flew open and Sophia was beckoned in by an elderly church helper to begin the process of scattering the aisle with a trail of pink rose petals that matched those in Carly's small bouquet.

'Are sure you want to do this, Carls, 'cause it's not too late to change your mind,' Lauren whispered into her friend's ear as they moved towards the doors that led into the church.

'I think it might be,' Carly whispered back despondently as the sound of the wedding march rose.

With that, Lauren took a tight grip of Carly's hand and they walked forward together.

As she and Lauren began their walk down the aisle, Carly felt underwhelmed by the bleak turnout. With Carly and Craig both being only children from small families, they hadn't managed to expand the guest list above fifty people.

On the right sat a handful of Craig's family members, the only instantly recognisable relative being May's sister Frances and third husband Ken, a retired scaffolder Carly and Craig had only met three times before.

On the other side of the aisle were mainly Carly's friends from Pinky Bingo, the rest a handful of people from her time working in children's social services. The only blood relative in attendance was Carly's cousin Amanda, who was joined by her partner Dane and their toddler Archie. Carly hadn't seen Amanda in years, and although it was nice of her to have made the effort to come, Carly had never much liked Amanda, a narcissist who had purposely walked Carly through a pile of dog poo blindfolded when she was nine years old.

As Carly and Lauren moved further forward, Carly looked ahead, and saw Craig waiting for her at the end of the aisle. He looked smart – for Craig – in a navy-blue suit and matching tie with a brand-new white shirt underneath, but his messy beard was in its usual state of messy and his unkempt hair in desperate need of a trim.

Unable to hold any kind of mature poise, he was standing nervously, fidgeting with his stubby fingers, his eyes darting constantly between Carly and their guests.

Panic set in. Carly's heart began to beat furiously inside her chest, against the letter held in her bra, against the words Jack had so eloquently put to paper, and it was then, as she stood halfway between her future and the church's exit, that Carly stopped walking.

On a day, in a church, which should have been packed to the rafters with friends and loved ones, Carly looked around and failed to spot anyone in the pews that she truly loved.

The two mothers she had been so fortunate to have loved were not there, and when Carly looked up at Craig, the only person she could think about was Jack, wishing with all her heart it was him waiting for her at the end of the aisle.

The wedding march came to a halt and the guests began to mumble in concern as they looked between each other and Carly.

'What are you doing?' mouthed Craig, his facial expression equal parts embarrassed and furious.

'I'm sorry, I'm so sorry,' said Carly, closing her eyes tightly as if building up the courage to jump off a tall building.

As Carly stood amongst wedding guests who meant so little to her, she came to the realisation that entering a marriage she didn't want would not only be disastrous for her, but also unfair to Craig. Although it was rare for Carly to feel anything other than contempt for Craig, she loved him just enough to do what she felt was the kindest thing.

Carly let go of Lauren's hand, hoisted up her dress, turned round and ran back up the aisle and out of the church into the open air.

Out of breath from running and adrenalin, Carly stood doubled over in the small overgrown graveyard of the church.

'Seriously, Carly! What the fuck are you playing at!' raged Craig as he stormed towards her.

Carly stood up straight, and clumsily pulled off her veil, letting it blow unmercifully in the wind, finally feeling as if a heavy, soul-crushing weight had been lifted from her.

'For fuck's sake, Carly, say something!' shouted Craig, making it evident that he was more concerned about his own humiliation than Carly's welfare.

'Fucking White Shirt! That's who all this is about, isn't it?' Craig nodded proudly to himself, as if he was a very clever man who had just worked out a very difficult equation. 'What? You wanna be with him? Is that it?'

Indeed it was true, Carly did want to be with Jack, but Jack wasn't the reason she didn't want to be with Craig. Their relationship had been dead in the water for years, their problems mounting up long before Jack had re-entered her life, and for once, Carly wanted Craig to understand her.

'You know I cheated on you ... and you ... we've ... never mentioned it again. Not once, not since that day at the hospital,' Carly shouted over the sound of a police siren coming from the main road.

'Great! So you wanna talk about it now! What do you want, Carly? What do you want me to do? Hit you? Scream at you, cry about it, call off the wedding?!'

'I want you to feel something, Craig! I want us both to feel something other than this stale boredom!' screamed Carly, waving her hands around and throwing her bouquet to the ground, finally losing her composure as she released all her pent-up frustrations.

'If you're so bored, then why did you come back!' Craig screamed, opening his arms and looking up at the heavens, searching for an answer.

'Because, I thought it was the right thing to do, which I'm sure at the time it was, but I can't do this any more, Craig! I can't carry on pretending! I can't stand in that church and vow to you in front of all those people to love you forever, when I don't.'

Carly and Craig went silent. They stood staring at each other with a look of defeated exhaustion, each knowing that their relationship was now in too derelict a state to ever rebuild.

'You don't love me?' asked Craig, his voice small as if he already knew Carly's answer.

'On some level I'm sure I do, but not in the way I'm supposed to,' said Carly, plagiarising a phrase she had once heard from Jack, it seeming to make for the most tactful response.

Carly watched as Craig gradually softened, his angry and frenzied state calming as he anxiously stroked his messy bread as he always did when he was feeling nervous.

'Don't you think we both deserve better? Don't we both deserve to be with people that can give us what we want?' reasoned Carly.

'It's been ten years, Carly. I … I don't … I wouldn't know …' Craig spluttered, unable to find the words to fully express himself, but Carly understood. The unhappiness she had felt for so long had never been one-sided. Carly and Craig had each been just too scared, or lazy, or both, to do anything about their failed relationship, and Carly took some comfort in realising that, for once, their feelings matched.

Feeling something that resembled pity for a man she had detested for so long, Carly moved towards Craig and placed her arms around him, hugging him tightly without revulsion, as they both finally laid down their weapons and surrendered their battle.

'I'm sorry,' said Carly.

Craig huffed his hot breath into Carly's shoulder. Carly waited, hoping Craig might make an apology of his own, expressing some kind of regret for the pitiful state they had both allowed their relationship to fall into, but nothing followed.

'What do we do now?' mumbled a defeated Craig, releasing himself from her hold.

'I er, actually have something I need to take care of …' squirmed Carly, feeling guilty about leaving Craig to clear up their mess alone, but desperate to get away.

'Oh great! So you run back off to White Shirt and leave me here to deal with all this!' ranted Craig, his softened exterior quickly hardening again, but before Carly had a chance to react, a calming voice of reason stepped in.

'It's okay, it's okay!' said Lauren, pulling Sophia from her hip and placing her down on the ground, the two of them having watched everything from the church's main entrance.

Lauren marched towards the pair with Sophia tottering behind.

'Don't worry, Craig, I'll help you sort it,' said Lauren, patting Craig on the shoulder, then turning her attention to Carly.

Lauren took Carly's hands in hers and beamed a smile at her best friend.

'I'm so proud of ya, babes,' gushed Lauren, before pulling Carly close to her, hugging her so tightly they each struggled to catch their breath.

'I've got this. You go!' whispered Lauren, assuring Carly all would be fine and willing her to seize the day.

'Thank you …'

Lauren pushed Carly's body from hers, keen for her not to waste another second, but before

Carly fled, there was one last act of decency she needed to carry out.

On her right hand, her engagement ring sat, waiting to be moved to sit alongside her wedding ring. Carly tugged at her ring, pulling it from her finger and exhaled a deep satisfied breath, as if to finally release herself from a tight set of restricting handcuffs and placed the ring Lauren's hand.

Lauren nodded in silent agreement, knowing to return the ring to Craig.

'Now go, before it's too late,' instructed Lauren.

Carly beamed a smile at Lauren, hoisted up her dress and ran with great vigour towards the waiting white black cab parked outside the church grounds.

There was a great amount of confusion caused when Carly jumped into the waiting bridal car, minus her groom. The chauffeur, a rather overweight grey-haired man, grudgingly agreed to drive Carly from Dagenham to north-east London, but not without requiring a full explanation, and not without informing her that chauffeuring runaway brides was strictly not included in his fee.

After thirty long minutes, an area Carly was gradually becoming more familiar with began to come into focus, causing her nerves to really crank up a gear. As she had no idea what Jack's plans were, there was every chance that he had already left for Cambridge, but that wasn't the worse fear lodged in Carly's heart.

What if he doesn't want to see me?

What if his letter was his own way of finding closure?

What if he has already moved on with some bohemian teacher type he grew close to at the staff Christmas party?

As Carly nervously tapped her foot on the floor, she tried to focus her mind on other things, a chore that was proving difficult with the constant drone of the chauffeur ringing in her ears.

'I feel for you, sweetheart, I do, but I've got another job I need to get back for in an hour, so I can't be waiting around, I'm afraid.'

'That's fine, I'm really just more concerned with getting there than I am with getting back,' said Carly, implying a subtle hint of *get a bloody move on!* 'Oh, you needed to turn left down there!' Carly yelped from the back seat, the cab passing the desired turning and heading back round a busy one-way system.

'Sorry, sweetheart. I can't go back, we'll have to go round again.'

'Stop the car!'

'What, I can't! It's fine, we'll—'

'STOP THE CAR!' yelled Carly in a frenzy that took both herself and the chauffeur by surprise, so much so that he did exactly as he was told.

The cab came to a sudden abrupt halt, the front tyres making the kind of scratching sound that would usually be followed by the sound of crashing car bumpers. Unconcerned as to whether it was even safe, Carly flung open the door and jumped out of the cab onto the pavement; and for the third time that day, hoisted up her dress and ran, faster and further than she had ever done before.

Hot, sweaty and with a dull ache in her stomach, Carly was fully aware she might have underestimated the weight of her wedding dress as well as the distance between Grandma Barb's flat and the one-way system. Her glamorously styled hair was now a windswept mess, her perfect make-up beginning to smudge with the aid of her excessive perspiration.

Exhausted and wheezing slightly, Carly made it to the black iron gate that led into the grounds of Grandma Barb's block of flats. As Carly fidgeted with the gate's latch, she heard the beeping of a passing car, quickly followed by a loud cheer, the fourth passing driver to cheer the crazy runaway bride in the last ten minutes.

Undeterred, Carly unlatched the gate, and ran through the smart grounds and down the concrete path. When she reached Grandma Barb's ground-floor flat, she furiously tapped on the front-room window on her way to the intercom and the buzzer for number 75.

After what felt like an eternity, a well-spoken elderly voice answered.

'Hello ...'

'Hi, Mrs Lewis, Barb ... it's Carly ... Jack's friend,' said Carly through gasps of breath as she doubled over, keeping her hands on her knees so as not to slump to the ground completely.

'Oh Cara dear,' said Grandma Barb, her voice almost breaking into song.

'Cara dear, how lovely to see you,' said Grandma Barb as she appeared at the flat's street door, looking anxiously at Carly. 'Is everything all right?' she asked, alarmed by the windswept wheezing bride at her doorstep.

'Mrs Lewis ... Barb ....is Jack there ...?' panted Carly, finally mastering the strength to stand and placing her hand on her left hip to steady herself.

'I'm afraid not, dear. You've just missed him. He left about fifteen minutes ago.'

Carly exhaled a loud annoyed groan, which hurt the back of her dry throat, and rubbed her sweaty brow in utter frustration.

She had run out of the church on her wedding day, jumped out of a cab onto a busy road, raced down the road like a crazed lunatic, and it had all been for nothing. Carly looked up at the cold grey sky, and felt foolish, with no idea what to do from here.

'Are you okay, Cara dear? Would you like to come in for a drink?' offered Grandma Barb, her solution to any problem, big or small.

Carly blinked hard and looked back at

Grandma Barb standing small and concerned in the metal doorway.

'No, no … But if you speak to Jack, can you tell him—'

'Tell me what?' interrupted a familiar voice.

Carly turned round, and to her amazement, there was Jack, holding his car keys and dressed in his usual smart grey jacket, but looking relaxed in dark blue jeans and a pair of dark blue trainers that served no athletic purpose.

Carly's mouth moved wordlessly as she blinked hard once again, half wondering if she was hallucinating.

'Jack,' she finally uttered, as if witnessing the sight of a ghost.

'Is everything okay, darling?' asked Grandma Barb, wondering why Jack had returned so soon.

'I stopped for petrol and realised I'd forgotten my wallet. I think I left it in the kitchen.'

'Wait there, darling, I'll go and check.'

As Grandma Barb disappeared back inside, Jack stood frozen, only able to muster half a worried smile at the sight of Carly looking so dishevelled in her wedding dress, delighted though he was to see her.

'What did you want to tell me?' Jack asked gently, rubbing the back of his neck apprehensively, unsure whether or not to approach Carly.

'I … just wanted … to tell you … that …' babbled Carly, realising she actually had no plan beyond turning up at Jack's doorstep, no idea as to what it was she really wanted to say.

Sweaty and flustered, Carly felt the bodice of her dress slip against her clammy skin and remembered that inside her dress she held Jack's letter.

'Here you go, darling,' said Grandma Barb, reappearing at the doorway with Jack's black leather wallet.

'I got your letter!' Carly blurted out, reaching inside her bodice and peeling the small crumpled envelope from her breast before Jack had a chance to move forward for his wallet.

'I got it this morning. And you know, I ... all ... I just wanted to say really ... is that I don't think you're an arsehole.'

Jack smiled and laughed inwardly, feeling a little bashful, if also a little unsure as to where Carly's frenzied state was headed.

'Actually, I know you're not an arsehole ...'

Jack raised his eyebrows, willing Carly to continue.

'... because arseholes, they don't write letters like this. And an arsehole wouldn't have looked after that smelly dog the way you did, or care about their grandma the way you do ... Or make love the way you do ...'

Carly saw Jack's cheeks flush with embarrassment, his eyes darting over to Grandma Barb standing in the doorway with no intention of offering Jack and Carly anything in the way of privacy.

'Sorry, Mrs Lewis,' squirmed Carly.

'Don't be, I'm pleased to hear he satisfies you, dear!'

'I know you think you're a horrible person, because of what happened to your friend. But no one's perfect, especially not me,' said Carly, rolling her eyes in reference to her jilting episode earlier in the day.

A silence fell.

Jack looked up at the sky, rubbed his hand over his head, and said nothing, much to Carly's frustration.

'Jesus, Jack, say something!' begged Carly, feeling foolish at having poured out her emotions.

Jack turned his gaze to her.

'Are you married?' he asked with the utmost seriousness, narrowing his eyes and holding his breath, fearful of Carly's answer.

Carly shook her head.

'No. I couldn't go through with it. I stood at the top of the aisle, and all I could think about was you.'

Jack finally allowed himself to breathe, as the deep black hole of sadness in his heart filled with light, clearing itself from his mind, allowing a promise of brighter possibilities to take its place.

'That must've been terribly inconvenient for you!' said Jack, through a stupidly happy smile he could no longer contain.

'It really was!' nodded Carly, matching Jack's

smile as the pair moved nearer to each other.

Bedraggled, exhausted and highly emotional, Carly was still a picture of beauty, and never in Jack's life could he remember wanting someone more than he wanted her. As their eyes met, Jack tucked a hand behind Carly's head and stroked his thumb over her lips before lowering his own to Carly's and lovingly kissing her, holding her body close to his, each of them losing themselves in their embrace.

Grandma Barb watched, suppressing the urge to clap, proud as she was that her grandson had finally found the kind of love he so deserved.

'I don't think I've ever been so pleased to have misplaced my wallet,' said Jack through soft laughter as he pulled his lips away, pressing his forehead against Carly's, when they each felt a hand on their back.

'Well I think it's imperative we go inside and raise a toast to your wedding day, Cara,' said Grandma Barb, showing no remorse for interrupting Carly and Jack's loving embrace.

'Oh, but I didn't get married,' said Carly.

With a beaming smile, Grandma Barb took Carly's hand in hers and squeezed it tightly.

'Exactly, Cara dear, exactly!' said Grandma Barb with a knowing wink and led them both inside.

EPILOGUE:

'Lauren, really it's fine, just let him take the picture!'

'Carls, this is the most important day of your life, you need to look perfect!' fussed Lauren as she arranged the pleats in Carly's gown.

'Okay, ladies, are we ready?' groaned Jack as he stood waiting to take their photo, slowly losing the will to live.

'Yes—'

'No!' protested Lauren, taking a length of Carly's long hair in each of her hands and draping it over her shoulders and gown.

'I'm so goddamn proud of you, babes!' gushed Lauren, the love and admiration she felt for her oldest and dearest friend overflowing once again as tears of great pride flooded into her eyes for what was maybe the fifth time that day.

'Oh Jesus, Jack, quickly take it before she goes again!' laughed Carly, rolling her eyes comically at Lauren.

'No, no, no, wait!' demanded Lauren, forcing her tears back before repositioning the black tassel on Carly's mortarboard for the final time.

'Right, okay, now we're ready!' confirmed Lauren as the two friends wrapped an arm around each other and happily posed for the camera.

'Right, let me take one of you two love birds before it starts chucking it down!' suggested Lauren, clanking in her high heels over towards Jack and looking concernedly up at the grey clouds that had settled above the university.

Jack happily handed his phone over to Lauren and took his place proudly next to Carly at the bottom of the university steps, they wrapping their arms lovingly around each other.

'I'm very, *very* proud of you, Mrs Lewis,' Jack said softly into Carly's ear, then kissed her gently on her temple just as the camera flashed and took their picture.

'I'm proud of me too!' Carly boasted coyly, letting her hands wander around the back of Jack's neck and lifting her lips to meet his.

'Good, you should be,' said Jack as their lips parted.

As Carly unwrapped her arms from Jack, the scroll she'd been holding fell to the ground.

'Hey, be careful, you don't wanna lose this bad boy! It's taken you long enough to get it!' said Lauren as she trotted over to the pair, handing Jack back his phone before bending down to rescue Carly's degree certificate and playfully tapping her on the forehead with it.

'Now, how are we going to celebrate your new credentials? I don't have to pick Soph up until

3 p.m. tomorrow, so I can stay out as late as I want!' said Lauren, hardly able to contain her excitement as she stood between Carly and Jack and linked arms with both of them, the three of them setting off to stroll through the campus, crowded with graduates and their proud families.

'Oh, well, I'm pleased you asked actually, because there's a seminar taking place not far from here, discussing the oppression of women in literature. It sounded really interesting, so I thought as you don't need to rush back home we could all go?'

Jack and Lauren looked at each other, bemused, not to mention morbidly disappointed by Carly's suggestion.

With neither of them wanting to be the one to quash her plan, they both began to splutter incoherent noises of agreement.

'Ha! My God, what do you two take me for!' laughed Carly, tapping her scroll on Lauren's shoulder and unlinking her arm.

'Last one to the pub's buying!' shouted Carly as she ran clumsily ahead as fast as her high-heeled shoes would carry her.

'Ah, there's the woman I love!' Jack called out, before running ahead to catch up with Carly, leaving Lauren behind for dust.

'Not fair, I'm in heels! And I don't know where the pub is!' Lauren shouted, her feet furiously clanking on the pavement while she awkwardly adjusted her dress, which was creeping up past her thighs as she ran.

Jack fast approached Carly, and as he did so, scooped her up off the ground. He threw her over his shoulder, at which Carly let out a yelp of giggly hilarity as Jack held her in place in a clumsy fireman's lift.

'It's okay, Lauren, I've got her! Run, first left when you get outside! Go! Go! Go!' yelled Jack, graciously giving Lauren a head start.

Lauren sped past the laughing pair and smiled widely at the sight of her dearest friend, so blissfully happy in the arms of the man she loved.

The End.

Printed in Great Britain
by Amazon

61739055R00225